By LaJoyce Martin

To Love A
BENT-WINGED
ANGEL

D1453584

By *LaJoyce Martin*

To Love A
BENT-WINGED
ANGEL

To Love A Bent–Winged Angel

by LaJoyce Martin

©1986 Word Aflame® Press
Hazelwood, Mo. 63042

Cover Design by Tim Agnew

Illustrated by Art Kirchhoff

All Scripture quotations in this book are from the King James Version of the Bible unless otherwise identified.

Printed in United States of America.

Printed by

Library of Congress Cataloging-in-Publication Data

Martin, LaJoyce, 1937—
    To love a bent winged angel.

    I. Title.
PS3563.A72486T6   1986   813'.54   86-7820
ISBN 0-912315-99-7

Dedicated
to
my children
Kevin, Angela, and Bethany

Contents

Preface

Back at the turn of this century, my grandparents, Robert Lee and Sally Rebecca Rhodes, staked claim on some government land in "the territory" of New Mexico. Grandma, separated from her family, became homesick, and Grandpa forfeited his land to return with her to Central Texas, oblivious of the underlying basin of "black gold" that would have brought them wealth.

In 1916, my husband's grandparents, Harlin and Julia Martin, staked their claim near Caprock, east of Roswell. The family lived in a dugout, and their menu included cornbread and water, antelope chased down in the Model-T, and a sampling of the neighbor's rabbit stew. Ironically, after the bitter sacrifice, Harlin sold the land and returned to Texas, not realizing the undiscovered minerals beneath its surface.

My husband and I fell prey to the Land of Enchantment in the early years of our marriage, spending two years just a few miles south of "Charles and Rebecca's land." Here I wrote my first story for publication, faced my first brush with death, and bore my first child. The country left its mark on my life.

As a girl, I lived in Cleburne from 1952 to 1959. I worked in the Johnson County Courthouse, a block from the old Liberty Hotel where Joseph roomed. I had the opportunity to attend the community church in Brazos Point, as well as a simple wedding in one of the nearby farmhouses. I watched the Brazos River in flood stage, overflowing the bridge near Five Oaks.

I was born in "The Springs," a city that sprouted its

wings and never got off the ground, and my parents, Donald and Lorene Berry, live in retirement two blocks from spring-fed Steele Creek where the Harris family picnicked.

The story is fiction, but the message is true.

Chapter 1

A New Home

"**M**ama!" Joseph ran toward the house breathlessly, staying on the path to avoid getting goatheads in his bare feet. "We got a letter!"

"Ye must be mistaken, Joseph," Martha said. "Couldn't be fer us. Fer th' neighbors prob'ly."

"Ain't we Henry an' Martha Harris?"

"Well, lemme see it!"

Charles had hoped that the letter would outdistance him by at least a week, preparing the way for the foster child. He had thought of no alternative if Martha refused Effie; Henry was his only living relative. But of course she would not—not with the offer he had to make!

"Read it, Mama, quick!"

"Don't be so itchy, Joseph. Prob'ly nuthin' of inter'st to you nohow."

"Henry and Martha: I am a. . . ."

"Here, Joseph, help me with these here big words!"

". . . .widower."

"You read it, Joseph."

"Henry and Martha," Joseph read, "I am a widower, left with a girl child, age three years the April past. I have a job on the west coast, and cannot take her with me at this time as much as I wish I could. If you will be so generous as to give her a home and good care until my return from California, I will square up with you in gold for your trouble. I shall make the employ well worth your time, dear Martha. I will be arriving on or about 10 September, 1878. Love, Charles."

It was a long dialogue for Charles in writ; he hoped it worked. Surely even the fretful, nagging Martha (as he remembered her) would be willing to shelter an afflicted child for a short duration in exchange for a sack of gold nuggets. *He would make it well worth Martha's time.*

On the swaying coach, Effie had cried until she was too weak to exert her lungs farther. Her active, intelligent mind fought the unsettling change from the hurt-proof protection of her mother's love to a hostile world of contest to survive. Struggle was not new to Effie, however, so struggle she would as Rebecca had taught her. At last, subdued and quiet, she lay on Charles' unfamiliar shoulder, reconstructing her small life. Rebecca had abruptly deserted her and now she must fend for herself.

"Need another blanket?" the solicitous stage driver asked.

"Thanks. The child's been sickly all her life," Charles explained. "Her mother passed on last week. . .I'm taking her to my sister-in-law until I can make a home for her myself."

"My sympathy to you and the little one. Haven't properly introduced myself; you were busy there. I'm Jim Collins."

"Collins?"

"Yes, sir."

"No kin to James Collins, by chance?"

"My father."

"What a coincidence! I'm Charles Harris. My father and yours were good friends."

"Your father was. . . ?"

"William Harris."

"Yes, I've heard my father speak of him many times. They met on the eastern seaboard, I believe. Is your father yet alive?"

"I wish I knew. I've lost track of him in life's shuffle. The last time I saw him was about five years ago when I struck out on my own."

"I see."

"Father was a roamer. I didn't understand it then. Mother died when I was a baby and he never stayed put after that. I could hardly wait until the government considered me an adult so that I could get me some land and be a squatter. I felt like a tumbleweed! But now that I've lost Rebecca, I know exactly how my father felt. . .why he couldn't be still. History repeats itself."

"And what took you to The Territory?"

"It was a lifelong dream of mine. . ."

"Were you married when you went?"

"Yes, sir. I was on my way there when I met *her*. I was 23; she was 19. I had no great plans of marriage, but when I met her, I knew I'd found one-of-a-kind."

"I've never met my one-of-a-kind."

"You'll know it when you do!"

"I hope so."

"By the way, it was your father who gave me a map of The Territory."

"It's a small world."

"Driving must run in the family. Does your father still drive a coach?"

"Father was killed by Indians on the trail, unfortunately. Died to save his passengers. I took up the trade. You might say he passed the torch on to me."

"You're still pretty young. . . ."

"The youngest driver on record."

"Like it?"

"Second nature with me. Gives me time to think."

"Time to think is what I *don't* need."

The letter to Martha preceeded Charles by several days. Martha, already overburdened with five small children of her own, received the unwelcomed news of a boarder with chagrin. "Thinks yer high-fallutin' brother that I'm a brood-hen?" she snapped bitterly to Henry.

"Now, there, there, Martha! The child jest might be a fetchin' sort o' mite that'ud steal away yer heart!" The pacifist approach was not working, so Henry added hastily, "An' remember th' gold Charles will bring you. . . ."

But nothing would molify the chafed Martha. Her thinking pattern was already at work peevishly sorting the extra washing, cooking, and cleaning. She envisioned a Brazos River of milk to separate, a Flat Top Mountain of laundry for the old black washpot.

For Charles, the gap between the devil's territory in New Mexico and Henry's farm in Central Texas was buttoning up mile by mile. As the coach neared the community of Brazos Point, Charles noted a well-kept cemetery in custody of the white clapboard church. Strange he did not notice the graveyard when he visited Henry before. But that was before death became his personal enemy.

If the child dies, as surely she will, at least she'll have the advantage of a civilized burying ground that her dear brave mother was not afforded, he reasoned. The thought soothed his grief-consumed mind.

Five Oaks at the fork of the road told him that Henry's place was next. Poor Henry! He had bogged down to a few acres of bottomland, never advancing any farther, feigning satisfaction with his stymied lot in life. What a gray monotony! A few pigs, a few chickens, a cow, and a wilted garden. Is that all life had to offer? *Maybe for Henry, but not for Charles Harris! His dreams would never let him stagnate!*

Ah, there it was! The Harris farm! The house was more dilapidated than he had expected; he would need to hurry back and build a new home for the family. Henry, looking much older and work-worn since Charles last saw him, heard the rumble of the coach and came down the path to assist with Effie's paltry baggage. Effie had fallen into a merciful sleep two stops back, her exhausted mind and body skirting the limits of endurance.

Martha was unprepared for the shock that awaited her. Henry occupied himself with analyzing his brother, seasoned and settled by the traumatic five years past, but Martha saw only the thwarted body of Effie. "Oh," she tactlessly cried in dismay, "What awful sin did yer Rebecca commit to be cursed by God with sech a child?"

Charles' first reaction to Martha's rude outburst was

fear—fear lest Martha utterly refuse to keep the defective bit of humanity that Rebecca had loved so desperately, thereby unraveling his travel plans into hopeless threads of lost ambition. His second reaction was anger, but he concealed it well.

"It was. . .it was the wilderness. . .lack of medical care. . .a long and difficult birth. . . ." His tongue stumbled on his teeth. "Of course you won't have to keep her long," he promised, regaining his composure. "A few short months at the longest. I will be returning soon with plenty of wealth for all of us. My job is waiting. I will make a comfortable home for my only child when I return, with no farther responsibility on your part. I'll thank you to take good care of her."

Five miniature sets of eyes gathered to focus on the object Charles held in his unaccustomed arms. Effie roused and, seeing the children that she felt no different from, managed a twisted smile. Martha frowned, determined that her own children should not be "contaminated with evil," instinctively stepping between them and the "impurity." Her stained apron failed to hide her secret; she was with child again.

Charles placed the helpless Effie on the trundle bed and began unpacking the items he planned to leave behind for her. Sensing that Martha was still unconvinced, he hurried through the protocol of instructions, so that he might be on his way before she had time to renege. He placed a Bible on the bed and an attractive china doll in Martha's hands.

"These belonged to my departed wife, Rebecca," he said, disregarding the hurt in his own heart. "In the Bible is a tintype photograph of Rebecca taken before we

16

were married. It is for Effie. . .in the event she should survive; Rebecca asked that she have the Book.''

Martha's emotions were so precariously unbalanced that she could hardly be considered responsible, and the china doll tipped the scales to Charles' advantage. Martha had yearned for just such a treasure for her two daughters, having been deprived of a real "storeboughten" doll during her own girlhood. Charles, in his haste, failed to mention the fact that Rebecca planned that her own child inherit the heirloom.

Martha's eyes hungrily feasted on the well-preserved georgette dress, finishing with the rich satin ribbon. *And Charles had just indicated that the weak child likely would not live long.* Verily, she looked as though she might not survive the night. The long trip would surely finish her off; children with evil spirits generally expired at an early age.

Curiosity caused the children to cluster around the bed and Effie made a garbled sound of greeting. Lacking prejudice or hostility, the children were delighted with their new cousin. They were busily adopting her while Martha's confused mind clung to the object of her dreams —the magnificent doll, neglecting her guard duty against evil spirits.

Charles studied Henry's children. These robust youngsters were his nieces and nephews, three of which had been added in his absence. Joseph, the oldest, must be about ten years old, "give or take a little." Charles remembered him from the last trip. He would be the kind with a frog in his pocket, and a yen for the fishing hole! A real boy! Charles liked the light of life in his sparkling eyes. The way he smiled at the delicate child revealed a big-brother protection that eased a father's fears. Ah, he could depend on Joseph to befriend Effie!

Matthew, holding to the loop on the side of Henry's overalls, must be about seven. Just a bit of a tyke on Charles' last visit, he had not changed much. Still serious and quiet, he reminded Charles of Henry in attitude and appearance. Henry loved all his children and could never be accused of showing partiality, but certainly Matthew was closest to his heels if not his heart.

A girl, the "spittin' image" of Martha, must have been born just after he left. He heard Martha call her Sarah. Judging from her size, it would not be long until she would be starting to school—if she could be detached from her mother's apron strings. She watched Martha closely, to see if it was proper to accept the newcomer. Doubt clouded her small round face.

Charles watched as Robert, an active lad of about four, darted out the open front door and ran to the coach to see the horses. Obviously an animal lover, he was carrying on an animated conversation with Jim Collins. Jim held him up to pet one of the mounts. He would be the kind that hated hats, coats, and shoes regardless of the weather. One could be sure that he kept his mother scolding and the hens squawking, with tail feathers flying. He was of a different world.

Charles' gaze locked on Dessie. A beautiful toddler with honey-colored ringlets and dimples, she flitted about like a butterfly. She must be just about Effie's age. *So this is what Effie should have been like. Effie should be walking. . .and starting to talk.* Small wonder Martha was taken aback by her appearance.

Charles followed Dessie with his eyes as she reached

out a chubby hand to touch Effie, blissfully unaware that Effie had a handicap. Martha snatched her back, and scolded, "Don't touch!" as if Effie had leprosy. Charles winced. Effie made a low cry, more like a grunt, her eyes registering fright. Just how much Effie understood, he did not know. *Too much, probably.* He would have a dual purpose for hurrying: to rescue Effie and relieve Martha. And the sooner he started, the sooner he would return.

Clutching his battered hat too tightly in his fist, he backed precariously toward the door, bidding farewell and thanking the bewildered Martha for the sitting job she had *agreed* to take upon herself. He patted the head of Joseph, slipping five Indianhead pennies into his hand. "Take good care of my angel." Then he left, before Martha could open her mouth to make comment or objection.

The revelation of Charles' departure came with the dissipating dust cloud kicked up by the wheels of the vanishing stagecoach. Martha looked about the room from the fancy doll to the crippled child on the bed, first helplessly, then accusingly, and lastly menacingly at Henry as if by his own contrivance, he brought this evil into her life for pure spite. But Henry donned a noncommital mask of protection, as was characteristic of him at such times.

An inner premonition warned Henry that a volcano was in the pre-eruption stages of Martha's tongue. He saw the usual evidence: set mouth, narrow eyes, arms akimbo. Sometimes he was able to escape the thunderous upheaval, but today he was the Pompeii at the foot of Mount Vesuvius to be buried alive in the hot lava of Martha's wrath. *Wise Solomon surely knew what he was talking about in the Holy Writ when he said it was better to*

19

dwell in the corner of the housetop than with a brawling woman in a wide house! Henry did not have a wide house, but he would "a heap ruther" been in the corner of the housetop just now—or anywhere else—than where he was.

"When did yer brother, Charles, say he was gettin' back?" Martha lurched as if to catch Charles' shirttail and bring him back until the matter could be duly settled.

"He. . .well, he actually said no 'zact date that I recall," admitted Henry, treading the dangerous ground perspicaciously.

Like a trap closing tightly on its victim, the full impact of her unwanted responsibility caught Martha. "D'ya know what this means, Henry Harris?" The "Harris" on the end of his name always indicated her furor, spelling trouble.

Henry shrugged (the only safe thing to do), embracing an unholy desire to be on a bouncing westbound wagon with Charles headed for a distant destination, gold or no gold, to flee the close confrontation with his irate wife.

"Means I'm stuck ta' home! Can ya 'magine me takin' that thing with me even ta *church?*" She pointed a sanctimonious finger at Effie and answered her own question with a gusty, "No, Siree!" Henry was grateful that she answered her own query; to open his mouth would be sheer suicide.

A feverish determination that the neighbors never know about the "cursed" child obsessed Martha, for she was a proud woman. If she must keep "it" for the next few days until "it" passed on to join the fate of "its" wayward mother, she would have to set forth some ironclad rules for the family. Rule Number One was: *Effie's presence in her home must be kept a guarded secret.*

Rule Number Two: *Her own children must not be affected by the bizarre behavior of the strange child.* This would take a united effort of both herself and Henry, who sometimes did not "tote his end o' th' log." Indeed, along with ignoring responsibilities, he had a bad habit of disregarding demons or spirits or Lucifer himself.

Then they must all pray for the child's death or Charles' decision to disband his foolish plan, and that he would return to make a home for the girlchild himself.

But alas, even an angel from heaven would have been hard put to stop Charles now. Necessity and ambition drove him mercilessly. If Martha could but hold her patience, he would make life a paradise for them all, educating those fine sons of Henry's in the college of their choice. Since he had no sons of his own, he would propagate the Harris name through his nephews, giving them the advantage of his wealth. The girls and Martha he would dress in finery. If dolls would make them happy, then the choicest of dolls they should have. The depressing poverty had worked adversely on Martha's melancholy temperament, causing her to be colicky. Ah, easily remedied, all this!

He wished he might have provided for Rebecca as he would be able to provide for Martha. But he would make it up to Rebecca through Effie, *if she lived until his return.* Charles the dreamer.

Henry had neither time nor talent for daydreaming. He was the practical one. The dasher of his reasoning power was plunging up and down in the empty churn of his resources, producing absolutely nothing with which to pacify Martha, growing more agitated by the hour. One thing for sure—he would have to get Martha to church;

he could not hope to live with her without at least a smidgen of "sanctimony."

"This is ever' bit yer fault, Henry," Martha said. Just where his blame began and ended in the whole matter, he had not pinpointed, but he was mixed up in the mistake somewhere. He had given it little thought, allowing that he would do a good turn for his brother, his only brother, by keeping his orphaned child. It had not seemed such a trial to him, sheltering an extra child for a few months. But then, women thought differently; at least *Martha* thought differently. His mind had not compensated for Martha's resentment, which he partly understood; they had both taken for granted that the niece would be a healthy, normal child. But she was a far cry from that!

Effie understood none of the turmoil that her coming had precipitated, being comforted by seeing other little people about her. One of them in particular, a merry little girl her own age with blue eyes and blond ringlets, reached out gingerly and touched her stiff arm while Martha was not looking. A bond of unspoken friendship was straightway formed. *Could a new home be so bad if she had a friend?*

Chapter 2

Memories

"*W*ill you be making the trip back with me?" Jim Collins asked Charles.

"Wish I could say I was, but I'll be taking the warm route to California. A man could get stranded in the mountains this late in the year, and I need to make time," Charles replied, adding, "A man as barefooted as I am don't want to take no chances with a rocky road."

Memories, he thought. *Memories are what I am trying to steer clear of.* How could it be that five years with Rebecca seemed no longer than a week, while the past week without her seemed like five years?

Flashbacks are not fair, he told himself, when the day he proposed to her came back to haunt him. It was the one impulsive decision of his life. "There are two kinds of tongues, Rebecca," he remembered saying. "A wagon tongue and a waggin' tongue, and the length of both are about the same."

She had laughed at his joke, not knowing that beneath his humor was a well-laid plan. That plan was to take his wagon tongue into territory too remote for waggin' tongues to reach.

"And the only mud-slinging I'll stand for is from the wheels of my wagon going west!" he had added. Then he saw Rebecca's lovely violet eyes wince with afterbirth pains from the fear born in her heart. "Then you're. . . leaving?" Her voice quivered. He could not bear to see her suffer like this.

"Yes! And I'm taking you with me!" He kissed her hand. It was his marriage proposal. He had never regretted it.

Rebecca's parents, whose ancestors were rooted in the rotting compost of the *Mayflower,* had not been pleased. He had swept into town and his genealogy could not be tracked to the local courthouse. His backdrop did not have enough light to suit them for the drama of marriage. He really could not blame them. This girl they were losing was one of a kind.

"Rebecca, a family tree without roots flourishes in the spring but dies in the winter," her mother had warned, but Rebecca had stood her ground.

"The same wind that blew Charles into town will blow him out," her father said. "The proposal was just another whim of his." But the romance had not blown over.

They wanted a big bash with wine and dining for their daughter's wedding to impress their society friends, but Rebecca insisted that the ceremony be kept simple. "I'll be just as married without all the fanfare," Rebecca said.

"But in years to come, you'll want beautiful memories. . . ."

"I'm not trying to impress anyone. I'll have Charles, and that's all that matters."

Shortly after the wedding, they learned of Charles' plan to take Rebecca with him to the ghastly wilderness country of his boyhood dreams. They had balked at donating their youngest daughter to the deceptive, youth-alluring frontier. "We can't let you go, Rebecca. . . ."

Rebecca had stood tall beside him, and said, "I'm Charles' wife now, Mother, and I will go with him anywhere on earth. I knew of his plans before we were married."

She was the bravest girl he had ever seen! For her journey west, Esther-fashioned, she required nothing but the essentials. Her mother insisted that she take some fancy dishes and quilts, and Rebecca did not argue, but she would have been satisfied with the clothes on her back, her Bible, and her last doll. "I'm taking the doll for our little girl," she told Charles.

She said her goodbyes without flinching. It seemed that her lace-trimmed upbringing only served to whet her appetite for the unfamiliar buckskin of the virgin territory. As the horses strained against the harnessing to give the wagon momentum, she gave only one backward glance to wave a cheery farewell to the two people responsible for bringing her into the world. *Had she any premonition she would never return?*

"You're the spunkiest girl I've ever met," Charles had patted her hand affectionately. "I've searched all my life for the likes of you." He had been afraid she would tire easily. He had taken her from chintz and velvet to the rough oaken planks of an unmerciful wagon. When the agonizing trip stretched from days to weeks, he watched for signs of homesickness in her; there were none. "I'm afraid you'll get too tired," he told her.

"Oh, Charles, this cannot be nearly so tiring as parties and balls and fake happiness. This is real *living!*" The look in her soft, expressive eyes made his heart do flip-flops.

Memories. Charles was not seeing the red schoolhouse or the white clapboard church or the Brazos River today. He was seeing the timberland with its black pasty mud give place to shrubby terrain paved with clinging caliche five years ago. This had melted into gentle grassland with rolling hills, finally ushering them onto the Great High Plains with its loose sand.

"Looks like the mud-slinging is all over," Rebecca had teased him.

"Thank heavens! And the waggin' tongues miles behind!" he laughed.

Jim Collins had asked him a question, hauling him back over the trail of years. "Sir?"

"I say. . .how long were you in The Territory?"

"Just short of five years."

"How'd the country strike you?"

"We had some rough days, but *she* loved it. Why, she could make the best jackrabbit stew you ever tasted! I threatened to invite the President in to sample it, but I figured he'd never be satisfied with Washington food again if he ever got a taste of it. . . And she'd run to the door just at sunset and say, 'Come quick, Charles—God's hanging out His *orange* curtain tonight,' or *pink* or *lavender,* or whatever color tinted the western sky."

"She never got homesick, huh?"

"Not once. We'd been on the land about three years when word came that both of her parents had died in a malaria outbreak. I thought she'd regret that she left them, but she was like the Bible's Ruth—she never planned to return to the land from whence she came. She said as long as she had me and the baby and God, that's all she ever wanted. She loved simplicity."

"Sounds like she was religious, too."

"Yes, she was. But not just *churchy* religious. It was deep down with her, a way of life."

I need to keep him talking, Jim thought. *It is helping.* "What. . .what took her?"

"I suspect it was pneumonia. I found her dead. She was never really strong after the baby got here. I thought I was going to lose them both when the baby was born. Rebecca had a hard time. The baby was so frail and tiny that I didn't think it would survive the first winter, but Rebecca's love refused to let the dim flicker of life smolder into darkness. Rebecca was a funny gal. You know what she said? She said, 'I brought along my doll for this baby girl, so she's going to live to enjoy it!' To her, it was as simple as that."

"Besides a good wife, then, she was a loyal little mother."

"Never seen a better. I knew all along that *something* was wrong with the child. I don't know when it first dawned on Rebecca that the child was not progressing normally. I noticed the prick of concern in her eyes, like a grassbur clinging to her worn skirt and snagging now and then on her patched cotton hosiery when she moved about. She'd put so much of herself into trying to get the little one to respond. . .to sit alone, to hold a spoon, to grasp objects. . .that when the truth could no longer be evaded, she went under."

"I've seen it work that way."

"I had my hands full keeping the wolf of hunger from the door, and wasn't as attentive as I should have been, but I'll never forget the night she broke down and cried so. She kept saying, 'But I *haven't* sinned, Charles.' I didn't know what she was talking about at first, but I finally got it out of her. She said babies with birth defects were supposed to be evidence that the mother had not been morally pure and a crippled child was punishment for the sin, or some such hogwash. I asked her wherever she heard such garbage and of course it dated back to some waggin' tongues in her home town. Superstitions never die natural deaths! Why, there was never a purer girl in the world than my Rebecca. The very idea!"

"I know all about those old wives' tales! We have an angel in our family that was born a spastic. I call her our 'Angel with Bent Wings.' She's my little niece and she's so special I wouldn't trade her for a thousand sound-bodied children! She's made of pure love and has brought us nothing but joy!"

Charles sighed. "I'm afraid life will be hard for my little Effie while I'm gone. I got the feeling that my sister-in-law is one of those 'curse of sin' believers. But Henry is my only living relative. I really had no choice. . . ."

"You'd best hurry yourself back then."

They reached the stage stop where Charles got off to connect with the southbound, bidding Jim Collins a safe journey. He found a seat apart, and closed his eyes, striving to will away the thoughts that came back to gnaw at his mind.

Memories. Perhaps Rebecca's parents had been right; The Territory was no place for a woman. She had given up so much for so little in return. He had planned so grandly for her and performed so poorly. She had passed quietly from a log cabin to a heavenly mansion, from mesquite bean broth to the marriage supper of the Lamb.

Charles supposed he would never marry again. Plucky women like his Rebecca were a vanishing species. Rebecca, who labored with the thread of hope, reaching for the eye of the needle of reality, knowing that if she found it she could mend her threadbare circumstances and add many miles to the worn sock of daily existence.

The driver put his head in the door. "Southbound stage leaves in five minutes. . .ladies first, gentlemen . . . ."

Chapter 3

Word from Charles

"*N*ow Effie's sick, an' I don't want none of ya catchin' what she's got," Martha warned her children. "She might even die. Her paw'll be comin' back fer her soon. 'Til then, keep yer distance. Ya'hear?"

The children, under Martha's stern gaze, stole out quietly, giving Effie a wide berth. Only Joseph remained.

"I've had ever' disease what are, Mama—chicken pox, 'n measles, 'mumps, 'n whooping cough, 'n all. I don't think what she's got would be catchin' fer a big boy like me. I'd be glad to help ya out with 'er." The five pennies weighed heavy in his pocket while his uncle's last request, *"Take care of my angel,"* echoed through the chambers of his soul.

Martha looked doubtful, but the burden of her unborn child sent a pain searing through her back. Summer was hastening into fall, and there were shirt collars to be turned and overalls to patch before school commenced; her two schoolage sons must look presentable.

Could Joseph be damaged by the exposure to the spirit-ridden child? Was there ever a case of demons being *transferred,* except of course, from the man in the tombs to the *pigs* in the Bible days? Was not an affliction of this sort a direct punishment for a mother who had soiled her chastity and tried to hide that sin? (And to think the unholy mother of this one had up and died!) Or maybe Charles. . . ?

"I could feed 'er fer ya."

"With th' onstart o' school an' crops ta be harvestin' 'round th' corner, I guess I'll have ta have help aw'right. But. . . ."

"I don't mind one bit. Honest, Mama."

Martha eyed Joseph sharply. She saw a handsome lad, a miniature of Henry's younger brother, Charles, a fact she willfully ignored. "Well, t'won't be fer long, an' I'll thank ya ta let 'er sickness not affect ya in any form 'ner fashin'."

"Yes'm."

However, with time, the warning Martha had issued wore off to dim print. Within a month, the segregation rule had been bent out of shape. Martha, laden with the duties of an expanding family, had scant time to supervise the children's preschool activities.

The smoldering volcano of her anger ceased its scalding overflow; only the residual ash remained. Life must go on, and Martha's first reaction to any life-altering situation was violent, gradually subsiding into a workable, though not always pleasant, rut. Henry berated himself for not remembering this quirk of Martha's personality, but in the heat of the eruption, he tended to forget that a volcano does not spew forever. Women were moody and complicated beings, keeping poor level-headed husbands like Henry in a headspin.

Harvestime brought daylight-to-dark chores. And while Martha wove her proverbial web in another corner, the small angels of mercy patiently began teaching Effie to communicate. She learned with extraordinary speed, having made marked improvement by the end of fall.

"Effie's learnin' to talk, Mama!" Joseph said.

But Martha was skeptical. "She don't understand ery a word yer sayin', Joseph. Might as wells save yer breath!"

"Oh, yes, Mama!" insisted Joseph. "Just listen to 'er say 'thank you.' " (Since beginning fifth grade, Joseph was making a conscious effort to speak "proper-like.")

"Say it, Effie," he prompted.

A two-syllable garble came from Effie's constricted throat in an indistinguishable "Ah. . .oooh."

"Fool boy!" reprimanded Martha, her patience thinning. "A dog could do thet!"

Undaunted by her pessimism, Joseph determined to have Charles' child walking and talking by the time he returned from the west. His wages, the pennies, still rode in his pocket. This was more money than he had ever had! He had been singled out by his beloved uncle to bear the responsibility of Effie's care; wouldn't Uncle Charles be surprised when she *walked* to meet him?

"I'll stay home with th' child an' let you go ta church th' Lord's Day next, Martha," Henry offered, when she, martyr-fashioned, threatened to drop from society's view because of Effie. The suggestion unnerved Martha be-

33

cause, for fourteen years Henry Harris had been a predictable man—and this she would not have predicted. She did not like anything that she could not foresee.

"The child is more my responsibil'ty than yorn," he said. "She's my only brother's child. Anyways, 'tis only fer a bit, while he's out west workin'."

Martha thought to protest the arrangement, but feared a house call from the deacons if her attendance record showed too many absences. And she wished a house call from no one! *Not a living soul* must know about Effie! *Oh, that Charles would hurry!*

Thus, on Sundays Martha went to church, but purposely left one other child at home to excuse Henry's empty pew. "Sarah has th' sniffles," or "Matt's puny ta'day," became standard answers that the parishioners came to expect. To staunch any suspicion that Henry was backsliding—and to assure that he kept his religion updated—Martha periodically stayed home with Effie and let him attend Sunday meetin'.

Before the grass "put out" in the spring, yet another child joined the Harris family, healthy and hearty William. Henry named this son for his father and carried the good news about the community with button-popping pride. Now he had *four* sons. How empty life would be without *sons*. Charles was to be pitied!

"Martha ain't hankerin' fer no company," Henry told the church ladies. "She'll bring 'em ta church fer ya'all ta see when she's up an' goin' again."

The older children became adept at side-stepping the work-swamped Martha, keeping Effie out of the range of her vision physically and mentally with numerous ingenious tactics so that during the genesis of adjustment,

34

Effie was spared the revelation of Martha's underlying hostility. With constant coaxing and encouragement from Joseph, Effie now managed a few faltering steps. This brought such applause from her young audience that she tried again and again, laboring feverishly to balance herself. She relished their praise, her eyes waltzing with excitement.

Effie's memory of Charles and Rebecca was drowned in the ocean of babyhood forgetfulness. Although her surname was the same as the other household members, she recognized from the onset that she was not counted worthy to be a Coat of Arms bearer for Martha's family, however infamous that family history. But being accepted by those her age, fed and clothed—though shabbily—she was more or less content during these primer days of her new existence. The beautiful preface of a mother's love was gone from her book of life forever, and she must now feel her way along page by page.

Joseph talked to Effie about her father, striving to keep Charles' portrait in her heart and mind until his return. "Your papa's eyes look just a mite like my papa's," he told her, "but his hair is blacker, thicker. He's lots taller and much thinner, and looks many years younger than my papa. You have a handsome paw, Effie!" Effie's small heart swelled with little-girl pride.

"And he's coming back to buy you pretty clothes and anything you want," Joseph promised with confidence. It was like a fairytale that Effie loved to hear repeated over and over.

However, when not a solitary word had been heard from the idealistic Charles in the space of almost a year, Martha's irritation shifted from a trot to a lope, then broke into an all-out gallop. "Henry, thet brother o' yorn done gon' an' *dumped* his retarded child on me an' hav' no plans o' returnin'." She flung the heated words at Henry, her only visible target.

"Now, Martha. . . ."

"Don't be 'now-Marthyin' me! Tain't you what has ta warsh th' dishes, an' scrub on th' backbreakin' rub board, 'n make all th' extry lye soap, 'n hominy, 'n. . . ."

"What ye want me ta do 'bout it, Martha? Go ta' Californey lookin' fer 'em an' draggin' 'em back by th' hair?" Henry's stolid temperament was showing wear around the edges.

"*What?* An' leave me behin' with these here hungry mouths ta feed? Why, Henry, I'm plum 'shamed o' ya. How could ya even mention sech foolery?"

"Well, then ya want that I take 'em all along with me ta find 'im?" An unholy boldness seized Henry.

"Henry Harris! (that last name again) Ya are th' aggervatin'est man a livin' this side th' Miss'ippi!"

"A fella might be happy ta move to th' other side."

"T'other side o' *where*?" Martha's cargo of thought had derailed.

"The Miss'ippi." Henry knew that he was provoking Martha beyond measure, but a "tormenting spirit" sometimes possessed him. Martha's badgering, like the pricking of long green thorns, goaded him to the precipice of profanity.

Being dominated by a different temperament, Martha was hard put to determine Henry's limits of tolerance, with a melancholy's inherent fear of pushing him over the brink. It would be tragic, indeed, to drive away the breadwinner with so many mouths to feed. So, instead of "chafing the strop until it broke," she turned on her heels and left, highly offended.

"That woman's gettin' powerful hard ta live with," Henry thought, knowing that if his prospecting brother did not send word of some kind soon, existence could get downright miserable. Of course, he never entertained a thought of leaving Martha and the children, since divorce was disgraceful and against his principles. He would just have to spend more hours in the field each day, out of her tongue's reach.

The one occasion annually celebrated with merrymaking by even the irritable Martha was Christmas; it was a gala affair at the Harris homestead. Henry traditionally chopped down a cedar tree, with Martha complaining all the while that dry cedar was a terrible fire hazard, and scores of small fingers strung endless strands of popcorn on the branches. This was a special year; Martha was unduly excited, since she planned to put the "store-boughten" china doll that Charles had left behind under the tree for her two daughters. They were now old enough to enjoy and appreciate a real doll.

Stockings in varying sizes hung from the mantle, each labeled so that Santa would make no mistake when he came down the sooty chimney. There was no stocking for Effie; Martha chose to ignore her presence.

"Effie needs a stocking, Mama!" reminded Joseph innocently.

Martha glared at him with such intensity that he squirmed uncomfortably. "Does a dog need ta hang a stockin'? Er cows? Er piglets?" Joseph did not understand, but the withering look that Martha gave him curtailed any further question or comment.

37

Poverty or no poverty, the children must have toys. Henry made a set of blocks for each of the preschool tots and wooden tops for the older boys. When he offered to include Effie, Martha objected that Effie would only "scatter blocks ever'where with 'er clumsy movements an' maybe hurt som'body." But Joseph, still championing Charles' cause (and without even consulting Martha), made a corncob doll for Effie, gouging out eyes, nose, and mouth with a knife "snuck from the kitchen." He dressed the doll in a wornout sock, and placed it under the Christmas tree with Effie's name printed lovingly on it.

A more appreciative recipient could not have been found. Effie's "Th-thank y-you," came out almost exactly as she planned that it would; it was another memorable milestone. The intelligible expression was Joseph's Christmas bonus; no other gift made him so happy.

In the exuberance of Martha's real doll presentation, her mind was sidetracked from the favors that Joseph and Dessie provided for Effie. Dessie unselfishly shared her blocks with her "goodes' friend." Unnoticed, the acts of kindness stood unprotested. Once again, Effie's appointed angel of mercy was on duty to spare her tender emotions the left out feeling on Christmas Day.

At the sight of the elegant doll, Dessie and Sarah squealed their delight. Martha took the girls aside for counsel. "Don't let Effie *touch* yer doll. She might tear it ta shreds in a fit o' palsy." The light faded from Dessie's eyes and she lost interest in the arrogant doll since it could not associate with Effie. She turned back to her blocks, greatly mystifying Martha, and casting a strange dampness on her spirits that day.

Martha was an excellent cook. Christmas dinner was

a picturesque outlay of chicken and dressing, candied yams, pumpkin pies, canned vegetables from the spring garden, and fluffy egg custard. Effie was not allowed to eat with the family at the holiday table (she might "break" something), but between Joseph and Dessie, she fared sumptuously.

Henry's pride and joy, an ancient victrola, grated at Martha's nerves, but she acquiesced to the "noise" that it made on this one special holiday. The snappy rhythm of the cylinder that Uncle Henry chose enchanted Effie; she watched with bated breath as he cranked the handle around and around to bring sound from the big flower-shaped bell. The music flowed through her thwarted hands and set the feet of her unfettered soul to dancing. Then, when the cylinder was changed to a slow, sentimental song commemorating Christ's birth, the melody plucked the strings of a just-emerging something deep inside, and her eyes smarted. How she wished *every day* could be Christmas, bringing gaity to the Harris hearth!

The letter from Charles, written in his usual freelance style, came the latter part of March, 1880. "Greetings to Henry, Martha, your children and my little lamb," Joseph read the salutation aloud to Martha.

"Haste it up, Joseph!"

". . .I have done much better than I anticipated though it took me longer than I expected. I now have enough gold to last all of us a lifetime, but am trusting that I have your permission to stay another fortnight so as to chance no foul weather on my journey homeward. How homesick I am to see you all—especially my angel! In the ensuing days, I will take farther advantage of the rare opportunity I have been afforded here. Martha dear, you will be paid abundantly and cheerfully for your faithful and loving services to Rebecca's beloved child, whom I hope is still alive and with us. I trust that you will be devising designs by which we may begin at once building you a new home; nothing you wish shall be denied you. Will arrive early summer. Sincerely, Charles.''

Effie received her first smile from the dream-intoxicated Martha that day. When Henry came in from planting, Martha met him at the door, flagging the treasured letter triumphantly.

"See there, Martha! I told ya Charles was honest!'' Henry could not resist the rare chance at I-told-you-so retaliation. But today, Martha remained unruffled and unperturbed; her mind was filled with illusions of vast wealth.

"I'll be gettin' a *modern* kitchen stove with a warmin' shelf 'n all,'' she boasted to no one in particular. "An' I want a warshin' machine with a wringer. An' new dishes, too!'' She finished with a flourish.

"Yes, yes, Martha,'' mumbled Henry, absentmindedly, glad to be free from her nagging. His thoughts were unleashed, too. "An' jest think! We can pay enough tithes ta build a whole *new* sanctu'ry.''

"Tithes?" Martha appeared to be doubting Henry's sanity. "Henry Harris, ya don't pay no tithin's on *gifts*. . .jest on what ya earn! *Charles* pays tithes on th' earnin's.'' Obviously, Martha would be handling the new finances. Henry retreated into his protective shell, but was not allowed to stay there.

"Ya don't 'spect yer brother's gonna 'spect me to keep *on* raisin' th' little invalid fer all this money he's bringin' us, do ya, Henry?''

"Naw, naw! Now Martha, ya know better'n thet! He's jest payin' ya fer what you *already* done! With my own ears I heard 'im say that when he returned, yore responsibil'ty would be over. Why, with all thet powerful 'mount o' money, he can hire all kinds o' maids an' servants ta care fer his Effie!" assured Henry, pursuing peace at a dead run. " *'Llow I might's well have a few days o' calm in this here life o' mine."* Henry chuckled at his own outfoxing ingenuity.

Days had never been divinely better for Henry. Martha carried her nose higher to church, surprising the usher by dropping a nickel in the collection plate. She cut patterns for dresses she planned to make of lush, colorful fabric on her new sewing apparatus. She was less stingy with last year's blackberry jelly, and cleaned off a shelf in the pantry for her new dishes-to-be, arranging for temporary storage until she could get a larger house built with her fancied china closet situated in the wall-papered dining room. She cast a disdainful look toward the water bucket and granite dipper.

"We'll shore have runnin' water in th' new house, won't we, Henry?"

"Why, of course, Martha! We'll take th' old bucket 'n dipper ta th' *barnyard!*"

Henry's days in field or woods mysteriously became shorter. Frequently, he came in before sundown to enjoy a peaceful evening at home. Tasty cinnamon rolls and flaky-crusted pies appeared often now. Martha found time to knit socks and houseshoes in happy, brilliant colors to match her mood.

Even Effie benefited. Although she was still treated as a Samaritan by Martha, the children were scolded less

41

for spending forbidden time trying to teach her acts that, according to Martha, she would never be capable of accomplishing. But since her coming played a part in their "good luck," the demons were temporarily ignored.

Joseph, sensing the unaccustomed tolerance in Martha, pushed his plan to have Effie "trained" to walk and talk for Charles. He confided these plans to Martha, and was permitted to spend extra time on his pet project, taking full advantage of the liberty. Effie was quick to catch the infection of goodwill, making commendable progress, stepping into the "healing waters, troubled by an angel," her vocal sounds becoming more distinguishable each week—sounds that expressed her inner joy.

"We had a letter from yer paw, Effie," shared Sarah. "An' he's comin' with a big heap o' gold an' buy us all sorts o' things. . .a buggy ta ride ta town in on Sat'day. . .'n a bran' new paddle churn. . . .'n a *peacock,* too!"

"Now when your papa comes, Effie," Joseph instructed, "you are to walk across the room to meet him. Come on, let's practice." He crossed the plank floor and Effie made her way to him haltingly, concentrating on each unsteady step. When she reached him, he let out a wild whoop of victory.

"And what do you say to him?"

"Da. . .dee!"

Another joyous whoop from Joseph.

Martha, milking Bossy in the barnyard, left her near-full bucket beneath the cow, and rushed to the house to see who was hurt. "What. . . ?" Seeing Joseph's radiant face, she stopped short.

"Look at her, Mama! She's walking! Come on, Effie.

Show her!"

Martha's scowl made Effie so nervous that she fell to the floor before negotiating her second step. Joseph rushed to help her up.

Martha turned and went back to the cowlot to find Bossy placidly eating hay with her rear hoof in the milk pail. "Jest go 'head an' be orn'ry!" she said to the impervious animal. "When I get my new house, I'll have milk delivered ta my front porch in *bottles*. An' I'll sell you to *Gertie Clark*!" She could think of no worse threat.

The happy confusion about a father she could not remember made little sense to Effie, but as long as Joseph's voice carried this excitement which evidently included her, that was all that mattered.

In the meantime, Martha settled down to wait for the fortnight to pass and put Charles on the stagecoach for his journey eastward with his magical gold; she dreamed of little else.

But Charles was never heard from again.

Chapter 4

A Special Day

"Somethin' ain't right at the Harrises!" Gertie Clark shook an accusing finger in the general direction of her husband, Deacon Clark.

"You're always jumpin' to conclusions, Gertie."

"*Conclusions*, nuthin'! It's plain as. th' nose on yer face, Clark. It's been *months* since Brother Henry and 'is wife attended church t'gether. Hadn'cha noticed? Of all people what ought to notice, should be th' deacon."

"Now, Gertie, you have no bunch o' children like Sister Martha does. You got no call to be talkin'."

"She *used'ta* get 'em all there!"

"But th' more she gets, th' more sore throats, 'n diarrhea, 'n diseases comes with 'um."

"They *couldn't* some of 'um be sick *every* blessed Sunday o' th' year, Clark. No. Mark my word. Somethin' is bad wrong. An' tis 'twixt Martha an' Henry Harris. When

45

she comes, he don't show up. When he comes, she stays'ta home. There's a skunk in th' woodpile som'where!"

"I'll thank you not to speak another word of it, Gertie!" The deacon issued the stern command, but Gertie Clark's fiction-prone tongue was not given to obedience. Unfortunate Deacon Clark had been called on the carpet more than once for violating Apostle Paul's qualifications of deaconhood in his epistle to Timothy. Pastor Stevens pointed out that an elder must "rule well his own house" and that his wife must be "no slanderer." But in spite of the possible repercussions, Gertie hurriedly set her type for her news release.

Summer, with its long stretches of sunlight, was welcomed by Martha, who feverishly filled the expanded days with preparations for Charles' return. One glance into the boys' room revealed enough work to fill an entire hectic week. The lamp, sitting on the night stand with its cracked marble top, needed its wick trimmed and globe polished. Why, the chimney was *black* with smoke! Negligent boys! Charles would need plenty light to study the house plans by night. The window, propped up with the stick she missed from the washpot, demanded rechinking before the pane toppled out. The patchwork quilt spread over the sturdy iron bed sorely needed mending in several places. The wooden floor begged a fresh oil-mopping. Such a mess! But with "deliverance on the way," one could endure temporary grievances.

Charles would have to share a bed with Joseph, while Matthew and Robert could sleep on a pallet on the floor until the weather turned cold. Maybe by then. . . .

When Charles arrived, Martha reminded herself, she *must* remember to put padding on the unaccomodating quiltbox lid that had been Effie's crude bed since he brought her nearly two years past. Even in cold weather, Martha never overstepped her "better" judgment and allowed Effie to share a single night's bedding with Sarah and Dessie. Of course, Charles would understand their crowded conditions and not question the arrangement.

"Martha!"

She turned to see Henry holding something behind his back. His boyish grin told her that the surprise was not an unpleasant one.

"Whatcha tryin' to hide from me, Henry?"

"I brought ye a wish book!" He held out the catalogue. Her rare smile reminded him of the first time he laid eyes upon her. It was her smile that fetched his heart.

"Why, thank'ya, Henry! Where'dya get it?"

"Th' postman gave it to me. I was out by th' post when he came by, an' he asked if'n I knowed a Ferguson in these here parts. I told him I didn't recollect no sech name. He said they'd onct lived acrost from Kopperl Community. Left no forwardin' address a'tall to deliver this here book."

"So?"

"So I said my wife'ud take it if'n no one else called fer it, seein's we was plannin' on buildin' a bran' new farmhouse this year, an' would be needin' to order some furnishin's fer it. He said you's much oblidged to it."

"*Farmhouse?* Why, Henry, ya should'a told 'im we's buildin' a *mansion!*"

"Now, Martha, you know I'm no braggart. It says in th' Bible tis better to be humble an' be per'moted than to be high 'n mighty an' be deflated. We're to let th' neighbors jedge what they think o' our new house, if 'n

47

when we ever get one."

"Henry, I'm feared yer makin' up yer own chimney corner scriptures."

"No, I ain't. 'Tis either in Psalms 'er Revelation."

Martha said no more, being more drawn to the wish book than the Good Book just now. Her eyes had long lusted for an uninterrupted look at a catalogue; she had never possessed one. She reached for it passionately, but was distracted by Joseph.

"Can I take Effie out on the front porch so in case Uncle Charles comes today?" Joseph's question caught Martha offguard.

She stiffened. *Someone might see Effie!* "No!"

"Why, Mama? It's warm enough."

"Th' neighbors might see. . .uh, she might fall off th' porch an' get hurt an' Charles would hold us to blame."

"I'm big enough to see after her. I won't let her fall."

"I said *no!*"

"Then can I take her out the back way and around in the yard. . . ."

"You can take 'er to th' back yard, but you're to *keep* 'er there. Hear?"

"What if Uncle Charles. . . ?"

"I'll call'ya when Charles comes. An' I wouldn't hold my breath till he gets here. He's never been on time anywhere in 'is life. Now be off, I got work to do." She clutched the catalogue hungrily.

However, her interruptions were not through. Sarah, hearing the conversation, asked, "Can we have a picnic, Mama? Huh, can we? Jes' this onct, please'm?"

"I'll be glad to fix up the biscuits and salt pork. That way, you wouldn't have to bother with cooking dinner,"

Joseph offered. ". . .and we'll be sure to stay out *back.*"

" 'N we could pick tomatoes 'n onions from th' garden 'n wash 'um at th' well," Matthew suggested.

"Don'cha be trompin' down my vines!" Martha warned—and this clue indicated that their picnic request was granted.

"What's that, Mama?" Dessie spotted the catalogue.

"That's my order book fer our new furniture 'n stuff. Th' good Lord knowed I'd need it, so He had th' postman bring it. Now run along!" Martha's heart was already buried in the wish book, her mind anesthesized with dreams.

Effie hoped she had heard aright; her heart tugged toward a brand new world without the confines of drab walls, and sunshine not canopied by a roof of rotting shingles. These commodities she had fantasized only in her most daring envisages.

Henry, incited by Martha's smile, and seeking an outlet for his goodwill, constructed a make-shift "sled" for the children to propel Effie about the place. *"I'll be favorin' Martha to keep th' youngsters out o' her bonnet whiles she enjoys 'er order book,"* he commended himself.

Five guides were ready to show Effie the world, with its pure country atmosphere, gentle breeze, and warm sunshine—as virgin to Effie as heaven's portals. *Could this be true?* She absorbed sight and sound with insatiable thirst.

Skin and sinew could scarce contain her spirit as it battled against fleshly confines, racing to explore this delicious new domain that lay about her, awaiting discovery. She was sure that if the sled had not moved when it did, she would have exploded.

"Let's take Effie to th' barn first, Joseph," insisted Matthew. "She wants to see ole Bossy."

"Want to see the cow, Effie?"

"Y-yes." Her head combined a dodder and a nod.

The sled was headed toward the barn, which was a three-sided hull thickly carpeted with manure, back turned to the north, the whole unit squawed a foot or more eastward.

Bossy stood chewing her cud, content to be shaded from the midday sun. Still chewing, she stretched a friendly nose toward Effie, bellowing her welcome. The frail child was seized with uncontrollable panic as the massive animal nuzzled her. "Uh. . .agh. . .ugh. . ." She struggled desperately to escape, eyes wild with terror, clawing frantically at Dessie.

"She's skeert! Effie's skeert!" shrieked the smypathetic Dessie, dancing to the rhythm of her own words. "She's skeert the cow's gonna eat 'er up! Take 'er away! Oh, *please!*"

Turning to the trembling invalid, white with fright, she crooned gently, "That ole cow won't hurt you, Effie— ner nobody else. She jest gives us milk fer our mush. She's a plumb frien'ly cow!" Effie faltered, wanting to believe the reassuring promise of Dessie, while at the same time desiring nothing more than to escape this frightful monster.

Robert, completely at home in the animal kingdom, held a fist filled with tufts of tender green Johnson grass toward the cud-chewing cow. "Look, Effie!" he commanded calmly. "She won't hurt you. She jest eats grass." Bossy wrapped her rough pink tongue about the weed, leaving Robert's fingers intact. But Effie's heart still grappled at her throat, and she was impatient to move on.

Robert lured the expedition toward the henhouse, reverberating with squawking fowls; it was his favorite spot. Less life-threatening in size than Bossy, the chickens nonetheless made Effie apprehensive as they fluttered about, vying for Robert's handful of corn.

"These are what makes our breakfast eggs," Robert explained, handing Effie a newly-laid reddish-brown oval. "An' old Shagnasty herself laid this egg. I can tell 'er eggs anywhere." Effie clumsily reached for it, breaking it with her uncoordinated fingers. "S-sorry," she stammered, near tears.

"It's okay, Effie. You didn't go to," comforted Dessie, while Joseph quickly buried the evidence of the mishap, lest Martha discover it and be angry.

"Let's us go where there ain't no scary animals," Dessie insisted. "I don't like Effie bein' 'fraid."

"What about Mama's workshop?" Sarah suggested.

"We'll go *by*, but we'd best not go in," Joseph said.

"That little rock buildin'," Matthew explained to Effie, "is where th' milk separator lives. Bossy's milk divides up, th' cream goin' one direction an' th' bluejohn another. Some crocks of bluejohn are in there now clabberin' fer cottage cheese. In th' summertime, Mama churns in there."

"An' a grindstone is in there that smashes th' dried corn to make it into powder for cornpone an' cornmeal mush," Sarah said.

"But sometimes Mama buys cornmeal from th' store," Dessie added.

"Yeah, sometime. When she has th' money, er somethin' to trade." The troupe moved away from the building cautiously as if it were sacred.

A mound of dirt blocked their progress southward. "This is our cellar, Effie," Joseph told her. "Mama keeps dried fruit, sweet potatoes, turnips, onions, and apples down there."

"D'ya think you could sneak down 'n get us a little fruit for our picnic lunch, Joseph?"

"Nope. Wouldn't dare. Mama might catch me and make us come in for punishment, and we're having too much fun. Right, Effie?"

"Y-yes!"

"An' when a stormcloud comes up, Effie, we have to run an' hide down in th' cellar in case a tornado might be comin." This from Matthew.

"An' I'm as skeert o' th' cellar as you are o' Bossy, Effie," Sarah shuddered. "Tornadoes don't skeer me none, but thinkin' o' th' bugs 'n snakes 'n spiders what might be down in there skeers me plenty!"

Effie's attention was stolen from the hump of dirt with its horizontal wooden door by Robert's abrupt appearance; he had lagged behind to pester the hens.

"Why don't we go to th' garden next? I'm gettin' hungry!" Robert was perpetually hungry.

"Effie'll like the garden!" The inanimate setting met Dessie's approval, and the sled was pulled and shoved on its way, jerking Effie heedlessly with each start and stop. But she did not mind; life had never been so exhilarating.

"Get you a tomato, Effie, but take care not to muss the vine. We don't want Mama mad." Joseph stopped on the outskirts of the tomato patch, abounding with rich, earthy aroma. Shivering with delight, Effie plucked the vegetable, only to have it roll from her grasp. Dessie patiently retrieved it for her. "And now we'll go by the well and wash it." Joseph tugged at the sled; fortunately, Effie was not heavy.

As Joseph lowered the empty bucket down into the stone well, a hollow splash resounded from below. Then, heaving the rope, he brought the container back to the surface filled with cold, refreshing water. Effie watched with fascination. On impromptu impulse, Joseph turned the bucket upside down, dashing the cold water over her bare feet. She wriggled her toes in an expression of delight; the cold water felt good. "Since you can't go swimming, we'll bring the swimming to you," Joseph laughed merrily.

"T-thank you!" Joseph never tired of hearing her say the first word he taught her.

"Let's us go to th' big tree fer our party," Dessie had played beneath the arms of the mammoth oak many times. "We can eat to *music*." The tree reverberated with the song of native birds. Effie loved their choir of mismatched notes, from the high soprano cries to the mellow baritone cooing. The live concert set the stage for Effie's first picnic, a memory she would carry in her bosom for a lifetime.

Away beyond, deep into the cedar breaks, Matthew said, lived bears and wolves and things that "eat'cha at night if'n ya go in the' woods by yerself without a gun." Matthew need reveal no more; the woods at once became Effie's dread enemy.

Sarah, the eye of her soul attuned to the artistic beauty of creation, pointed out the plant life to Effie, plucking the delicate flowers of intricate design and naming them. "This is a dandelion, Effie. . .an' this a buttercup. See th' yellow cup it makes? An' here's th' bluebonnet.

It makes a wee blue bonnet, just like a really Sunday-go-meetin' bonnet." She giggled and so did Effie, a real girlish giggle that came out exactly like it started out "way down in her middle." The happy sound of her own laughter surprised and pleased her.

"Effie, you're so busy learnin' ye dunno if'n yore warshin' 'er hangin' out." Robert grinned.

"T-thank you!" Joseph rewarded her expression of gratitude with a proud smile. *Now wouldn't Charles be surprised at how much his angel had learned in his absence?*

Back in the sanctum of the house, Martha was thumbing industriously through her catalogue, her mind inflamed with desire. Except for sleeping William, the children were dismissed from her thoughts. She skipped hastily over the pages of clothing, purses, shoes; these would come later. She *did* plan to have a church outfit that would incite the wagging tongue of Gertie Clark, but first things first. . . .

She passed up the showy jewelry, pictured with enticing allurement. It did not hold her interest—just yet. Anyhow, Pastor Stevens frowned on adornment.

She hurried through the obscene pages of men's underthings, her face burning with shame. She would have to hide the publication from the girls' view. The newfangled baby clothing scarcely caught her attention. Furnishings for her new home were her priority. The dishes . . .ah, yes! The fabulous blue willow pattern would give Brazos Point's "society ladies" something to talk about. She would need service for twelve. Marking the page with a piece of tattered ribbon, she allowed she would ask Joseph or Henry to assist her in filling out the order sheet;

it would be wise to do that right away.

She needed a large silver coffee urn, now that there would be plenty of coffee. Terribly expensive, these. But Charles had a bottomless purse. There would be muffin tins to buy, an angel food cake pan. . . . She ran out of ribbons to mark her places and tore strips from the worn cuptowel. Deeper and deeper she plunged into her fairy-land of illusion. Only William's crying brought her back to reality, motherhood—and poverty.

The back yard had been crisscrossed time and again, leaving sled marks pressed on the face of mother earth, disturbing her fresh summer make-up. "Are you getting tired, Effie?" Joseph asked.

"N-no!" Looking into her weary eyes, Joseph knew she was stretching the truth. He must take care not to overtire her, with her daddy's arrival pending any minute now.

"But what about th' woodshed, Joseph?" asked young Dessie. "We hadn't been there yet."

"That'll be our last stop for today." More heaving, shoving, and pulling got the entourage to the woodshed. Joseph focused Effie's attention on the low-built log shed with a rusty-hinged door made of crude planks. "This is where Papa keeps the firewood for the cookstove and the fireplace," he told her. "It's close to the house, so Mama doesn't have to go far for wood in the wintertime if it snows."

"Mostly she sends me or Joseph anyhow," Matthew said. "An' we keep th' woodbox inside th' back door of th' house filled up for her. She don't much go to th' wood-shed herself."

Joseph rushed the tour to a conclusion. "We need to

go in now, and let Effie rest,'' he insisted. But Effie's heart had fallen captive to the miniature log house, peaceful and inviting. She looked back once more to the conforting structure, a strange longing calling from the depths of her soul. Could it be that her subconscious mind, rapidly adding a sixth sense, had honed in on the part this woodshed would play in her future?

Chapter 5

The Three R's

By midsummer, the vigil for Charles that sent feet scurrying to the door at the sound of every passing wagon had ceased.

Exposure to sun and wind brought strength and health to Effie's frail frame. Throughout the days of Martha's whimsey of filling out order blanks, the youthful tutors had educated the alert Effie bit by bit in an earthly manner. And yet, as she grew older and wiser, and watched the children don their Sunday best clothing, heavy with starch and meticulously ironed wrinkle-free with the black flatiron, leaving for church each Lord's Day, she knew she was missing out on a deeper, more infinite something in life.

"See that Bible on th' mantle?" Dessie pointed and Effie's gaze followed.

"Y-yes."

"That b'longs to *you*."

"M-me?"

"Yes. Your Paw left it fer'ya. It b'longed to yer Maw, Joseph said. Someday when ya learn to read real good, you can have it!"

"O-oh! T-thank. . . ."

"It's not me fer to say thank-ya's to. It's a'ready yours, you funny little goose!" Dessie laughed fondly.

What did it all mean? When Dessie whispered, "We're goin' to church ta'day, Effie," it was simply taken for granted that everyone knew what church was all about!

When the smell of autumn's breath filled the air, Martha slowly roused from her summer's dream, and with that awakening became increasingly alarmed that Charles had not yet arrived.

"What if Charles *never* ever returns, Henry?"

"I dunno, Martha."

"What'll we do with 'is crippled-up child?"

"She's bein' no great bother, Martha. Don't eat enough to keep a bird alive. I can eat less myself. . ."

"Bother 'n eatin' ain't th' trouble, Henry!"

"Then what's problemin' ye, Martha?"

"You ain't realizin' that we can *never* ever go to church all t'gether anymore, er have th' neighbors in, er. . ."

"Why, I don't see why not, Martha!"

" 'Cause 'o what people'd say, that's why! We'd be th' talk 'o th' whole countryside—havin' an afflicted child with evil spirits in our home. . . ."

"I don't sense no evil spirits nowhere. . . ."

"*You* wouldn't, Henry Harris! Cause you ain't

spiritual ner discernin' enough to sense nothin'!'"

"Well, I ain't turnin' my own brother's flesh 'n blood into th' woods to starve!" The unspiritual Henry stormed from the room.

Post-mortem rites for Martha's dead dreams of wealth were postponed as long as possible. She vacillated between accusing Charles of maliciously murdering her fondest hopes or burying her very soul beneath the heap of broken promises, with Henry roped in as accomplice. She towed the brothers into her self-made court and condemned them almost daily for what seemed to Henry an eternity.

Henry held her at bay with fragile "what-ifs" and "maybes" until any chances of Charles returning was a ridiculous fantasy. *"It's mighty risky to possess anything as precious as gold, especially in th' amount that Charles had,"* Henry told himself. *"I'd 'a been surprised if'n he had escaped th' rugged western territory with either his life or his money!"* Yet he fed Martha's illusion for his own self-preservation, knowing full well that the gold would not have made her completely happy; riches in themselves never made anyone happy. "Wealth's just another of Solomon's vanity trips," the preacher said, and he may have been tossing his sermon Harris-ward.

No, it would take more than wealth to change Martha. It would take some great miracle of God, some awakening. He did not fathom how God could do it at all without starting with all new "dust."

A strange set of circumstances shielded Effie from the hurricane of Martha's wrath. Twin boys were born prematurely, and Martha's energies were expended nurturing the babies to their proper weight and health, with no time left for reflection. Martha named her identical sons Chester and Alan after her political idol, Chester Alan Arthur. Henry made his usual proud announcement at church, and Martha's absence was excused for weeks without question.

Henry paused to pray in the field each day. The twins must survive! If they did not, Effie would likely bear the blame for bringing the omen of death to the household. Poor, innocent Effie! What was to become of her if Charles had met an unfortunate end?

"I'm proud to name my boys fer Mr. Arthur, Henry. I sure do b'lieve he's playin' th' game fair 'n square up in Washin'ton. Paw said he was a good gener'l in th' war, tho' he were on th' Yankee side."

"T'aint b'comin' fer women to discuss politics, Martha."

"Maybe t'aint, Henry, but since bein' President sort 'o jest fell in his lap all et onct, it must 'o been God's Will fer him to be our leader," she asserted as though personally in cahoots with God on matters of the nation's destiny.

" 'Tis only a matter 'o yore opinion, Martha."

"I say th' Good Lord lifts up who He will and lets down who He will."

"Sometimes."

"Sometimes? Henry, are you disputin' th' Bible?"

"No. Remember twas th' *people* what put King Saul in as leader, not God's doins."

"You ain't *fer* President Arthur?"

"Don't put words in my mouth, Martha. I jest ain't fer you discussin' politics like a brazen woman in my house! I ain't downin' ye fer namin' the boys fer th' President. . . Them's good names an' they'll be right proud to grow up bearin' a worthy name, but keep yer tongue out 'o a man's world!''

Martha had no more than gotten Chester and Alan through their babyhood difficulties and on the road to soundness when she gave birth to yet another little boy whom she named Arthur.

"Now we have th' 'whole President' in our house,'' she boasted, thereby letting Henry know she had not forgotten politics. "An' thet's th' last o' th' Harris crop.'' She said it with finality.

With nine children to underwrite (not counting Effie), Martha had no immediate time for ferreting out evil spirits, letting the proverbial "crumbs from the table'' fall to Effie as best they would. The young children commanded her total and constant attention; her hands were busy washing diapers, her mind concocting menus that balanced supply and demand.

She reminded herself periodically that the unwanted child of the vanished Charles Harris had *not* become an accepted part of the family, or even a welcome houseguest —yea, never would. The problem was only put on a mental back burner to be dealt with at a later date. It took superhuman strength to deal with demons, and best leave them unruffled until one could carry through with the job. If they were tackled and not conquered, they'd be "tougher" the next time, like a half-broken bronc. Martha did not presently have that kind of strength.

In the midst of the population explosion in the Harris household, or the "arrivin' o' th' President in three persons'' as Henry put it, Dessie started to school.

"I'll teach you ever'thing I learn jest as fast as I learn it!'' she promised Effie, and it was hard to determine which was the most excited on the first day of school—she or Effie.

Effie could now walk and talk haltingly, thanks to the preseverence of Joseph. And true to her promise, each of Dessie's daily lessons was shared meticulously with the knowledge-hungry Effie, and although she spent her days in loneliness while Dessie was away, the dividends were worth the sacrifice.

Dessie taught fervently and with patience. Effie learned to read with amazing speed, but the writing lessons were a disaster.

"Hold th' chalk like this," Dessie showed Effie the technique time after time. But each of Effie's unyielding fingers moved independently of one another, resulting in broken chalk which often missed the slate entirely. The long-suffering Dessie neither scolded nor condemned, unobtrusively slipping the shattered chalk from view.

Numbers were mastered so easily by Effie mentally that Dessie vowed she must have a " 'rithmetic brain." Verily, Effie was a math genius, frequently assisting her young schoolmarm in finding elusive answers. "Your head's faster'n my slate!" laughed Dessie.

Effie looked forward to each lesson with breathless eagerness. Her craving mind raced years ahead; she ached to try her reading abilities on the books Joseph and Matthew brought home. If Dessie would only teach her faster . . .faster. . . .

"When you learn th' big words good, Effie, you can read th' Bible o' yourn on th' mantle," Dessie reminded, jerking her head in the direction on Rebecca's treasured Bible. Effie's heart leaped with excitement. *"Oh, hurry, Dessie! Please do!"* her inner being cried out. *"I want my*

Book! I want to read every word of it! I've never had anything of my very own!"

No price was too great to pay to learn to read her Book, including the one thing she most detested about the school year the monthly hair-clipping sessions.

"Come, Joseph, Matt, Robert. . . . It's time fer yer Papa to cut your hair." The boys were lined up in chronological order, and as each lad's turn came, a tin bowl slightly larger than the water dipper was turned down over each shaggy head while Henry's shears clipped away, trimming to the rounded pattern of the bowl's outer rim. It was quite becoming to the boys, but alas, Martha insisted adamantly that Effie be included in the barbering ritual.

"Get Effie's, too, while yer at it, Henry. There's no time fer me to fool with 'er tangled, matted hair." Even Dessie's offer to take the full responsibility of brushing Effie's hair each day did not change Martha's demand. Indeed, it appeared to strengthen Martha's decision. Effie's silent tears went unheeded.

How Effie hated it! Sarah and Dessie were not subjected to the humiliating bowl haircuts, but were allowed to keep their beautiful feminine tresses that held bows and ribbons, were entwined into braided "pigtails," or left free to fluff about their shoulders. How Effie envied them! Why must she be made acutely aware of her "difference"—the difference that forever excluded her from the precious privilege of going to school like Joseph, Matthew, Sarah, and Dessie? And they took it for granted! Why, just yesterday, Joseph fretted because he *had* to attend school, and would have been tardy or absent had not Martha threatened the hickory stick treatment on his backside. To think that he would rather be in the field helping Henry than reading his books was beyond Effie's comprehension!

Even Sarah balked at reciting. She had rather be doodling on her slate, drawing silly pictures of the objects around her. *Ah*, thought Effie, *if only I had their chance, I would never waste a moment!*

Dessie cleverly arranged Effie's lessons to correspond with Martha's evening chores outdoors. But one fateful afternoon, Martha came through the back door into the house with her egg basket on her arm. She was red-faced and flushed with agitation; Robert had shirked his duty of giving the hens their mash. Dessie had no time to hide the evidence of her teaching scheme before Martha burst into the sitting room. Dessie was caught in the very act of giving Effie a spelling lesson.

"Dessie, whatcha doin'?" Martha's dark eyes narrowed.

Dessie was an honest child. "I was teachin' Effie to spell from my blue-back speller."

"Yore teachin' Effie nuthin' et all," Martha corrected. " 'Cause Effie can't learn nuthin'. Yore wastin' yer time, thet's what yore doin'!"

Effie's mind froze into solid panic as Martha glared at Dessie. Had she known how to pray, she would have bombarded heaven with foundation-shaking distress signals. Her eyes riveted to the Black Book on the shelf and her soul gave a piercing cry: *"Oh, please, Aunt Martha, you don't understand! I must learn to read my Book!"*

I'll forbid any farther lessons! Martha thought. But no, perhaps the repetition, even falling on dumb ears, might aid Dessie in learning herself. After all, Dessie showed signs of being the most scholarly of all her children, "bellyachin' least o' all" about homework. The teacher had sent a note commending the studious Dessie for her accomplishments, polishing Martha's pride and inflating her ego. A high standing in the community was one of her priorities. What could it hurt for Dessie to say her lessons aloud?

Thus Divine Intervention kept Martha from extinguishing Effie's one bright flame of hope—the hope of learning to read the "big words" that Dessie said were in the Black Book.

Phonetics were arduous for Effie's disobedient tongue, but she was able to make the initial word sounds with a degree of accuracy. "Baby" became "Ba-"and if she paused and started anew, she could add the "-by." Dessie became "Day" and Sarah "Say." The second syllables were sometimes added, but more often left off entirely. When she had mastered the whole of the alphabet verbally, Dessie gave a victory whoop and Effie's lopsided smile made a "fetchin' match" for the laughter in her eyes.

"Yore not *dumb*, Effie!" she encouraged. "Why, yore plumb *smart*! If'n I ever be a teacher, I druther have brains like you have to teach on than smart-alecky kids that talk back an' don't 'ppreciate books none."

"T-thank you!"

"When I'm a teacher, I'll tell 'em 'bout th' very first one I ever taught to read. Yes, a teacher is what I plan on. Bein' a teacher'd be plumb *fun*!"

Impatient Effie could learn only as fast as Dessie and her primary books advanced, and that seemed *painfully* slow. What if Martha, in a dark mood, should decide that

Effie had had enough "educatin'?" What if the "big words" were never mastered at all, and she was never able to comprehend the message her Book held for her? Oh, perish the thought!

Matthew, now studying fifth grade books, was steady and methodical. He laid aside his country dialect more slowly than Joseph, but the metamorphosis was taking place. As he changed, he felt that everyone about him should change, too.

" 'Tain't long till we get out 'o school fer summer," Dessie commented one day.

Matthew looked up soberly. " 'Tisn't 'tain't, 'tis 'tisn't!" he corrected.

"Matthew's tryin' to teach yer teacher," Dessie laughed to Effie. "Teachers have to be teached, too!"

Instead of going to school, the day before Joseph's fifteenth birthday, he went directly to the field where Henry was plowing. "I'm bored with classrooms and lessons and teachers, Papa," he told Henry. "I've had enough schooling for a lifetime!"

"Does seem ridiculous to hav' to hire help in th' fields when I got a strappin' boy 'round to lend a hand," Henry admitted. "But I daresn't think yer mother'll hear to it."

Late spring had produced a warm afternoon. Martha checked on the cheesecloth bags hanging from the clothesline, dripping with wet, milky whey. When all the moisture had seeped out, the clabbered milk would be crumbly cottage cheese. Then she fetched her dishpan of early English peas and situated herself on the front porch in her favorite cane-bottom chair for the task of shelling them. Ah, the front porch. . .one of earth's most delightful spots, with its saggy, posterior-shaped chairs and aged porch swing! Always sheltered and shady, it stretched the full length of the house, offering a magnificent view.

Pea-shelling time provided Martha a sorely needed hour of reflection. The three babies were napping, Effie was feigning sleep to placate Martha, Henry had taken William with him to the field, and the other children were in school.

There had been little time for Martha to consider the destiny of her fastly maturing children and now, comfortably parked, she pulled out the mental brick and mortar with which to build her hopes for their future, and went to work.

Joseph will be a leader-hopefully a politician. She reviewed his charisma, his personality, his quick wit and amazing ability to sway people "like his Uncle Charles" (she quickly dismissed that last evil thought). She could picture him now strutting down the streets of Fort Worth, dressed to the hilt with his stovepipe hat and shiny black "President Arthur" shoes. He would be going to finishing school, of course, when he completed the local grades. She would sell off part of their land, if necessary, to get him to his destination (or better said, *her* destination).

Why does Matthew have to be so much like Henry? Henry never would " 'mount ta much" and Martha was determined to bend Matthew toward more ambitious inclinations. He did have a knack for music, according to the school master, and although Martha had little music-appreciation built into her fiber (she considered practicing on a musical instrument a waste of time), she was aware that musicians and conductors were highly accepted in social circles, their popularity on the rise. She might even try to buy a piano if Matthew showed sufficient interest in the idea.

Sarah, without doubt, will be a famous artist. The thoughts of her first daughter made Martha look inward. She must see that Sarah was not a child bride as she herself had been. She would not be "bound under the yoke" of a man who did not appreciate her finer points. Few women, if any, had made history with their paintings. . . it was mostly *men*. But it was high time that history be updated. Move over Michelangelo. Here comes Sarah Louise Harris, the first famous woman painter— *daughter* of Martha Harris.

Robert will surely be a doctor. She had watched him in his apprenticeship, splinting the bones of his wounded animal friends with gentle hands. Many a bird, rabbit, or squirrel had been nursed back to health. Bosque County only had one part-time physician, who was always in the wrong place when needed. Doctors were in great demand, with the need for more increasing every year. Robert Samuel Harris, M. D., the shingle would say. *Son* of Martha Harris.

There is no question what Dessie will be! She'll be a school teacher. She actually *enjoyed* pretending to teach the incapable Effie, and if an "object" on which to practice gave her more satisfaction than an empty chair, then so be it. Dessie's marks in school had always been superior; she had a passion for books. Since early childhood, she had disdained girl-toys like dolls. Remember the meager attention she had paid the splendid china doll, preferring to play school with her mute, but unprotesting pupil? Well, teachers were revered creatures, too. So let Dessie grow up to be the successful schoolmarm that she wished to be and teach right here at Brazos Point.

William? Why, William is as sure to make a parson as the apple tree makes little green apples! She chuckled at the thoughts of him imitating the preacher to amusing perfection, getting "anointed" with fervor as he threatened that all sinners would "split hell wide open, spreading sparks all over eternity." Even Parson Stevens called William a "little preacher boy." Preachers were reputable, too, although Martha was often offended at Reverend Mr. Stevens when he stepped on her toes. The Right Reverend William Paul Harris, D. D. *Son* of Martha Harris.

What the "President's boys" might attain in life was still hidden behind their babyhood antics. Their talents had not surfaced; the building of their lives would be reserved for a later pea-shelling episode.

Martha wished that more of her children had been female to "even the score." She had an overplus of boys. But one had to accept God's will in all things.

Now there was the witless child of Charles' whom she would never accept, but would have to find some answers. . . .

Through the screen door, Effie could hear the green peas plinking into the dishpan in a systematic pattern. Martha paused in her reverie to straighten her back, casting a fixed, intent look into the woods teeming with new life, but seeing naught of it.

Henry and Joseph rounded the corner of the porch, talking earnestly in low tones. Martha's heart gave a leap of premonition; it was not time for school to be dismissed. Seeing Martha and not expecting her to be on the porch, the two stopped abruptly, looking at her sheepishly.

"Whatcha doin' outta classes, Joseph?"

Henry hurried to Joseph's defense. "He's no bookish boy, Martha," he pointed out. "He's been wantin' to quit school, so I allows t'would be better fer him to help me than that I should have to hire help. Lawsy me, I can't afford no hired hands 'round here at prices they charge now!" Then he added as a postscript, "Some have brain 'n some have brawn, ya'know. Joseph wants to try his brawn awhile!"

Henry could feel Martha's mental darts puncturing his back as he and Joseph left to fell logs to build another pigsty.

Into the woods walked Martha's dreams of presenting the world a President, a Senator, or a Governor in the bodily form of her eldest son. Joseph Lee Harris, Farmer, Wanderer, Nobody. *Son* of Henry Harris!

Chapter 6

An Unforgettable Summer

"Pardon me, Son," the big man reined his team to a stop. "Could you tell me how to get to a place called Brazos Point near Five Oaks."

"Yes, Sir," Joseph smiled. "You've found the place. We're not a town, really. We're just a few farms splashed over a two-mile area, with a church and a school."

"Good farm land?"

"Real good, Sir."

"My name's Gibson. We bought some land next over from some folk by the name of Clark. Supposed to have an old log house on the place that we hope is livable. Would you happen to know that location?"

"Sure, Sir. I'd be glad to direct you to it."

"Do you have a horse?"

"No, Sir."

"Ride up with us then," Mr. Gibson insisted. "You'll

find us real neighborly. If you people ever have need of a horse or wagon, what's ours is yours." Joseph liked this man at once.

The wagon sagged under the weight of Mr. Gibson's family and household items. It looked as though another pound would be its undoing, but Joseph climbed aboard. He could not tell exactly how many children were hidden beneath the canvas of the wagon.

Newcomers considered the community modern. There was no post office, no store, and no smithy, but the small church, with its arms locked about a well-kept graveyard, and a typical red one-room schoolhouse made the land enticing to settlers.

The nearest town was some twelve miles to the west, known as The Springs, where most of the Saturday shopping and business transactions were negotiated. County records were kept at Meridian, nine miles farther on.

The Harris farm was a convenient three quarters of a mile from the river; a packed earth road, like a dirty wrinkled ribbon twisted its way to the water. The road became muddy ruts when badgered by spring rains, but was seldom inaccessible. A covered, rickety wooden bridge hung precariously over the rushing waters, its condition telling one that every trip across it was an adventure that might or might not be successful. Except for the rather steep banks on either side, the water itself was shallow enough for wading at the crossing.

In the summertime, it was to this river that the Harris boys took their homemade fishing gear, caught grubs and grasshoppers, or dug worms, and worried the fish on down the river or onto their hooks. Martha did not fret, since there was no danger of them drowning. It was, in fact, a relief to have them from underfoot, and they occasionally caught enough fish for a mess.

About midsummer of Effie's seventh year, Henry enlisted Joseph's help with hoeing the cotton, leaving the fish and fishing to the younger siblings. Robert and William hounded Martha to let them go to the river, but Martha felt that they needed a chaperon.

"Neither o' ya'd be strong enough to drag th' other'n up th' bank if'n ye got hurt," she objected.

"Sarah could go with us, couldn't she?"

"I'll take 'em, Mama," Sarah offered, seeking a scene for her painting. "An' Dessie can come along too."

Out of her mother's earshot, Dessie said, "Effie's old enough to be seein' th' world, too. Let's us take 'er on th' sled!" So without consulting Martha, the well-worn sled was dragged from its resting place and Effie was loaded for the trip.

Effie looked worried. "What's botherin' ye, Effie?" Dessie coaxed.

"S-Snakes?"

"She thinks there's snakes runnin' all over!" laughed Dessie. "Land sakes, Effie, there's not many snakes a'tall, an' what there is, is as skeert o' you as ye are o' them!"

Of two things Effie was terrified: the woods that contained the bears and wolves that ate human beings—and snakes. Martha had issued grim warnings about the snakes, described by Dessie as slithery creatures with poison-filled fangs. The most fearsome of reptiles was the cottonmouth water moccasin that made its home at the river. If bitten by one, "Ya'd never live to git home," Martha said. The blackish viper with white inside its mouth had a heat detector system for finding warmblooded prey. Some were "as long as yer arms can reach." "Be careful," Martha cautioned. "Several o' these cottonmouths has been killed 'round th' river this year."

The Harris cousins remained undaunted by the talk of snakes and wolves and bears. "We ain't skeert," Dessie scorned. Effie supposed that the ability to run from danger would produce bravery, but as halting as she was, she would be "got."

When no snakes peered through the broomweed with menacing fangs, Effie relaxed. Three-quarters of a mile seemed a very long journey! Pulling the sled without Joseph's assistance was no easy task. "Effie, you're gettin' *heavier*," Sarah commented. "We're gonna hafta stop n' rest!"

"Why don't we have recess from sled tuggin' at th' school, so Effie can see where her teacher goes fer learnin'?" was Dessie's suggestion. Pushing, pulling, heaving and laughter brought them to the shade of the schoolhouse; the river was just beyond.

So this is where Dessie got the wonderful knowledge! In trance-like rapture, Effie thought of the many books hidden deep in the bowels of the red building waiting to be digested. If she could gain entrance to the padlocked door, she would gladly spend the rest of her day—or the rest of her life—right here, looking, reading, absorbing, leaving hobbies as unimportant as fishing to the others. Ah, that would be unspeakable delight!

The Indian Paintbrush curtsied in the soft west wind and the birds scaled the harp, playing a sweet summer song. The prickly nettles of Martha's malice were far away. With his hand substituting for a wind vane, Robert nodded his approval. "This is th' day fer fishin', all right! 'Wind from the east, fish bite least; wind from th' west, fish bite best'."

"Where'd'ya learn that bit o' po'try?" Dessie asked.

"Paw's almanac." Robert was thrifty with words, wasting few. "Let's go."

The descent down the bank left Effie breathless. Robert stationed himself at the bottom of the incline to stop the sliding vehicle, while Sarah gave it a slight shove with her foot from the top. "Catch'er, Robert!" Dessie hopped on and rode down with Effie. The effect was that of riding a tall slide; Effie had never had such fun!

"Here's a good place fer Effie," William pointed to the shade of a salt cedar where she could watch him and Robert fish while Sarah sketched and Dessie skipped rocks across the shimmering water.

Robert's first fish, a tiny blue-gilled sunperch, brought squeals of joy. He threaded it onto his stringer, rebaited his hook, and repeated the process. William tangled his line on brush and logs; he had not learned the strategy. Sarah reveled in her own world, intent on her landscape while Dessie collected rocks and searched the bed of the stream for arrowheads. The cadence of the undulating water together with the warm sun reflecting from the pebbly white beach soon lulled Effie to sleep.

Dessie was tugging on her sled when she awoke. "We gotta go, Effie," she said. "To'day's rushin' quick to get to ta'morra." The four maneuvered the sled to the bank's edge, but with exhaustive tugging and pulling could not hoist it up.

"Let's us all push *hard*," suggested Robert. "One, two, three, PUSH!" But the sled did not complete its journey. Halfway up the incline, it went cascading down again. For a full hour they struggled, dragging, lifting, coaxing the stubborn piece of wood. The sled behaved like an adamant stone.

"We're not quite strong enough," Dessie admitted finally. "Best ye go get Joseph whiles I stay with Effie."

Sarah went along with Robert and William to help get the fish, fishing gear, and her art supplies home. She planned to confide Effie's predicament to one of the strong-muscled men-members of her family and ask that he assist in Effie's rescue, bypassing Martha. But unfortunately, Joseph, Matthew, and Henry had gone to The Springs to help Mrs. Gibson, the new neighbor, load some furnishings into the wagon. Henry took several bushels of peaches to sell, too. When Sarah asked their whereabouts, Martha said that it would be very late, or perhaps on the morrow before they returned.

"Where's Dessie?" Martha asked immediately. When she learned that Dessie had been left at the river, she was wroth, demanding that Sarah and Robert return for her without hesitation. The very idea of leaving a child that young alone at the river! The more she considered it, the madder she became, and in her inflamation, issued an awful verdict: "An' if'n yore not returned by sundown, I'll call th' County Sherif' ta lock'ya all up in th' jail!" It was the worst threat that her raging mind could think of. No one questioned how she would notify the sheriff or where the jail was located, but "sufficient unto the day was the evil thereof." Robert and Sarah scrambled back to the riverbed as fast as their legs would carry them, leaving William to Martha's mutterings.

Dessie refused to leave Effie until a savior could be

found. "She's skeert to stay all by herself," she said stubbornly.

"If'n Effie's skeert 'er not skeert, you gotta come home with us anyways!" argued Sarah hotly. "Ma'll put us in th' jail if'n you don't come and quick. I'm skeert a' Mama!"

"Well, I *shain't* leave Effie!" Dessie sat down firmly and refused to budge. "An' you can't *make* me neither!"

"Come, Robert. We'll just hav' to drag 'er," Sarah said resolutely, aware that the sun would soon be dropping into an amber glow beyond the horizon, precipitating the jail-sentence.

Sandwiched between the older brother and sister, a screaming, kicking Dessie was hauled up the ridge and down the clay road. She cried all the way to the farm.

Martha stood akimbo, waiting; when the children were within sight, she marched herself angrily to meet them. "Dessie!" she scolded harshly, "You shut up thet bawlin' n' squawlin' right this min'it!" Crises took advantage of Henry's absence, but she was ready to take the bull by the horns.

"B-b-but Effie's alone at th' river, an' *skeert!*," blubbered Dessie, her emotions out of control, still trying to free herself for a lunge back to the creek.

Why Dessie had not come home with Sarah, Robert, and William was now clear to Martha, and it infuriated her the more! To think that a child of superior intelligence, a child of Martha Harris, would risk her life for a feebleminded waif was preposterous! She—Martha Harris—had left the problem of Effie on the back burner until it had fermented!

Dessie kept crying, begging, pleading for someone. . .

anyone. . .to go to the river and bring "poor, skeert little Effie" home. Martha eventually wearied of her tears and sent her to bed without supper, but the snubbing continued into the night. Dessie fought away sleep with every possible thought-weapon, then fought barehanded by twisting and turning, sitting up, and counting stars; it was a bitter battle, but she meant to be awake when the menfolk came home!

Martha, entertaining a trace of guilt over the stranded Effie, reasoned that she, being a homebound mother with a tiny baby, could do absolutely nothing about the misfortune of Effie. The Bible said that all things work together for good to those who love the Lord (and certainly she loved the Lord) so this must be working for some ultimate good. She even convinced herself that a passing traveler might find Effie before Henry returned from The Springs. No one would know to whom she belonged since Effie could not communicate and she would be taken to an asylum, which is where she really belonged anyhow. Thus pacifying her conscience, Martha went to bed and to sleep, snoring loudly as usual.

Nightfall began a reign of terror for Effie. The full moon, which should have been a solace, only increased Effie's ability to see the tormenting things about her, distorting harmless shadows into objects of evil intent. Across the river, on a distant rise, stood the community church, silhouetted against a starry background. The moon swept her magic wand of light across the old cemetery, cradled in the lap of the churchyard, stirring the tombstones to ephemeral sentinels of the night. These marble guards, in assorted shapes and sizes, left Effie weak with fright; she had not noticed them in the light of day.

Effie waited and waited, assured that her rescuers were on the way. Surely it would not be much longer! Where was Joseph? Where was Dessie? They would be here any time now! An hour passed. . .two hours. . .three hours. . . .

The temperature that day had hovered near ninety degrees and Effie had suffered mild sunburn even in the protection of her shaded haven. Her campsite in the draw was still stifflingly hot. A demanding thirst joined forces with the gnawing hunger in her spent body. She crawled to the edge of the water for a cool drink. But alas, the lack of muscle coordination and physical strength almost ended her life when her head jerked forward, submerging her face in the shallow water. Frantically, she willed her elbows into the rocky shore to lift herself, tearing away tender flesh. She held her breath until her lungs rebelled. A determined upward surge saved her, and she fell back to the safe rocky shore, with only the water on her face to quench her burning thirst. She dared not try again, though; death from drowning would come quicker than death from dehydration. She rolled back to the comfort of her familiar sled, not expending the energy to try to walk or crawl.

She had scarce layed down, her heart kicking a staccato against her ribs from fear and fatigue, when a low, ghostly sound arose from the thicket to her right and above, causing her heart to almost quit completely. *"Oh, why didn't I just go ahead and drown?"* she chided herself, shaking violently. That wolf—or was it a bear?—was close by, and would surely find her. Again and again, the mournful cry bounced off the walls of the canyon, until

Effie was faint with dread. Her fuzzy mind cleared. She must try to escape! Where could she hide? And she must make no noise in moving about!

She eased cautiously off the sled onto the crunching gravel, wincing at the sounds made by the movement of the rocks beneath her. Breathlessly, inching her way on her belly, she sought shelter beneath a squatty shrub near the rushing stream. At least, the roar of the water would overpower more fearsome sounds. She hid herself beneath the bush, tears of relief slipping down her cheeks unbidden. She had escaped the terrible "thing"—while the innocent hoot owl never knew what jagged pains her nightcall sent ripping through a little girl's breast.

Time was now measured by eternities, not hours. How many eternities she had been in her harbor of safety when she saw the monstrous snake, she did not recall. It was dangling from a nearby limb, slowly making its way toward her. Its sensory system was seeking out her warm blood! The brilliant light of the moon showed that it was dirty black, without question a water moccasin.

A squeezing pressure that clutched Effie's insides made it hard to breathe, but to succumb to panic would be sure death! The moment of frozen fear passed, replaced by frantic reasoning; she realized that she had but moments to react. Time! Time! If she just had time! She suddenly remembered the rock she had pushed aside to make herself comfortable, knowing that she could not grasp or lift it and hope to win with the snake suspended in the air. Even if she had a stick, she doubted that she could maneuver it accurately.

Yes! That was it! If she could reach the limb the snake was on, pull it down and release it, it might fling the monster to the ground with enough impact to daze him until she could get the stone. It was worth a try!

She thrust herself into a sitting position, graduating to an awkward kneeling stance and reached for the limb. *"Oh, hands, please do work right just this once,"* she implored. Carefully, carefully, with singular concentration, she aimed the curved fingers of her right hand for the grasp, ready with her left hand to knock the fingers loose if they should lock. Then grab she did, flipping the snake to the rocky ground below with stunning force!

Now, neither fighter nor foe were idle. Effie wrapped her awkward hands around the heavy rock. To lift it required every ounce of her leaking strength. The venomous creature opened its lethal white-lined mouth, the epitome of a miniature death angel from the tombs.

A new emotion boiled in Effie's being. It was anger! How dare that wicked beast to attack her! What right had he to strike? This was her world, too. She had as much right to be here as he did. She had not harmed him; she had provoked him in no way, until *he* became aggressive! The anger gave her a blind determination to win in the battle for her life. Clumsily, she heaved her rock directly at the reptile's head, burying the mini-death angel beneath the hard, cold stone she had thrown.

After killing the snake, Effie sat down weakly and broke into great beads of sweat. Then she lapsed into tranquil unconsciousness. The moon, like a child at play, slid down the velvety wall of sky.

Back at the farm, Dessie had fallen into a restless sleep in the newborn hours of morning, but dreamed of Effie and awoke crying. Martha came checking and scolding, padding back to bed, unhappy about the interruption of her sleep, not sharing Dessie's concern.

When Mr. Gibson's wagon pulled into the yard shortly after daylight, Dessie did not wait to dress. She ran desperately, gowntail flying, to her father's arms, almost incoherent with grief. Henry, heartsick with worry, implored her to slow down and tell him what tragedy had taken place in his absence from home. Joseph, climbing from the tailgate half asleep, stumbled to his bed by way of the open window, missing the scene.

"Effie! It's poor little Effie!" sobbed Dessie. "She's been down et th' river all night long, an' nobody could fetch 'er up th' steep bank. She's there still. Oh, Papa, please! Please- Will'ya *please* go fer Effie? She's so skeert! Please, Papa?"

No parent with human heart could resist such a compassionate plea from a weeping child. "Why, 'course I'll go, Dessie. You jest get on yore dress 'n bonnet an' come along to show me where she is."

Nor had a child ever dressed with more haste. Dessie returned, bonnet strings hanging and sash dragging along behind, before Mr. Gibson had time to turn the horses around. Seeing Dessie's distress, he paused. "Something the matter, Mr. Harris?" he asked solicitously. Henry chuckled; Martha would be *mortified* if a neighbor learned about Effie.

"No, Mr. Gibson," Henry told himself it was not actually a lie. "Nothin' serious. Th' child's pet is missin'— follered 'er to th' river yesterd'y. Wants that I go lookin' fer it."

"I'll give you and the lassie a ride to the river bridge," Mr. Gibson offered, and Dessie was climbing on the tailgate before he finished his sentence. Anything to get there faster!

When Henry had properly "much obliged" Mr. Gibson, he followed Dessie down the slope. But Dessie stopped and wailed in anguish. Effie's sled was empty; Effie was *gone*.

Chapter 7

Illness

"She's gone, Papa! Effie's gone! Somethin' got 'er!"

Henry was a softhearted man. Resurrected from the tombs of yesteryear, a boyhood memory of a lost puppy triggered an empathy for his distraught daughter. Besides, Effie *was* a human being, and even though Martha considered her "not very bright," she was the child of his only brother. He must find her! Charles would give his life to find Dessie if the role was reversed.

"Now, now, Lamkin," comforted Henry. "Dry away those tears so's you can see to help me hunt 'er."

Henry studied the sled's surroundings, finding the trail in the gravel disclosing Effie's efforts to drag herself across the bank. When evidence led to the water's edge, Dessie fought hysteria. "Maybe she fell in th' river an' drownded!" she cried plaintively.

"Th' water's too shalla to drown in right here," Henry

told her. "If'n she'd a' fell in, she'd still be here. An' she ain't! Th' water's not swift enough to carry her no-wheres." They followed the tracks made by Effie's rolling body back to the sled.

"Where could she be, Papa?"

Henry's mind searched the avenues of possibilities. *Could a wild animal have taken her body to his lair?* This seemed unlikely since there was no evidence of blood or struggle. On the other hand, the child probably was not capable of resisting any force that came against her.

"We'll find 'er. Don't you worry none." Or was he merely postponing a bitter finale by all this brave talk?

Another spoor led to a clump of vegetation, but Effie, concealed amongst the foliage, was not visable. Verily, it appeared that she *was* "gone" as Dessie had concluded. At last a feeble idea occurred to Henry. "Call 'er name, Dessie," he suggested. "If'n she's sleepin' nearby, maybe she'd hear you, an' make a noise."

Dessie tearfully walked up and down the creekbank, calling, while Henry combed the region for farther clues.

"God knows where she is, Papa. Could we pray an' ask Him to help us find 'er?"

"Why, sure, child!" Henry bowed his head, but Dessie tumbled to her knees on the pebbles. *The girl could not have traveled far, unless. . . .*

Henry saw the snake, its head crushed beneath the rock, and walked toward it, puzzled. Effie began to rouse; someone had called her name from a great distance away! She could scarcely hear them; she had a sensation of being in a hole in the ground with the sound coming from the top. As the shores of reality came into focus, she recognized the voice as Dessie's, but failed to comprehend why Dessie would be calling for her or where she was. She opened her eyes with concentrated effort, seeing only the green leaves above her. She had been sleeping, but she was not in the corner of the room on the quiltbox at Martha's house. How strange! What did it all mean?

Turning her head slowly, she saw the black snake, and remembered. The cottonmouth moccasin! She lurched and gave a distorted cry, like the whine of a wounded animal. Dessie and Henry heard it and zeroed in on her location curtained with greenery.

"Papa! Papa! God answered our prayers!"

The dead viper told Henry the whole horror story. Poor little tyke! What a battle she must have fought! To be victor in such a combat for her life, the child certainly must have more intelligence than Martha gave her credit for. Dessie, overjoyed to hear the weak cry, disregarded the black monster, dead or alive, and flung herself down beside the reclaimed Effie, smothering her with reassurances.

"I'm so sorry, Effie! Papa jest now got home to come git you. I prayed all night long that God would watch over you. I'm so glad He did!"

Henry gently lifted the frail form from the bushes and carried her home, with Dessie trailing the empty sled behind. Martha, having suffered a disturbing night fighting both her conscience and sleeplessness, was still snoring when they arrived at the farm. She never asked how Effie managed to get home; indeed, she chose to ignore the subject. "The Will Of God" did not work out quite as she had planned that it would. She was still burdened with Charles' illiterate child.

Dessie hastened to bring Effie a drink of water, holding the cup to her parched lips, then returning to the cupboard for bread and jelly. "Poor little Effie. Yore most nigh starved," she fussed, mother-like. If guardian angels were sent in the form of seven-year-olds, here was one.

Effie's disturbing nightmares did not cease for several weeks; she was unable to sleep the night through without agonizing fright. When she cried out, Dessie slipped from her bed and patted her until she was calm again.

Fall came, restoring the beloved reading lessons, hated haircuts, and tolerated Dessie-absences during school hours. V-shaped formations of honking geese flying south warned of an early winter, unusual for Central Texas. When it blustered in, dressing the world in dazzling white and hanging frozen crystal teardrops from the trees, Effie could never remember being so cold! The quiltbox, emptied of its contents, failed to provide enough quilts to suffice, and thus divested of its volume, made Effie's sleeping quarters even colder. Effie started out with two of the priceless commodities of warmth, but was disfurnished when one of the "reg'lar Harris children" complained of the bitter chill in the house. Effie felt sure she would have frozen to death had she not been in the corner of the room that housed the fireplace, the faint radiation of dying embers reaching her berth.

How she escaped catching her death of cold was nothing short of a miracle. She shivered and shook until her bones ached and her teeth hurt from the frigid air. A plea for more cover was sent from her icy lips to a God she did not know. When the snow piled high against the windows, she longed for but one hour of summer's warmth to escape winter's prison.

Dessie heroically shared her flannel petticoat with Ef-

fie. "I know you must be nigh to freezin'," she sympathiz-
ed. "Wish I had a bed o' my own, an' I'd give you one
o' my own quilts. But Sarah would surely miss a coverlet
an' squeal to Mama. Then I'd be in trouble shore."

"Y-yes," agreed Effie, thankful that someone at least
understood. Dessie wore the warm petticoat in the daytime, and slipped it on Effie at night. It helped some, but
not enough. The biting cold reached through the scant
protection, holding Effie in its miserable grip. Would the
blizzard never end?

Childhood diseases ran rampant that fateful winter.
The chicken-pox made its rounds, starting with William.
Measles came next. Effie patiently accepted the illnesses,
laying in her corner quietly without complaint, trying to
make as little trouble for Martha as possible.

Corked bottles labeled "blue flag root," "hoarhound,"
"witch hazel bark," "snake root," "sassafras," and "blood
root," sitting on Martha's medicine shelf, got a thorough
work-out. She religiously believed in foul-tasting herbs.
Effie hated the taste of them no less than the other children, but when Joseph came with the spoon, she knew
that he had taken her welfare to heart and she trusted
him. She wondered, however, if the disease itself could
possibly be any worse than the medicine.

Effie lost her first tooth during the winter. "Look at
you!" Dessie held the looking-glass for Effie, not wanting to risk any chance of the mirror being broken, bringing Martha's superstitious seven years of bad luck. "You
look jest like yer teacher now!" Dessie already had both
front teeth missing, and the sensation of being "just like
Dessie" left Effie exultant.

Dessie painstakingly wrapped the tooth in an old

89

stocking for her, tucking it away under her thin pillow. When the delinquent tooth fairy had not touched it with her magic wand by the end of the week, Dessie took matters in her own hands. She traded her yellow hair ribbon for a piece of taffy candy at school, and slipped that into the stocking in place of the tooth. Martha missed the ribbon and scolded Dessie soundly for her carelessness, but Effie's joy at finding the candy left by the fairy outweighed any scathing words Martha could have uttered.

One miserable day in January, Dessie came home from school too "tired" to teach Effie her reading lesson. She leaned her head against the bedpost, swept with dizziness. Effie touched her hand; it was hot and her lips were brilliant red, the color extending to spots on her cheeks. Martha put her to bed with a terrible tasting tonic. But the next day Dessie was worse. . .and the next and the next. None of Martha's home remedies were working.

Martha grew panicky. When a malady lurked near her habitation, she went on a speedy soul-searching expedition. Was God punishing her for something? Had she inadvertently erred in some way? Was she slacking in her prayers? Had she missed too much church lately? Ironically, her cold attitude toward Effie was not given any consideration in these deep searches.

Henry caught a ride into town with Mr. Gibson for medicine from Dr. Brooks, but the medication did nothing to alleviate Dessie's symptoms. Her weight grew lighter, her wrist pulse fluttered, and she begged for more quilts. She was cross; her voice fretful.

Effie was scared, perhaps more scared for herself than for Dessie. If anything should happen to Dessie, she could never, ever learn to read her Book. "Oh, Dessie, please do get well!" She yearned to say the words aloud. "And if anyone must die, let it be me!"

Still Dessie's condition worsened. She tossed, moaned, and muttered on her bed. Martha sent word to Dr. Brooks to please come at once, and waited with trepidation for his arrival. And just before the early winter sundown, the crunch of wagon wheels on the frosty ground in the yard announced that he had come. Effie was shuttled out of the front room, but lingered near a doorway to hear the "verdict."

Dr. Brooks, swamped with similar calls and cases, shook his head wearily. "A regular epidemic," he sighed. "We can only hope for the best—and pray. I suspect pneumonia in this case." He left a sedative. *Pneumonia.* That awful word. The child killer. Effie cried silently, enchained in sorrow, while her cherished teacher and friend walked through the valley of the shadow of death.

Dessie's fever was stubborn and the remedies slow. Her heart throbbed slower and slower; life was running out breath by breath. The death angel and Dessie's guardian angel fought at the foot of her bed, each determined to win. Martha kept the hot water bottles (as well as her heart search) going constantly, rubbing Dessie's inert feet and hands to help "circulation," muttering snatches of prayers.

Effie's broken heart again implored the God she had never met to spare Dessie, her only hope for an education and access to the Book's message. Selfish request though it was, an angel of mercy doubtless bore it to heaven's portals, for slowly, slowly the fever abated. After hopscotching in and out of consciousness for many days, Dessie opened tremulous eyelids and called for Effie. Effie struggled to her side and touched her hand; it was damp with sweat, the fever gone. Martha, relieved to the point of tears and wishing to humor Dessie, allowed Effie to stay beside her. Effie tried crudely to tuck the covers about Dessie's feet with little success; Dessie understood and smiled wanly.

"I-I n-no doc-tor!" Dessie comprehended Effie's attempt to speak.

"I think my spine is most nigh worn clean through, Effie," she said. "I been bathed most threadbare, an' I'm tired to death o' beds! Wisht it would rain mud on me an' get me plum' streaky!" Effie laughed. It was easy to be happy now that Dessie had taken her hand from death's doorlatch at last.

The weather had warmed appreciably, along with Martha's spirits. The whole dreadful incident that happened that afternoon was a slip-up on Martha's part. Gertie Clark had heard through her niece, the substitute schoolmarm, that "one o' th' Harris younguns" was at the point of death. And since she was a member of the newly appointed visitation committee to visit the ill churchfolk of the community, she deemed it her obligation to pay a call to the Harris farm. She took her position seriously. . .and haughtily. The visit, too, might enlighten her on the problem "twixt Henry an' Martha Harris."

Martha was expecting no one, least of all Sister Clark, when the knock came at the front door. No noisy wagon or horse's whinny had forewarned her of a prospective caller. She had not even heard steps on the front porch. Sister Clark squeezed past Martha and entered the sickroom before Martha had presence of mind enough to hide

Effie from her view.

"Jest came to call. Heared that one o' yorn were turrible sick," the large, pushy deacon's wife expostulated, as if reciting her memory work. "I'm on the committee fer. . ." her voice spun to a thin thread and broke off, knotting in midair when she saw Effie standing statue-still beside the recovering Dessie who was still abed.

"Who? . . .What?" Gertie Clark's mouth dropped open. The object of Gertie's shock dawned on the horizon of Martha's befuddled mental processes with a sudden jolt.

"I. . .I didn't know you had *that*. . .er, her, I mean. . .what a *pity*!" lamely finished the accusing Gertie with a wise, knowing look.

Flustered, Martha felt she must offer some explanation for Effie's presence in her home. Without premeditation, she had no time to conjure up a credible story.

"Unfortunate, yes," Martha agreed, with downcast countenance, realizing that the secret of the "cursed child" would be out through the lips of the church gossip. "That's Effie, the child o' my husband's lawless brother."

Gertie Clark misinterpreted Martha's embarrassment, and showed even more dismay. "Then you are openly admittin' to me, Sister Harris, that this child was born of sin?"

"By all means! Why should I deny somethin' so fer certain?"

"Seems to me you'd at least try to hide it."

"Thet's what I've been doin' fer more'n five years now."

"But, Sister Harris, I'd 'a never thought it."

"Well, you might do me a favor to keep it quiet." Martha's anger was rising. She had never been fond of the deacon's overweight wife anyhow, and today's visit was doing nothing to add points to Gertie's score sheet.

"God always punishes them who sin, don't He?" Gertie's voice was preachy and she looked directly at Martha who made the mistake of dropping her eyes.

"Thet's what th' Good Book says. Jest sorry I'm th' one havin' to raise a product o' sin. . ." Martha was obviously still confused.

"Had'ya thought perhaps thet's th' reason th' t'other one's been so sick?"

"Oh, no. It has nuthin' to do with my Dessie, I'm sure."

Gertie was not through with the interrogation. She now had the verbal reins, chauffering the chariot of conversation with Martha as her passenger. "What happened to th' father. . . Brother Harris's wild brother?"

Martha, her sixth sense out of commission, fell right into the tattler's trap. "He was in New Mexico when Effie was born, but went to Californy, an' hain't never been heared from since."

Sister Clark clucked her tongue in a shame-shame sound. She had found the "skunk in the woodpile." Now maybe Deacon Clark *and* Pastor Stevens would believe her when she told them trouble was "a-brewin." She had her guns loaded with scandal and was ready to get away from here and fire them.

"I'm sorry fer yore illnessess an' misfortunes, Marthy Harris, but th' way I see it, you deserve it all if'n what you told me is true," she said, pressing her bulky frame out the front door, and flouncing arrogantly off across the yard.

Martha stood staring after Deacon's Clark's heavy

wife, perplexed. She had addressed her as "Marthy Harris" instead of "Sister Harris" when she departed. Was that an unofficial disfellowshipping from the church? Gertie had obviously left offended, and it all seemed to center around Effie. She had actually given little attention to sick Dessie, the professed purpose of her visit. Whatever could be the matter?

Perturbed, Martha tried to reconstruct the previous conversation in search of answers. Sister Clark had entered abruptly, announcing her reasons for the call. . . she had then mentioned being on some sort of committee . . .then she had seen Effie standing by Dessie's bed. Of course, seeing Effie was unsettling. Martha could well remember the first time she saw the thwarted child. . .the chilling feeling of something iniquitous. . .that was understandable. She could not blame Mrs. Clark. Then something in the deacon's wife's beady gaze had made Martha speak up. Let's see now. . .she had told her that Effie belonged to the wayward Charles. Sister Clark seemed taken aback that Martha would admit that Effie's mother had undoubtedly been a sinner. . .and she had asked why Martha did not conceal "it," and Martha said that she had tried to keep "it" a secret all these years. The deacon's wife had asked so many nosy questions. Why, none of them were any of her business, anyhow! The very idea! What did it matter who had brought Effie to Texas?

Martha's heart froze in horror! Supposin' Sister Clark misinterpreted Martha's information. . .supposin' she thought. . . .oh, but she *couldn't* have! She could not have possibly presumed that Effie was *her* child, fathered by Charles, could she? Standing in the doorway, with Gertie a vanishing speck in the distance, Martha's face turned from red to white. Martha had failed to mention anything about Rebecca. How stupid of her!

Should she run after Sister Clark and try to straighten out this awful mess? But then, what if the deacon's wife thought no such thing? She would think Martha was accusing her of evil surmisings. Then Martha would be churched for sure. Oh, what a miserable situation!

Martha's mind was a jumble. The only logical thing to do, she concluded, was to keep Effie safely out of sight so that any rumors would spread no farther. And it might even be wise to stay out of public view herself until she was certain what would come of today's visit. One thing for sure, Martha was most unhappy with the "Marthy Harris" coolness that emanated from the church's foremost gossip. Days of mental chaos followed.

It was spring before the last trace of illness departed the premises. Martha had the excuse she needed for evading Deacon Clark's wife and the public eye; sick children kept her home from church. It had been a trying winter for Martha. But Effie had survived the harsh, cold winter and was learning to read some nice, big words!

Chapter 8

Sunday Meetin'

"*T*is chicken today an' feathers tomorrow!" piped wizened little old Brother Rogers. His ample wife threw him a loaded look and he caught it, muttering nonplused, "Looks never killed nobody!" The henpecked man's wit and humor never failed to intrigue Matthew, who made it a practice to be within hearing distance at church gatherings like this one.

Fifth Sunday dinner-on-the-grounds needed no formal announcement; these eat-togethers were an immutable tradition of the Brazos Point Community Church. "How many fifth Sundays are they this year?" was Robert's first question when the new almanac arrived at year's onset. Counted and marked months in advance, these magic days meant a feast of plenty after the morning service.

Benches, pulled from the interior of the sanctuary,

were lined up face to face in the yard (weather permitting) to hold the stockpile of goodies. Myrt's cobbler, Gertie's sour dough bread, Martha's white leghorns, and Sister Stevens' dumplings evaporated into the chipped ironstone plates.

Even though Martha had not been to church for months now, when May's Sunday number five arrived, she sent her contribution as usual so that her family could honorably enjoy the church social.

"Mama sent this here food," Sarah bore the heavy platter of fried chicken to Gertie Clark, while Robert held the pot of hominy.

"Why didn't she come 'erself?" Gertie gave Sarah a cold look of scrutiny.

"She had to stay home with Ef-. . .uh, we think Dessie might be prob'ly takin' th'. . .th' *itch*." Slow of thought pattern, Sarah mouthed the first thing that entered her mind. Robert punched her with his elbow and frowned.

"Tutt-tutt," Gertie Clark scorned.

Sarah placed the food on a cloth-covered bench and moved away gingerly. "Mama'll sure be mad about that *itch* story," Robert whispered. "*Itch* is somethin' shameful!"

"She'd a been madder if'n I'd told 'bout Effie!"

Gertie Clark's righteous indignation flared. How long would Pastor Stevens suffer hidden sin to prevail? Today's incident proved that the leprosy was spreading to the Harris children. Martha was actually *teaching* them to lie. Like the Bible said, when the tree was rotten, so was the apples! Of course Sarah, away at school on the day of the house call, did not know that she, Gertie Clark, *knew* her mother's "secret."

Martha's disposition took a turn for the worse with the decline of her church attendance. Her lacerating tongue cut deeper, her warmth toward Effie dropped to a glacial zero on the thermometer of affection. After all, Martha reasoned, she would not be in this mess had it not been for Charles' unwanted child. Her soul became barren and empty, her spirit eroding into deep canyons of bitterness, while the underlying reason for her withdrawal went unconfessed. Henry knew nothing of Gertie Clark's visit, and was sorely troubled. After several months of excuse-making, it became obvious to him that she was purposely evading the House of the Lord. And that was not good.

"Now, Martha, I'm a'goin' to stay home with any o' th' sick 'n ailin' ones the Sunday next an' let you go fer some spiritual nourishin'," he insisted at length.

"Never you mind, Henry. I'm readin' my scriptures an' prayin' right here at home on th' Lord's Day. You are th' one what's supposed to be th' spiritual leader 'o this house, anyhow."

"But folks keep askin' . . . ."

"I'm not respons'ble fer what folks ask er think. I'm mindin' my own business an' they can mind their'n!" Her voice rankled with gall.

Henry found the load of the family's spiritual health weighing heavy upon his shoulders. He had always believed that the salvation of children took a united effort, and sensed that, trudging the path alone, he was losing ground. Dessie found various and sundry complaints to stay home with Effie, and since the winter of her close brush with death, Martha had become lax in disciplining the child.

No one would have thought of taking the "Harris seat" at church. Their name was so indelibly branded on it that open theft would have been a greater crime than taking another's pew. Henry lined his offspring up on the wooden bench beside him. Sarah, in her mother's absence, sat between Matthew and Robert in an effort to keep them from talking or pinching during the lengthy sermons. One or all of the "President's Boys" took to the pallet and slept through the whole of it.

Pastor Stevens gave little regard to the needs of the children of his congregation, expecting them to function spiritually as adults. Indeed, the newly formed Sunday School Union ired him. "The Scripture says 'tis for you and your children," he quoted. "That means the same gospel is for both ages. It never said anywhere to split up families and teach adults and children in separate groups. I don't read where Jesus separated the children from the rest when He taught the Sermon on the Mount. Children should worship with their parents, so the parents will be responsible for behaving them. There won't be no 'classes' in my church as long as I'm the pastor!"

Childless Deacon Clark agreed with him wholeheartedly. "Sunday School is of th' devil!" he thundered. "When th' church goes modern, th' church goes to hell!"

Since Martha's hibernation, Joseph made a habit of slipping out of church while all heads were bowed for prayer. With dismissal time memorized to a fine art, he slipped back in while heads were bowed for the benediction. Aware of the problem, Henry was hesitant to question where he went or what he did during the church service. After all, Joseph was "approachin' seventeen" and Henry figured, "If'n we ain't done our homework on 'im, 'hits too late now."

For months, the music in Matthew's bloodstream drew him to the fine old ornate organ. As antiquated as the organ itself, "Sister Myrt" sat on the round swivel stool Sunday after Sunday, pumping away at the stiff treadles.

"Don't know what keeps Sister Myrt from havin' leg cramps, the way she pedals that thing," Matthew whispered to Sarah.

"She 'ort to have plenty of muscles by now. They say she's been playin' it fer nigh on to forty years," Sarah whispered back, anticipating a snap of Henry's fingers to gesture silence. The wheeze of the organ saved them.

"What keeps her legs from gettin' tangled up in her skirts?"

"I dunno."

One Sunday after church, Matthew made his way to the front where Sister Myrt was folding her ineffective music; she could not read a note, playing entirely by ear. Matthew supposed the music was there to make an impression. "How old are you, Sister Myrt?" he asked, probably the most tactless subject he could have chosen.

"I think, young man, that is none of your business," she retorted, forgetting the good blessing she had received during song service.

"I was jest wonderin' if'n you was ever gonna retire. Thought I might apply for yore job." Matthew's fingers had been telling him that he could play the instrument, and he was "hankerin' " to give it a try.

Sister Myrt considered herself absolutely indispensable and the thought of someone usurping her role had never crossed her mind. Now a mere slip of a kid was threatening her position! Never fond of Matthew, she liked him even less.

"Nothin' but a *sissy* boy would *ever* play an organ!" she spat. Her ruse worked. Had the musical apparatus been a viper, Matthew would not have shunned it more. From this moment on, he diverted his attention from the hymns to the preacher's blond-haired daughter, Pauline.

Neighbor Gibson's freckle-faced teenage son, who sat two seats up from the Harris row, was included in Sarah's "watchin' and prayin'." A study of the headstones in the cemetery outside also helped her "endure to the end."

Only sermons about animals held Robert's attention. His mental pictures were colorful during the dialogues of the prodigal son's pigs, the dogs that nursed the poor beggar at the rich man's gate, the sheep rescued by the shepherd, the little spoiling foxes, and the talking donkey. But when the preaching settled down to Paul and Silas, the whinny of a horse or barking of a dog outside drowned out the sermon. "I'm glad God included animals in His Book for Brother Stevens to preach about sometime," he told Henry. "If I was a preacher, I'd preach about them every Sunday."

William was never bored with the preaching, whatever the text; he lived for it. The preliminary parts of the service might find him talking, wiggling, or turning, but when preaching time came, he sat entranced. Had Henry allowed it, William would have been Pastor Steven's most avid "Amen-er." Parsons Stevens, not overly fond of any children save his only child, was partial to William. In William, he had an admirer and it boosted his ego. William committed to memory many of Brother Stevens' favorite scriptures, and had asked permission to be baptized.

"You have to wait 'til you're twelve years old," Martha insisted. "Twelve is th' age of 'countability with God." Her notion, unsubstantiated by chapter and verse, was never contested.

When Dessie infrequently went to church, she enjoyed the testimony service best. "Everybody got to preach a little bit," she said to Effie, "an' many o' them can out-preach Brother Stevens!" Some of the more repetitious testimonies were familiar to Dessie; when certain ones got up, she knew exactly what to expect. She had, in fact, composed a speech of her own and tried it, fully expecting Sarah to pull her back down to a sitting position. During a very short lull, she jumped up and said it real fast: "I love th' Lord tonight, 'cause He first loved me." She sat down abruptly, and felt the color crawl up her neck and splash all over her ears. She had said "tonight" and it was daytime! She would never "testify" again!

Henry, not a demonstrative Christian like Martha, was sincere and worshipful. "He has a whole orchard o' th' fruit o' th' spirit compared to Martha's blighted harvest!" Gertie told the deacon. This shining truth could not be tarnished by its bearer, but the deacon felt threatened by Henry who was appointed by Brother Stevens to be part-time usher. It was his duty to pass the collection plate in the absence of Deacon Clark, and the deacon made sure that was seldom. Like Sister Myrt, Deacon Clark mortally feared loss of position.

The collection of tithing distressed Henry. Martha's method of figuring earnings at the Harris household never left any "profit" to pay tithes on. Henry's idea would have been to take the Lord's part off the top, but evidently Martha's view was taking it off the bottom, with the bottom of the family's purse missing.

And so Martha stayed at home each Lord's Day, fighting her battle with no weapons. Henry attempted in vain to put the puzzle together, becoming more confused when he found a piece missing. At one time, he was sure that Effie was the problem, but he had offered repeatedly to stay home with Effie and let Martha attend the services and she had refused his offer time and again. Convinced that he was not seeing Martha's inner linings, only the outer wrappings, Henry grew all the more perplexed. He struggled on in a cloud of turmoil.

The parson never missed asking about Martha and whichever child happened to be ailing, and requested that the congregation have special prayer for her and the sick one. But after many absences, he began to question the excuses. Something did not ring true. What was amiss in the Harris home? Being pastor, he must make it his business to find out where the "sin was hidin'."

Chapter 9

Pastor Stevens' Visit

"You say, Sister Clark, that you suspect *sin?*"

Pastor Stevens began his investigation at the worst possible source. Sister Clark was head of the visitation committee and she should know if the illnesses in the Harris household were authentic or supposed. Blanketed in her best holier-than-thou atmosphere, Gertie Clark hinted of sin in her initial sentence.

"I'd never be guilty o' confidin' secrets to nobody on earth," she said piously, "but pastors have a right to know about problems that are disturbin' th' whole o' th' flock."

"Of course, Sister Clark." Pastor Stevens fidgeted, waiting for her to get to the point.

"Th' matter's so delicate 'n touchy, I didn't know if'n I should come direct to you with it er keep it to myself in prayer, but in the future, I'd be happy to bring things straight to your attention if'n you want. . . ."

"In the event of a soul straying, that might be the best." Each of Pastor Steven's sheep meant fleece, and although Martha had never been a financial asset, her nickel a month did help some.

Sister Clark lowered her eyes and fumbled with her hands sensationally, setting the stage to open the curtain on her dramatics. "Pastor, there's *definitely* sin."

"In what form, Sister Clark?"

Gertie feigned embarrassment. "Well, you see, pastor. . .ah, er. . .there's a child o' sin in the home that none of us knowed anything about."

"Where did you get your information, Sister Clark?"

"I *personally* visited th' home, Pastor. I *personally* saw th' child."

"But Sister Clark, with so many children, why would another. . . ?"

"Th' child is one of those kind, Brother Stevens. A product o' sin."

"I'm sorry, Sister Clark, but I don't hold with the general idea that all sickly or deficient children are products of infidelity."

"Oh, but pastor, you haven't heard me out."

"Then kindly explain your unusual conclusions."

"I asked Sister Harris. . .ah, Marthy. . .about th' child, an unfortunate little girl."

"And what said she?"

"She said that th' child was fathered by a wild, immoral brother-in-law of hers," Sister Clark faked reluctance to share such shameful tidings.

"You mean she admitted to the sin of adultery?"

"She did. With Henry's younger brother. And without remorse, it seemed to me."

106

"And she has tried to hide her sin?"

"She told me that she had tried to keep th' birth of th' child a secret for th' past six years."

"I don't understand. . .no one would have known that the child did not belong to her and Henry. Why did she feel she must. . .?"

"Reveal it to *me*? I couldn't answer that, but she asked me not to tell nobody. But I actually didn't make her no promises. . . ."

"Sister Clark, this is a very serious charge."

"Yes, sir, it is! Don't you know it has weighed on 'er conscience all these years? And she knew that if people saw th' child, they'd know. And *I* was th' unfortunate one to discover her sin, quite by accident. I had gone to make a simple sick call like my job with th' church calls for. It amazes me that Marthy was able to come to church an' shout. . . ."

"Perhaps she feels forgiven. I read in the Bible where Jesus forgave an adulteress. He that's forgiven much loveth much."

"Forgiven? She didn't so much as mention repentance for her ungodly deed. Paul said 'godly sorrow worketh repentance,' but she wasn't one bit sorry. She's a genuine hypocrite if ever I met one. Why, pastor, it's a wonder God ever blessed our little flock a'tall with such a flagrant sinner sittin' right in our midst actin' sanctimonious. Why, it's a wonder to me God didn't strike Marthy dead. It's a wonder. . . ."

But Pastor Stevens had heard enough. A visit to the Harris home in the immediate future was a must. If Sister Clark was prevaricating, which he feared she had a tendency to do, he would have to deal with *her*. He groaned.

Being a pastor was not always a pleasant task.

Martha got wind that the pastor was coming; the news leaked through by way of the pastor's blond-haired daughter. Matthew was elated, hoping the preacher would bring the girl along. He had a glad eye for Pauline.

Martha had been both expecting and dreading the visit, but decided to make the most of it in an effort to convince the pastor of her virtue as a Christian, wife, and mother. She put on her best saintly front. Forewarned was forearmed her Paw always said. She made her sought-after cinnamon rolls, and donned her prettiest apron keeping a nervous watch on the sinister sky.

The clouds were banking in the southwest like smoke from a recalcitrant forrest fire. Under normal conditions, Pastor Stevens would have scrapped his visitation plans on such a stormy night, but Sister Clark's report had eaten at his peace of mind like termites.

Off the kitchen, Henry built Martha a narrow pantry in which to store her flour bin, sugar barrel, and other cooking supplies. It had one small high window for ventilation and was curtained off from the rest of the house by a heavy muslin drape. This room, just wide enough for a cot, was Effie's "hideout" when company came. Martha could chance no more experiences like the one with Gertie Clark; her nerves would not bear the strain.

Immediately after supper, Martha moved a cot and quilt into the stifling pantry. It was sultry and Martha propped the small high window up with the stick she used to punch her clothes in the washpot, allowing fresh air that smelled of rain from the approaching clouds to pour into the tiny branch of the kitchen. Then she explained to Dessie, thinking it useless to explain anything to Effie, that this would be Effie's "room" for the duration of the evening until the parson took his leave.

"I'll stay with Effie," Dessie offered.

But Martha set her foot down. "Pastor Stevens will want to visit you, too, since you are one o' his church members." This made no sense to Dessie, since the pastor had ignored her all these years. "An' you're to make no mention o' Effie durin' th' pastor's visit," she warned, leaving Dessie to wonder why.

Effie rather liked having her own room. She decided it would not be a bad idea to have this room all time. The light faded early, the afterglow of sunset curtained behind the approaching clouds. The drumming of thunder echoed in the distance. Martha lighted the coal oil lamp. The flicker of flame teased by the wind cast clandestine shadows on the muslin curtain and Effie chuckled at the drama. She was having fun! It would suit her if the parson would come more often.

Effie heard Pastor Stevens when he arrived. Did he bring Pauline, his beautiful daughter that Dessie told her about? Or quiet-as-a-mouse Mrs. Stevens? Effie's hearing was acute and nought but a thick curtain stood between her and the rest of the house. No, Pastor Stevens did not bring his daughter; he was alone. Matthew would be disappointed! Effie had no way of knowing that he had purposely left his family behind, not wishing to expose them to the evidences he hoped his visit would produce.

Martha fussed about, hostess-like, making the pastor comfortable. She apologized for her long abstention from church services and the sermons which she knew were most edifying and well-delivered. She served the delicious rolls on her best ironstone saucers.

Pastor Stevens looked about furtively, confused. "Are all the children well?" he asked, and Martha presented them to him properly. Then he had an idea; he would ask Henry to show him the house, with its bedrooms. Thus, he would discover the disabled child abed in one of the adjoining rooms.

"I see you've added to your house," he congratulated. "I'd enjoy seeing the additions, the fruit of your labors." He hoped his voice was matter-of-fact.

The Harris homestead was an unpainted wooden structure with many appendages, malignant with lean-tos that had been added on here and there to house the growing family. Henry was not the most famous carpenter in Bosque County and the whole affair faintly resembled a woodpile that had fallen and sprawled. After the treacherous winter with its near-death illnesses for the children, Henry had hurriedly added a second stone fireplace, though winters of long duration were rare. The three older boys' sleeping quarters were shifted to the remodeled loft, easing the main floor congestion.

"Be glad to show you around!" Henry offered eagerly, needing no forethought. "Martha, hold th' lamp fer Pastor an' myself. He wants to see our humble abode." Martha cheerfully brought the lamp, calling attention to the new fireplace and explaining which bedroom belonged to whom.

Pastor Stevens felt a wee bit deceitful; it was not the "abode" he wanted to see at all. And after the thorough tour, he was even more baffled. There was not a shred of evidence that Sister Clark's story was true! And she had been so convincing! Would the head deacon's wife deliberately make up such a character-smudging untruth?

And what would her motive be? Jealousy? Envy?

When the kitchen was inspected, no attention was called to the pantry, and Effie, comfortably cloistered, spent her time watching the gathering clouds, making no exposing sound.

Pastor Stevens had another idea. "Nine children must be a great blessing," he said, watching closely for hints of a blush of shame on Martha's countenance. "I am blessed with only one, and the deacon has none."

Martha did not redden, and Henry responded guilelessly, "Yes, we're thankful for nine healthy olive plants— though sometimes we have to *prune* them." He laughed easily, no trace of guilt inhibiting his humor.

So that settled it. Henry and Martha were not having marital problems, Martha had carried on no affair with Henry's trespassing younger brother, there had been no infidelity on the part of either. The children were honest-to-goodness sick every Sunday. With that many children and the rampant illnesses of the past dreadful cold, that was plausable.

Then what about Deacon's Clark's wife and her ungoverned tongue? Her slander must be stopped! Martha must never learn of it! Pastor Stevens did not admit it to himself, but he would rather have faced blatant sin head-on than confront Sister Clark with the lie she had told on this good Harris mother. Trouble was bound to arise from a confrontation and Deacon Clark was the church's best tither! Pastor Stevens' mind was churning so that he could scarcely attend to what Henry was telling him. "Martha an' th' children come first, but now that th' house is expanded, I hope to be able to get me a team an' wagon come fall."

111

Would he have another cinnamon roll, Martha was asking politely. "Uh. . .what's that, Sister Harris?" Yes, he believed he would. He'd never tasted better. Martha thought he must be very mind-weary indeed.

"Sounds awful weathery out, Papa," Joseph said. The storm was raging violently outside before Brother Stevens' senses were aroused to it. The tempest in his soul overpowered the natural elements. He was hardly aware that the wind shrieked, rain pelted in irregular gusts, and a deafening clap of thunder announced that the fierce front had arrived.

Effie had been watching the fireworks in the sky for an hour. The lightning cracked across the black heavens like breaking ice, splintering in all directions. The air was humid, heavy with danger. Fright had crept upon her gradually and now she cowered on her cot, afraid to stay where she was and afraid to leave. On the scale of trepidation, she feared the wrath of Martha more than the wrath of God.

Presently, above the immense roar of the storm, she heard Martha's urging. "We must get to th' cellar quick, Henry! I think it's a tornado!" She peered out at the boiling clouds, intermittently pointed out by the crooked fingers of lightning.

Pastor Stevens, imprisoned by the weather at the Harris home, looked about furtively. Martha was urging the children to move toward the back door for a hasty exit to the storm cellar, giving no thought to the occupant in the pantry. But Henry and Dessie had not forgotten about Effie.

"You jest go on," Henry spoke into Martha's ear while the roar grew louder. "I believe I'll stay above ground this time. Th' storm'll blow past in awhile." Martha, near panic, could not fathom Henry's hesitation. "The parson will come too, of course," she offered, thinking Henry might suppose she intended to leave their special company alone. But still Henry objected.

"Henry, I *hear* th' tornado! Hurry!" she implored.

"Take th' children an' go, Martha!" Henry suggested with maddening calmness and a gentle push. "The preacher can go, too, if he wants. If'n a twister takes me to glory, it'll be a fine ride! I'm ready to make th' trip!"

Henry must be getting senile at forty! Well, he could get blown away if he wished, but it was her duty-bound obligation to protect the children, and so she scuttled them off through the drenching rain to the protective underground shelter, a frightened and bewildered Brother Stevens trailing along with them in his utter confusion.

The rain was pouring in the window about Effie in torrents, soaking her cot and coverlet. She pulled herself as far from the opening as possible. Then the hail began, sending marbles of ice bouncing off the windowsill, coming menacingly close to hitting her. A tornado! What had Dessie said about tornados? They were whirling, swirling funnels that took you high into the air, depositing you in a remote place, more often dead than alive. Sometimes the whole house went along with you.

Effie pushed her damp mop of wind-ruffled hair back from her face. Would this be a repeat of the tormenting night on the river? The shifting winds had blown out the lamp, leaving terrifying darkness. The back door slammed shut with finality. The whole family had gone to the cellar, forgetting about her. Effie was unaware that Henry and Dessie had lagged behind and slipped, unnoticed, out of line. When Effie felt a small hand touch her in the dark, she cried out in fear. "It's jest me, Effie," Dessie comforted. "Fer mercy sakes, child! Yore bed is all wet." Effie cried tears of relief.

"I'll call Papa to put down that winder! An' if'n th' old tornado wants to blow us away, we'll jest go to heaven together!"

Henry removed the prop that Martha used to hold the window open, and went for Effie a dry quilt. Dessie, fumbling about in the inky blackness, brought her a cinnamon roll.

"Mama, where's Papa?" whined William when the occupants of the underground shelter were settled into crowded sitting positions.

"Isn't Brother Harris amongst us?" worried Pastor Stevens. He pulled his feet up to spare the trampling of his shoes, but it was useless.

"Henry must still be topside," Martha said, flustered.

Pastor Stevens lived through a one-night eternity. He could only hope that Sister Clark never learned about his stay in the cellar near Martha with Henry elsewhere. But to ask Martha and the children not to mention it would make matters worse, as if he had something to hide. Into what tangle Sister Clark's tongue would twist the facts of this stormy night's lodging if she got wind of it would defy anybody's guess. She had already proved her maliciousness on the unsuspecting Sister Martha Harris.

It was the most miserable night of Brother Steven's life. For a full half the hours spent in the dark, cramped quarters, someone sat on his feet, tormenting his corns. Not accustomed to small children, he was annoyed when the President's boys, missing the comforts of their own bed, whimpered and whined the whole time. The sounds of hail beating on the cellar door was amplified, startling the children, and the entire episode was nothing less than nerve-wracking.

In the semi-darkness, with only a lantern for light, Martha did not miss Dessie at all, supposing her to be "amongst the stuff." Dessie was basically a quiet child. Sarah knew that she had stayed behind with Henry—and knew why—but held her peace, secretly wishing she was in her own bed, too, tornado or not.

As the storm clashed on toward the north, leaving behind a gentle, pattering rain, Effie fell asleep, full of sweet rolls and contentment, and did not awaken until the light of morning tugged at her eyelids and the pastor's voice, sounding strained, was bidding Henry adieu.

Chapter 10

The Book

"*I*'ll fix you some breakfast a'fore you depart," Martha offered, scraping the bowl of her goodwill and finding just enough hospitality to spread to the edges of Pastor Stevens' visit.

"Not wanting to be ungrateful or rude, Sister Martha," he returned, "I beg to be excused. I'm right anxious to get myself home and see what damage the storm may have layed to the church and check on the welfare of my good wife and daughter." The pastor's greatest ambition was to escape unscathed.

She handed him a basket of eggs, depleting her alabaster box of generosity. "I'll thank ye, then, to take these to Sister Stevens."

"My pleasure. And may we count on seeing you in service the Sunday next?"

"I'm perdictin' that 'bout half these younguns'll come

down with the croup after that exposin' night in th' wet cellar, Pastor." As long as Gertie Clark "ruled the roost" at church, Martha had no intentions of returning.

A pastor with no answers took himself home, and life on the Harris farm reverted to its drab pattern of work and sleep.

Henry made a low stoop at the back door with Effie in mind. This she mastered easily, spending the dragging days of summer out-of-doors. "H-how l-long?" she asked Dessie.

"How long to what?"

"S-school!"

"We're 'bout halfway 'twixt th' behind school year an' th' ahead school year."

"O-oh."

The hours until the onset of school were stretching into miles of unbearable forever in Effie's impatient soul until Robert found the brindle-colored female cat, large with kittens, and brought it home with him. The animal made the slow-motion hourglass perform miracles.

"Can I keep 'im, please Mama?" begged Robert.

"He's a *she*, Robert," corrected Martha. "An' we can scarce feed th' useful animals we got, let 'lone a stray cat!"

"But she'll eat mice, Mama. Paw said onct we needed a good mouser."

"Cats causes ringworms."

"I'll fix 'er a place in th' woodshed where there's plenty of mice, an' she won't bother Alan er Chester er Arthur none. I'll see that she don't."

"Looks like she's fixin to multiply."

"I'll give th' little 'uns away to all my friends if you say."

Robert wheedled and Martha conceded, not knowing why and lacking the telescope of foresight to look into the years ahead when she would be forever thankful that she had granted the boy's simple request.

Robert named his cat 'Lasses'n'Butter and introduced her to her new home in the woodshed; she understood and purred her gratefulness for a place to bear her young. Effie hovered nearby, checking on the cat frequently and becoming Robert's cohort.

"I'll give you one of 'er kittens, Effie," he promised. "An' you'll have first pick 'cause yer helpin' me to take care of 'er."

"T-thank you!" A delighted Effie smuggled scraps from her own meals for the feline to add to the mouse diet while Robert coaxed a tin of fresh milk from Bossy each evening.

Effie arose early the following day to see if Lasses had brought her the hoped-for arrival. Here it was again—the sensation she had felt the first day outdoors on the sled. If Lasses did not hurry, there would surely be an Effie-explosion. But Lasses lay quiet and still, asleep.

Fortunately, Effie's patience did not suffer a lengthy test. Lasses had scarcely got her house in order when Effie heard the soft mewing of hungry babies on the third morning as she approached the door of the shed. Effie had never seen more beautiful creatures! How would she choose her child from the fluffs of fur? She stumbled out, finding Robert in the cowlot. "B-babies!" she pointed, and Robert bounded to the shed in running leaps. Effie limped along as fast as her lumbering limbs would carry her.

Three of the five kittens were small replicas of their mother. One was black and white, and the other a downy

gray. With the approval of Lasses, Robert inspected each
of the litter one at a time. He influenced Effie's choice
by dropping the wooly gray baby into her lap; it was deliberate. The kitten nuzzled her hand, becoming a thief
on the first day of life, stealing Effie's heart.

"W-why eyes. . .?" Effie made a gesture of closing
her eyes tightly.

"You mean, why are their eyes closed?"

"Y-yes."

"They were born with closed eyes. They'll open 'em
in 'bout ten days."

"O-oh."

"Whatcha gonna name yer baby, Effie?"

"N-name?" She had never owned anything that
merited a name save her corncob doll that Joseph had
made, worn to shreds long ago.

"Sure. He has to have a name, and he's your very
own!"

"S-socks."

Robert roared his approval. Socks looked for all the
world like Henry's worsted gray socks! "Now I dunno if'n
she is a boy er a girl, but I don't s'pose that matters to
you, does it?"

"N-no."

"Socks will want to stay close to Lasses for a few
weeks til he gets weaned, but someday it'll follow you
'round outside in th' yard."

"O-oh, t-thanks!"

Effie spent rapturous hours in the woodshed watching
the playful litter. In her eyes, Socks was superior in every
aspect. No cat ever boasted a more doting mistress.

Relief from boredom embodied itself in four inches

of squirming appetite, occupying Effie's time and energies. But not even her affection for her lovable Socks could supersede her consuming desire for the fall lessons to begin.

Dessie, more anxious to teach Effie than to learn herself, looked forward to a higher grade. But would Effie have the mental capacity for advanced learning? When the assignments became difficult, could she hurdle the obstacle of retaining in her mind what her hands could not formulate on the slate?

Initially unsure, Dessie's mind was eased when the tougher lessons only served to goad Effie's photographic brain to greater perception. She digested every particle of information Dessie could feed her, searching the empty slate for more. After a few such lessons, Dessie was convinced that Effie was near-genius and had she not been foiled by a hindering body, there was no telling what she could have attained. Dessie was proud of her scholar; she had outdistanced her teacher and was ready for advanced material.

School had been going less than a month when Dessie announced, "I think you're ready for your Book now. Would you like to give it a try?"

"P-please!" The end of a lifetime of waiting came into view.

"I'll tell you what I'm gonna do. When I leave for school in th' mornin', I'll lift it down for you. You can study it all day while I'm gone to school. When I come home, I'll see what you've learned."

"T-thank you!" Excitement sent first hot and then cold shivers through Effie's body. Fourteen more hours. How could she possibly wait until morning to clutch the

Book to her heart—her own mother's Book, sacred and precious? She lay awake far into the starry night. When Dessie first told her about "making a wish on a star," her first wish was to be able to learn to read her Book. "T-thank you," she told the star, for lack of a recipient for her gratitude.

She willed herself to sleep, but tossed convulsively, dreaming of opening the Book and finding big, complex words written in a foreign language, beyond her comprehension. She wept bitterly in the dream, awakening with a start to find Dessie beside her.

"What's th' matter, Effie? Are you sick?"

"B-bad d-dream."

Again she slept and dreamed that Martha banished the Book from her and donated it to the deacon's wife, who was pointing an accusing finger at a page near the center. None of it made sense and daylight brought welcome respite from the nightmares.

"I should keep you home to help me today," Martha told Sarah. "You could at least watch the little'uns." Martha planned to make hominy from dried corn in the old black washpot. The kernels had to be washed again and again to remove the ashes; it was a monumental task.

"But I have a test today," Sarah excused herself.

After breakfast, Dessie slipped the Book into Effie's lap before gathering her books for school. "See how much of it you can read," she whispered.

The busy day for Martha, with time in especially short supply, left Effie and her beloved Book in blissful solitude. With a wildly beating heart that made her temples throb, she opened the pages at random. Actually, the Book seemed to open to the spot of its own accord, as if the leaves were accustomed to spreading here, awaiting the reading of the exposed portion of scripture. Several verses were bracketed with ink, imploring to be read.

Shaking with emotion, Effie let her eyes absorb the printed words: "In my Father's house are many mansions . . ." M-a-n-s-i-o-n-s. Whatever could that word mean? ". . .If it were not so, I would have told you. I go to prepare a place for you. And if I go and prepare a place for you, I will come again, and receive you unto myself; that where I am, there you may be also."

Why, that was not complicated at all! It was very understandable, in fact, except for that one big word. Someone was going away to make a place for the reader of the Book. Just who that Someone was she had not determined yet, but she supposed that she would know more about it when she had read farther. She would mark the place and ask Dessie about that one word; the rest posed no problem. She looked at the top of the page to learn where she was reading. John, Chapter 14. That was simple enough, and easy to remember besides.

Likely her own mother had put the markings there. The verse must have meant something special to her. Was that where she had gone when she left this world? To this place that Someone had prepared for her? Effie yearned to join her there! But first, she would need to find out where the place was located and how to get there.

Ah, here in the Book with a "5" beside it was a person as uncertain as herself. Somebody named Thomas was asked the same question that had bothered her: "Lord, we know not whether thou goest; and how can we know the way?" A good question!

Effie read on feverishly. Printed beside the number

"6" was the answer. "Jesus saith unto him, I am the way, the truth, and the life. . . ." Then this One named Jesus was the solution to the puzzle. Verse fourteen caught her attention: "If ye shall ask any thing in my name, I will do it." She had so much to learn about the Book, about Jesus, and about the place He had gone to prepare! She wished she might read the entire contents of the Book through in one day, but that would be impossible.

"I will not leave you comfortless: I will come to you," the 18th verse said. And Verse 27 was breath-taking! "Peace I leave with you, my peace I give unto you: not as the world giveth, give I unto you. Let not your heart be troubled, neither let it be afraid."

Effie was still reading in the Book of John, stumbling over hard words, pondering the meaning of others, reluctant to turn from the rich and comforting verses that Rebecca had loved and marked, when Dessie came home from school. Effie's eyes were bleary, and her arms ached from holding the Book, but her heart bubbled with joy. She had thought of neither eating nor checking on Socks all day.

"You've read th' Book *all day*?"

"Y-yes."

"You didn't even stop to *eat*?"

"N-no."

"Do you find it that interesting?"

"Y-yes!"

"What's it like?"

Effie placed her hand on her heart. "S-so g-good h-here!"

"The words are not too hard for you?"

"S-some. T-this?"

124

Dessie bent to study the baffling word pin-pointed by Effie. "M-man. . ."

"M-a-n-s-i-o-n. Mansion."

"W-what?"

"I've heard Brother Stevens say it, but I don't know what it means, either. Mama's too busy to ask. I'll write it on my slate and ask my teacher at school tomorrow. She'll know."

"T-thank you!" A whole day lay between her and finding out where her mother lived.

Dessie liked what the book was doing for Effie. Poor little girl! She needed a spark of sunshine in her life! Dessie fell to wondering what would become of Effie when she "grew up" and all the other Harris children were married and gone. A leak in Martha's attitude let Dessie know that Effie's condition frustrated her mother more as time went by. She had overheard words like "demented" and "demon possessed."

"I'll just take 'er to live with me forever an' ever when I'm grown 'an have my own house," Dessie resolved. "An' I wouldn't be a bit ashamed of her. I wouldn't care who saw her at my house, neither! She maybe has a bent-up frame on th' outside, but inside she's all straight! That's better'n bein' straight on th' outside an' all bent up inside any ole day!"

Dessie wrote "m-a-n-s-i-o-n" on her slate and took it to school with her; Effie was still asleep when she left, exhausted from the long hours of laborous concentration. When she awoke, she found that Dessie, not yet habited to handing down her Bible, had forgotten to fetch it from the mantle before she left for school, and the Book lay prone, a recipient of Effie's imploring gaze.

Even Socks did not fill the vacancy that day. The soul-hunger, awakened by a taste of yesterday's Bread, gnawed through the creeping hours. How is it that she felt so empty without the presence of the Book weighing against her frail arms?

At last, Dessie burst in, excited. "I found out about the word, Effie! It's 'mansions' an' it means great big beautiful homes with *ever'thing* you could ever think 'bout wantin' in 'em! They are heaven's houses, all made of gold 'n pearls 'n precious stones!"

"T-they r-real?"

"Oh, yes! More real than this house right here made of brown boards 'n square nails." Dessie knocked on the wall with her fist to emphasize her point.

Effie grew pensive. So her mother went to heaven to claim her mansion that the Book had promised her. Why, she was there right now enjoying her house of gold!

"M-my m-mother t-there."

"Sure she is, Effie! Someday we'll get to see her! Aren't you glad she left you her Book? It's kinda like a map to help you find th' place!"

"O-oh YES!"

A nameless longing overwhelmed Effie—yearning to know what Rebecca was like. If she could have seen her mother's lovely face! How did she look? What was her voice like; how did the touch of her warm hand feel? All she had to remember her by was the mark of a pen in her Book, but oh, that was *something*. . .something tangible. She had not found the picture, hidden in the Bible's flyleaf.

Chapter 11

Matthew's Revelation

"*I* need to have a talk with you in private, Sister Clark."

The more Pastor Stevens tried to unsnarl the tangled threads of Sister Clark's allegations, the tighter the noose looped about his own neck. Martha had not returned to church. Could it be possible that she was aware of the dregs of the cup of mud Sister Clark had stirred? Joseph's interest in spiritual matters was plummeting. He had been such a promising young man, but of late, his seat was mysteriously vacant after the initial prayer.

Pastor Stevens called Sister Clark into conference with all intentions of setting the record straight, avouching Martha's innocence. He was treading on thin ice, reprimanding the head deacon's wife, his counsel being accusatory. A barehanded battle with a live rattlesnake would have been no less dreaded.

"Ah. . .Sister Clark, I notice that our good neighbor, Sister Harris, has dropped from our church attendance altogether. The Bible says if a man be overtaken in a fault, ye which are spiritual restore such an one *in the spirit of meakness*: considering thyself, lest thou also be tempted. I believe that you could help our church by apologizing to our dear and beloved Sister Harris for the. . .er, ah. . .falsehood. . .the Bible says if ye have aught against your. . . ."

"Now, Pastor Stevens, I'll *swear*. . .no, I mean I'll *affirm*. . .that I told you th' truth, th' whole truth, an' nothin' but th' truth, the God of Heaven bein' my unbiased Judge."

"But Sister Clark, I personally investigated the case. Brother Harris, an honest and upright man in all his dealings before God and our community, told me that he had but nine children and all nine of them were properly accounted for in the home during my visit."

"Of course, *he* has only nine children, Pastor! I never said he didn't. But *she* has *ten*!"

Pastor Stevens thought hard, trying to adjust into focus the exact conversation at the Harris home. Come to think of it, it *was* Henry that spoke up about having nine healthy "olive plants" he called them, that needed pruning now and then. Perhaps he did not feel it his obligation to prune Martha's illegitimate ch. . . . No, he must *not* let Gertie Clark predispose his thoughts like this. She was doing exactly as he had determined he would not allow her to do!

He tried again. "It is unfortunate that I am forced to dispute your word, Sister Clark. But I spent a whole night. . .er, ah. . .I meant to say, I called at the Harris dwelling one evening and saw no such child as you depict. In fact, I toured the whole premises, including the cellar!'' Pastor Stevens was unmistakably rattled, almost irrational. His face reddened, agitating him farther.

"Pastor Stevens. . ." It was said with a pitying, mother-soothing-a-child inflection, ". . .the child may have been temporarily housed somewhere else, or sent away for medical care. Had you ever thought of that? I know whereof I speak! I'm sorry this has upset you to such an extent, but I do understand that an errin' sheep is a great trial to a carin' shepherd. In some cases, however, th' strayin' sheep is deliberate in its wanderin' an' wants no help. That's Marty Harris' case I feel safe in sayin'.''

"But I have no evidence other than your word, and the Bible says in the mouth of *two* or *three* witnesses.'' Pastor Stevens relied heavily on the Bible when cornered.

"I'm sorry that you can't believe nor trust th' wife of your head deacon not to tell an untruth, Pastor. An' I realize that 'unconvinced against his will, a man is unconvinced still,' '' quoted pious Sister Clark, probably supposing that she, too, was quoting scripture right from the Bible's pages. "You don't *wish* to believe that sin could escape you for six long years with you not bein' in close enough communion with God that He would reveal it to you. Pastor, it shows carnality on your part.''

The parson flinched; she had hit a sensitive nerve in his very soul. She had voiced aloud the thoughts he had wrestled with for many wakeful nights since the revelation of Martha's "wrongdoing.'' His study, a curtained off section of the parsonage bedroom, had become a battleground of sweat and tears.

"Sister Clark, you are telling me that you *knew* there

was sin before your visit to the Harris home?"

"I genuinely felt it each time I shook Marthy's hand at church for th' past six years! I knew something was wrong. . .and you didn't?"

"Well, not exactly, so to speak."

"You mean you didn't feel an evil spirit when she testified an' when she shouted—like she was trying to cover something up an' was just shoutin' to make others think she was livin' a holy life?"

"Uh. . .well, no, I never. . . ." If word got back to the Harris family that he, Pastor Stevens, labeled Martha with the sin of hypocrisy, the church would lose the entire Harris family, a hard-working, stable unit that for years had been an integral part of the farming hamlet. He was dangerously close to falling into Gertie Clark's trap where she wanted him instead of she in his. How did this happen? *Careful, careful,* he told himself. He detested dealing with women!

"I would suggest that you pray for th' gift of discernment, Pastor. You are sorely in need of it."

"And I would request you to refrain from gossip."

"This is not gossip! It's cold, hard facts that you are refusin' to face for fear of losin' membership. It's what my paw always called a *compromiser.*" The deacon's wife was getting bolder. Conversation this out-of-hand could cost a minister his position.

"Well, I won't entirely close my mind, Sister Clark. I will investigate this thing farther, though frankly, I don't know just now where I will begin to get to the root of it."

"The pitiful child's name is Effie Harris. Marthy asked me to keep it quiet, but since it's come down to my very pastor doubtin' an' questionin' my word, I'm obliged to speak up er be accused of bold-faced lyin'!"

"Now, now, Sister Clark. Let's not jump to conclusions. . . . I wasn't actually accusing you, you understand . . .I was just. . .you know. . .well, I just have to be positively certain in these delicate and reproachful cases. . . ."

"You have the girl's name now. Check all you want to! Good day!"

Gertie Clark was visibly miffed. To what consummation it would reach, Pastor Stevens could not predict. He was certainly in a hornet's nest now! If he must choose between losing the Clarks and their generous tithing and loose tongue, or the large, faithful Harris family who brought no financial rewards, and were reportedly hiding sin, which would he pick? Of course, he might have no choice at all; he might lose them both. Worse than that, he might be the one ousted!

In an unsuspecting moment, he had caught his Pauline flitting her long eyelashes at Matthew at the conclusion of a recent church service. He had considered the personable, popular Joseph as a match for his daughter, but the slow, methodical Matthew, so much like his father, had not crossed his mind.

Matthew. . .there was his answer to this perplexity! He would enlist Matthew's assistance in some small repairs about the church, and. . .why had he not thought of that before?

He announced to Mrs. Stevens and Pauline that Matthew would be taking supper with them on Saturday after a work day at the church, and saw a slight color rise in Pauline's cheeks. Then it was not his imagination!

Matthew proved to be a willing guest, a willing helper.

Pastor Stevens rather liked this diligent worker, built of solid muscle, while sixteen-year-old Matthew deemed seeing Pauline worth any amount of hard work. With muscles straining to get out of the confining shirtsleeves, he sat across the table from her, grinning boyishly. Pauline lifted her intense blue eyes now and then, casting an approving look in his general direction, while the beguiled Matthew could not have told what delicious food was on the table, especially prepared for him by Pauline's silent mother. Pauline's attention was by far more delicious than the table furnishings.

Pastor Stevens, highly pleased with Matthew's skillful work, nonetheless remembered his ulterior motive for soliciting the boy's help. So serious was the matter, that unless Matthew could help him out of his dilemma, Pauline might soon be miles removed to a new parish.

"How's the family, Matthew?" Pastor Stevens began customarily, feeling his way along.

"They're fine, thank you, Pastor," answered Matthew properly in his fine, mellow voice that especially pleased Pauline.

"No sicknesses?"

"None at present, sir."

"Let's see now—you have eight brothers and sisters in all. One older and seven younger. Is that correct?"

"Yes, sir."

This is getting me nowhere, thought the parson. There was no dishonesty to be found in Matthew. He would tell the truth if sure death awaited him for doing so.

"Your family is kind of overbalanced with boys there, isn't it?"

Matthew laughed a rich, hearty laugh. "Yes, sir.

Guess it's kind of hard on my maw, not having more girls to help her out in the house."

"Just two sisters, huh?"

"Yes, sir. Sarah and Dessie. And Dessie's pretty young yet to take much of the responsibility for chores."

Pauline looked at her father strangely. Surely he *knew* how many were in the Harris family as long as they had been in his church! She had never heard her father ask such impertinent questions just to make conversation. Had he forgotten how to relate to young people entirely? She felt she must come to the rescue of her groping father, so she spoke up. "Big families must have lots of fun!"

"It's lots of *work*," Matthew looked into her eyes and hoped the drumming of his heart could not be heard, "but we have our good times, too, of course. I especially enjoy Christmas."

Brother Stevens was still floundering and had eaten almost nothing. "Have some peach cobbler, Matthew."

"It's apricot, dear," from Mrs. Stevens, her first words since her initial hello to Matthew.

"Pardon me," he muttered, nervous and flustered, and Pauline worried that he was ill. Matthew took the pie that was passed to him.

"My favorite pie!" He smiled at Pauline's mother.

Pastor Stevens sat up straight, resolute. He might as well beard the lion in his den and get this thing over with for better or for worse. Let the results be as they might, he could bear this mental torture no longer.

"Do you have a little sister named Effie, Matthew?" Pastor Stevens did not take his eyes off the boy so as to be alerted to any possible deception or embarrassment.

Pauline shot her father a puzzled look.

"No, sir. Effie's my cousin," Matthew answered truthfully, unabashed. Martha might be unhappy, but lie he would not. "She's a cripple and my uncle brought her to live with us when she was about three years old. He couldn't take care of her by himself after her mother died. They lived out west." And then he added, as if to ward off any prejudices, "She's a real sweet little thing!"

Weak with relief, Pastor Stevens rested assured that he had learned the truth about Effie. It would have been his pleasure to hug Matthew then and there, but instead, he asked for a second helping of everything on the table, completely baffling Mrs. Stevens. He had not eaten so heartily for days. Pauline was convinced that fathers were the most complicated creatures of God's creation.

So this was why Martha had been absent from church —to care for a poor, lame niece who doubtless was unable to leave her sick bed to be brought to the Lord's house! Where, oh where, did Sister Clark get the idea that the child was borne by Martha Harris? Just some more of her mixed-up suppositions! If she could not stir up rancid batter and bake it into a lopsided cake, she would never be content!

Pastor Stevens, fortified with his information, was willing for Matthew to depart any time, but Pauline had other plans. The family drifted into the sitting room where her piano dominated the decor. Matthew ran a calloused hand over the smooth, black finish of the musical instrument.

"Do you play it?" he asked Pauline.

"I'm learning. Papa takes me to a tutor in The Springs once a month for my lessons."

"You like it?"

"I love it!"

Pauline shared his love for music; it was too good to be true. Matthew's rough fingers itched to touch the milky white keys. "I've always wanted to learn myself," he admitted.

Pauline sensed his inner longing. "Try it."

"Don't know a thing about it."

"Let me show you. This is Middle C. They're in alphabetical order from A to G. Every other note makes a three-note harmony, like this." She hit the keys of C, E, and G, producing a pleasing sound. Then she played a selection from her music book.

Jumping up, she said, "Here, sit on the stool and try it. Reading notes is no harder than reading words, really. And music is a universal language."

Matthew was her eager pupil, grasping the chords with unbelievable perception. Brother Stevens, amazed, changed his mind about the boy being "slow." Why, this boy had talent! Someday he might make a great musician for the church, replacing the inept, outdated Myrt. Now that he had the Harris problem resolved, he could look far into the future with confidence that he would remain on as pastor of the community church.

More robust boys should take up music; it was not an art for sissies. History's most famous pianists had been men, composers like Mozart, Haydn, and Clementi.

Pauline was at Matthew's elbow, almost touching it. When she bent to show him a new note or chord, her golden hair fell in ringlets about her shoulders and he could smell her intoxicating perfume. Two hours melted away before he roused to the time of evening, announced by the striking of the grandfather clock near the door.

"I didn't realize it was so late!" he said. "I must be getting myself home. Tomorrow is the Lord's Day!" Church had suddenly taken on a new dimension.

He would barely get home in time to do his chores before dark. Martha would scold. But he did not mind today. He hurriedly took his leave, but not before Pauline had invited him back once each month to share her piano lessons. She touched his hand lightly. It could go without saying that his feet hardly touched the ground all the way home.

Chapter 12

A Wonderful Discovery

"*I'*m sorry I forgot to get your Book down from the mantle for you Friday," Dessie told Effie. "I'll try to remember from now on."

"T-thank you."

Dessie did not forget again, and Effie decided that it might be best to start with the very first sentence of the Book and read all the way through to the last word. She might thus better understand its contents, though she doubted anything could be more clear and beautiful than the mansion verse Rebecca had marked.

When the Harris children had left for school, Joseph and Henry for the harvest fields, and Martha to the clothesline, Effie reverently lifted the front cover.

And there, bonded by heat and time to the inside fly-leaf of the Bible, was Rebecca's portrait, smiling up at Effie! Beneath the picture, printed in small calligraphy, were the words: Rebecca Ann Franklin, June, 1872.

"Oh, *Mother, Mother!*" Effie buried her face in the Book's cover and wept. "You did leave me a memory!" She sat spellbound, gazing at the face that smiled at her. "You are beautiful. . .*beautiful!*" Tears of joy obscured her vision of the picture, and she quickly wiped them away with the tail of her dress.

The photograph was clear in every detail; Effie felt as though Rebecca shared the room with her, rejoicing in the happy reunion of mother and child. Her hair was dark and wavy, almost black, and two small bows of ribbon graced it. Her eyes were dark, too, and filled with a dreamy light. A smile played at her lips in spite of the solemnity required by the city photographer. Seated on a couch of velvet, she wore a little light-colored summer dress with dainty lace trim and a flower on her shoulder. Her hands—they must have been tiny and kind and soft, with a touch like silk—were folded on her lap. Very slim and strikingly pretty, she looked quite young. Effie guessed her to be about seventeen years old when the picture was taken.

Time stood still as Effie stared at the daguerreotype, communicating in her heart with the departed mother. Martha's noisy feeding of the three boys in the kitchen did not disturb her reverie; Effie had no appetite for earthly food. Her starved spirit feasted. What would it have been like had this sweet mother lived? There would have been smiles, encouraging words, and a goodnight kiss every night. Life would have been a little heaven on earth.

"Can you see me down here from your golden mansion in heaven, Mother?" she asked in her heart. "Aunt Martha wishes you had lived to keep me or else took me with you. Dessie and Joseph have always been kind to me, and I think I've just found a new Friend since I can read our Book—the Friend that made you the mansion. But I haven't seen Him yet. I hope to see Him soon. I feel better to know where you are, and that He's taking good care of you. . . ." The heart language went on and on, and for the first time, Effie regarded herself as a real girl who once had a beautiful human mother, instead of an insensitive animal underfoot in Martha's way.

No treasure could thrill her more than this one, but might there be other pictures in the Book? Reluctant to divert her eyes from her mother's face, she left the picture long enough to search farther. The next page simply stated in large print: HOLY BIBLE and underneath, Presented to: Rebecca Ann Franklin on: Her 16th birthday By: Mother and Daddy. Effie supposed that her grandmother made this entry. *Grandmother?* A real grandmother?

The print, which she planned to read every word of when her search was through, stopped and started at unsuspecting times. Some books were long and others were short; some were more like poetry. Bottled up elation caused her to want to laugh and cry at the same time.

Near the middle of the thick Book, she found her second surprise, the Family Register. The writing was so delicate that she relegated it to those soft, kind hands in the picture. She tried to imagine those hands holding a pen, carefully and evenly making the entries. Oh, glory! She had a heritage! She had a genealogy! Here was proof before her very eyes:

This Certifies That

Rebecca Ann Frankin
and
Charles Andrew Harris
were united in Holy Matrimony
on the *23rd* day of *July*
the year of our Lord Eighteen Hundred and *Seventy-Two*
by *Rev. W. D. Hollingsworth*
Witness: Mrs. Mary Elizabeth Franklin Browning
Witness: Mr. and Mrs. R. L. Franklin

What charming names! Rebecca and Charles' names belonged together! Now whoever was Mary Elizabeth Franklin Browning? Was she still alive? She supposed that Mr. and Mrs. R. L. Franklin were Rebecca's parents. Were her grandparents yet living? Questions outran the answers in Effie's race for knowledge about her "forgotten" family.

The next page supplied more pertinent pieces to the puzzle, the facts falling together to make a sunshiny scene that lighted Effie's life.

Husband's Genealogy

Name: *Charles Andrew Harris*
Date of Birth: *May 13, 1850*
Date of Death: _____

The rest of her father's genealogy was left blank except for Henry Joseph Harris listed under "Brothers," with no birthdate given.

Wife's Genealogy

Name: *Rebecca Ann Franklin*
Date of Birth: *March 7, 1853*
Date of Death: _____
Father's name: Richard Luke Franklin
  Born: April 6, 1810   Died: August, 1876
Mother's name: Margaret Elizabeth Franklin
  Born: Nov. 6, 1815   Died: August, 1876
Brothers: Johnathan Donald Franklin
  Born: Sept. 25, 1843   Died: Dec., 1864
Sisters: Mary Elizabeth Franklin Browning
  Born: August 31, 1839   Died:

Record of Children

Name: Effie Rebecca Harris
Date of Birth: April 24, 1875   Died:

A birthdate! Effie knew the date of her birth! Now Dessie could celebrate with her! What a loving, thoughtful mother to write it all down. There was room for other children that never came. No entries were made after Rebecca died, and Effie had no way of knowing exactly when that was. Effie was still pouring over the pages of genealogy when Dessie came in from school. One look at Effie told her that a tremendous discovery was waiting to be shared.

"What'dya learn today?"

"B-bout M-mother!"

Dessie laughed brightly. "I know the story of Rebecca is in the Bible. I heard Pastor Stevens preach about

141

it. But it's not *your* mother, Effie. It's Isaac's wife that had the twin boys named Jacob and Esau!"

Effie struggled to make Dessie understand. "M-my mother!"

"Your mother was *named* for the Bible's Rebecca like my mother was named for the Bible's Martha." Effie paused to wonder fleetingly how anyone as unkind as Aunt Martha ever managed to get a good Bible name. Her own mother, a real princess, deserved such a name, but Aunt Martha. . . .

"H-here!" Effie pointed to the tintype.

Dessie caught her breath in a gasp of delight. "Why, Effie, she did leave you a honest-to-goodness picture! How wonderful! Now you can feel like you've seen her for yourself, can't you? You know what she looked like!"

"Y-yes!"

Dessie studied the picture. "Effie, you'd 'a looked just like her if'n you hadn't been all bent out of shape." It was a compliment and received as one. Effie beamed.

"An', lands sakes, she must've been *rich* as a queen! Just look at that garb o' lace! Like right out of a wish book! An' a real *velvet* chair!"

"Y-yes!"

"If she'd a' lived to raise you, Effie Harris, you'd a never spoke to poor little ole Cousin Dessie in her flour-sack dresses!"

"Y-yes I w-would!"

"If your Paw had come back from Californey with all that gold, might none of us spoke to anybody. Th' good Lord knows what's best."

"Y-yes." What Dessie said made sense, but Effie could not help wishing the Lord had "known best" to leave

Rebecca with her suffering child.

"It's a mighty fine photograph, Effie. I can just tell by lookin' that she'd 'a made th' sweetest auntie in th' whole world for me!"

"S-see." Effie turned to the family records in the middle section of the Bible. Dessie, a history buff, was interested in any family tree, hers or anyone else's. The entries fascinated her.

"Oh, Effie!" she cried exhuberantly. "How lucky for you! Your wishing star must've been workin' overtime!"

"Y-yes!"

As Dessie pursued the informative pages, Effie pointed to the unfilled lines of Charles Andrew Harris, her own father. "N-nothing."

"My paw will know," Dessie assured. "Charles was Papa's younger brother, remember. We'll ask him when he comes in from th' field this evening."

"P-please!"

"Look. Your Grandmother and Grandfather Franklin must have died together. Isn't that strange? Both of 'em died in August of 1876, when you were just one year old. Maybe they got killed in an accident er somethin'. It would be kind o' nice to go up to Heaven together with someone you loved, don't you think?"

"Y-yes."

"Johnathan Donald Franklin was your mother's brother. Isn't that a pretty name for a boy? I might like that to name my own boy. Let me get my slate and figure up how old he was when he went to Heaven." But Effie, with her " 'rithmetic brain" had already figured it in her head. "T-twenty o-one."

"Look at the dates. He must've died in th' Civil War.

143

Th' war stretched from 1861 to 1865, remember, an' he was soldier-age. Lots an' lots of soldiers died. Isn't it just too bad, Effie, that nice uncles like Johnathan had to die because some people got mad at some other people an' started fussing an' shooting? I don't know why ever'body can't just *love* ever'body else!"

"Y-yes!"

"Your aunt, Mary Elizabeth, married someone named Browning. It doesn't say here what her husband's name was, so we don't know if'n he's dead er alive. Accordin' to th' birthdates, she was lots older than Rebecca, your mother. Here, let me subtract it on my slate." Again Effie outcomputed Dessie with her capable brain. "F-fourteen y-years."

"She was nigh grown 'fore you mother was even born!"

Effie nodded.

"And it don't say if'n she had any kids er not, so you'll never be able to know if'n you have any Browning cousins."

"R-right."

"Oh, *Effie*! Here's your *own* birthday! Now we can have a party ever' year on April 24! And Effie Rebecca, you now know what your mother looked like an' you even have her *name*! Did you know that your middle name was Rebecca?"

"N-no!"

"Well, you've learned who you are today! An' since Joseph remembers your Paw an' told you what he looked like, you have a whole treasure of family memories!"

"S-so *g-great*!"

"An' we'll find out about our Harris grandparents this

evening when Papa comes in; I'd like to know about them myself."

"O-okay."

Dusk was dimming the celestial lights when Dessie solicited the Harris family history from her father. She waited until Martha began bathing Chester in the tin washtub, heating water in the teakettle on the woodstove to add for Arthur and Alan.

"Effie's history page in 'er Bible is left blank fer her daddy, Charles. Can you tell us about our Grandma an' Grandpa Harris, Papa?"

"There's not much to tell. I was might nigh grown up when Charles was born," Henry said. "We lived on a big plantation way back east. Our mother, whose name was Sarah Ruth, fer whom I named our Sarah, died when Charles was born. Our father, William Joseph, for whom I was named an' we named William an' Joseph, tried to raise Charles hisself. But Charles was a rowdy youngster, always restless, an' I allowed that not having a mother didn't help matters none. Dad grieved fer Mother an' drank too much wine. He finally sold th' plantation to get away from th' memories of her. He gave me my part o' th' money an' I bought this place here in Texas. I don't know what Charles did with his'n. Paw an' Charles kind of roamed 'round, not putting' down no kind o' roots. Charles came by here on his way north somewhere; he didn't know where Dad was an' I supposed he was huntin' him. I don't know where Charles met Rebecca. He never stayed in one place very long. We don't know what ever happened to Paw, whether he's dead er alive, but he'd be most nigh seventy years old by now. I 'spect he's dead."

145

"T-thank you!" Henry jerked his head up with a startled expression. Effie had spoken distinctly!

"I never did see Rebecca, but I always wished that I could have. She must have been a special woman!"

"S-see picture?" Effie shoved the Bible toward Henry. The portrait was inside the front cover.

"Oh! You have her picture? Now I recall Charles sayin' when he left for Californey that there was a picture in th' Bible taken of Rebecca just before he married her—an' that she wanted her child to have it! But I never gave it another thought all these years!"

Henry studied the picture, and Effie thought that a mist clouded his eyes. "What a lovely lady!"

"What's this, Effie?" Dessie found a small, flat weed in the Bible.

"T-trash."

"No, no. It's a pressed flower. That's th' custom with keepsakes. Look! It's a piece of th' flower she was wearing in th' picture. Maybe Charles brought it to her an' she wanted to 'member it forever, so she pressed it between th' pages of her Bible. That's the way Maw does!"

"O-oh!" Effie touched the brittle flower lovingly. Was this actually a fragment of the flower that once lay on her mother's breast? Life suddenly seemed so *real.*

"Th' picture of Rebecca is stuck to th' Bible, but it'll come loose without tearin'," Henry pointed out. "I'll take it out for you an' you can keep it with you when th' Bible goes back to th' mantle for th' night."

"O-oh, t-thank y-you!" *She is really sayin' words,* Henry decided. And a grateful little soul she is. If 'er bent wings could be straightened out, she'd look a powerful lot like 'er gorgeous mother!

Henry carefully removed the picture from the flyleaf of the Bible and handed it to Effie, who clasped it to her heart hungrily with the help of her crooked fingers.

Just before going to sleep, she put it to her lips for a mother's goodnight kiss.

Chapter 13

The Prodigal Son

"Socks is sure growing, isn't he?" Joseph stopped on his way in from the field, stooping to scratch the kitten under the chin.

"Y-yes." Effie sat in the shade of the big white oak; summer's heat had carried over into October. Joseph found her playing with Socks, watching him chase his tail, swat at imaginary objects, and tumble in the fading grass. The opportunity he sought to talk to Effie presented itself.

"Effie, I know life has been hard for you here." Joseph dropped backwards to a sitting position onto the dry grass, circling his knees with his arms. "Superstitions die slow. Mama still holds in her mind to the old law of Moses that sins of parents are visited on their children to the fourth generation. She cannot forgive you for the wrong she believes your mother committed to cause your physical disability. I don't believe it that way. That's dark age ignorance! I hope I live to see the day when all the hogwash about God cursing people with crippled children is forever dispelled. Why would evil spirits want a lame body anyway? Seems to me they could get a whole lot more accomplished through a good, strong, healthy body! Why, Effie, you couldn't even cuss, or dance, or play cards, or hurt anybody! You're as innocent as a mockingbird!''

Effie giggled, amused by Joseph's expressions.

"We don't all live in the same kind of a house. Your body is just the house you live in; it isn't the real *you*. I've seen beautiful houses with wicked people living in them, and I've seen tumble-down shacks lived in by very beautiful people. It's the same with this flesh. The house doesn't really count. It's who lives inside!"

"Y-yes!"

"I'm sure you had a good, Christian mother, clean and lovely."

"T-thank y-you!"

"And I know Mama disliked your father, because when she gets angry with me she says I act just like my Uncle Charles. She says I even look like him. Am I so bad looking, Effie?"

"N-no!" Effie wished she could say that she thought Joseph very handsome, but her language barrier made it difficult, so with her eyes she revealed her thoughts of admiration.

"I declare, Effie!" Joseph laughed. "If everybody communicated with their eyes like you do, we'd have no need for talking at all!"

"T-thank y-you!" Praise from the idolized Joseph was the highest of rewards.

"I'm going to make a trip soon, Effie. I'm eighteen now. I stayed to help Papa through the peanuts and maize; couldn't leave him in a lurch. It's been the best year we ever had. Most of the work is behind and he can finish up without any problems. Matthew is old enough to help out the rest of the harvest. I've been borrowing a friend's horse on Sundays while Papa was in church and riding north to the main stage crossing that runs from Stevenville to Cleburne. I've met a driver that remembers Uncle Charles. He's going to take me out to the old stompin' grounds as he calls it. I want to see where Charles and your mother lived. I need to get going before the weather turns."

"M-miss y-you!" Effie fought back tears.

"I'll miss you, too, Effie, but it's something that's eating on the inside of me. I'll be back someday. Don't you cry now. You just keep you chin up and keep on being brave for me. . . ."

"O-okay."

"And I'll have lots and lots to tell you when I return!" Effie watched him disappear into the back door to wash up for supper, wondering if Martha and Henry knew of his plans. Joseph *eighteen*? It did not seem possible!

Meanwhile, Pastor Stevens, congratulating himself on his profound wisdom in solving the Clark-Harris conflict, called Sister Clark aside to share the good news of Martha's innocence. Surely she would be as gladsome as he to learn that a good sister's name had been exonerated.

"Thank you for your concern, Sister Clark," he began pleasantly, "but I did check farther into the mysterious Harris case, and *finally* got to the bottom of it. The child, Effie, of whom you spoke to me, is indeed a family member. . . ."

"See. Jest like I said!" Pastor Stevens ignored the interruption.

". . .She is a niece of Sister Martha and Brother Henry. Her mother died when the child was very young and the father, unable to care for an ailing child, brought her to Martha."

"And where, Pastor, did you get your information from?"

"From Matthew Harris, a member of the immediate family!"

"Ho! Ho! Just as I thought! Brother Stevens, you are surely th' most easily deceived man I've ever met. 'Tis a most uncomely trait in a preacher! Certainly you must know that this is th' very story Martha has concocted to cover her sin!"

"But Matthew is as honest as. . . ."

"Oh, for a fact, he is, Pastor. How should he suspect that his own mother's story is a falsehood?"

"I believe his story to be true and. . . ."

"Anyone who tries so hard to help a sinful woman dig a grave an' bury her sin when its hand is stickin' out in plain sight, must be hidin' somethin' hisself!"

Brother Stevens shuddered. Gertie Clark had found out about the night in the cellar! How could he absolve himself now?

"But Sister Clark, I. . . ."

"If t'was just *me*, t'would be different. But at th' fifth Sunday meetin' last May, Sister Myrt was standin' right beside me when th' oldest girl, Sarah, told me a mighty coverin' up lie that her mother had told her to say. 'In th' mouth of two er three witnesses' is your favorite candy-stick, an' I've got th' witnesses."

The pastor's respite was short-lived. He put his thoughts in reverse. What had Matthew said? It *was* vague. An uncle brought a crippled child from "out west somewhere." There seemed to be few substantiating facts on either side. Sister Clark fit the Bible's description of a contentious woman; Pastor Stevens was butting his head against a stone wall.

"Just you wait, Pastor. God's judgments will fall on Marthy Harris. She won't get by with these lies forever. Th' leprosy of sin is spreadin'. You can fool man, but you can't fool God. Like I say, judgments is comin'!" Gertie haughtily excused herself.

Joseph chose to leave on Sunday. Martha thought he went to church and Henry thought he stayed home. Before nightfall, he was headed west, following a magnet in his heart.

Martha discovered his absence after dark. Supposing that he took Sunday dinner with some of the church folk, she asked no questions. Those church members who had eligible daughters especially favored Joseph, who was quite popular and always in demand. Joseph *was* good-looking, even if he did resemble Charles Harris. Martha fell to wondering what she would do with Effie when Joseph married "into society," which he would surely do, and she had to receive callers.

Joseph had never brought a girl into the home to make introductions; of course, it was because of his embarrassment at Effie's crippled condition. Joseph could not be blamed for his chagrin; some disposition would have to be made of Effie eventually. The children needed to feel free to bring their friends in for popcorn and candy. They had not had a taffy pull since Effie arrived! She must confront Henry with these particulars. A man did not understand the complications brought on by an unwanted child. He was not being fair to her own maturing children to expect them to go elsewhere for fellowship!

"Did Joseph take dinner with friends from church today?" she casually asked Henry, trying to hide her growing concern as darkness claimed its rights against the receding light.

"Well, not that I know of. He didn't even go to church today."

"He *didn't?*"

"No. I thought he stayed home with you."

"I thought he went to church with you."

"He was up at breakfast this morning."

Martha's panic was mounting. "Robert, you climb up to th' attic an' see if'n he's up there sick er dead." They waited in silence as Robert mounted the ladder. He came back, shaking his head.

"He ain't up there, an' his clothes 'n longhandles er all gone, too."

"You want that I go a'lookin' fer him, Martha?" Henry offered. "I could check at all th' neighbors' houses."

Prideful Martha was unwilling for the neighbors to know if Joseph had chosen to leave home. She could hear the clicking of Sister Clark's tongue now: "Did you know Joseph Harris ran away to th' city jest like th' prodigal son in th' Bible? Probably wastin' his life in riotous livin' there 'stead o' *righteous* livin'!" Martha had her pegged word for word.

"Let's wait, Henry," Martha suggested calmly, much

154

to Henry's surprise. "I 'spect he'll show up in 'is own good time! He's visitin' somewheres, maybe some girl, an' forgot to watch th' time. He's eighteen now, you know, an' not a baby anymore. He's probably jest tryin' to be a bit independent!"

Henry's concern was for Joseph's safety. "Best I go lookin' to be right sure, though, Martha. If'n he's not at th' neighbors, we'll know for sure he's someplace else."

Still Martha objected. "Let's get in no fizz, Henry. Simmer yourself down. Chances are he'll be comin' back tomorra' when he gets hungry fer his maw's cookin'. Campin' out fer a night'll be a good way to learn him a lesson. After a night o' batchin', tain't fun no more. East 'er west, home is best!"

But the morrow brought no Joseph. Nor the next week, or month. Only Effie knew what had happened and where he had gone. A first norther brought a chill to Central Texas all the way from Canada; Dessie's swollen eyes revealed her distress when she came to give Effie her schooling.

"W-why c-cry?" Effie asked solicitously.

More tears, held in the reservoir of Dessie's soul, overflowed into puddles. "It's gettin' cold, Effie, an' I don't know where my brother, Joseph, is. Oh, Effie, maybe he's somewheres *cold* or *hungry*. Or maybe he's *d-dead*! I pray for him every night, but what if'n he's hurt er sick an' can't get back home to us? What if'n he's killed? What if'n he. . ."

"N-no! S-top!"

"I can't stop. I love Joseph!" wailed Dessie.

"H-he's al-right!"

"How can you know he's all right, Effie?"

"H-he t-told m-me."

"He came back and told you while I was gone to school an' Mama was washin' an' Papa was in th' field?"

"N-no."

"Then when did he tell you, Effie?"

"B-be-fore."

"Joseph told you that he was leavin' before he left?"

"Y-yes."

"And he told you where he was goin'?"

"Y-yes."

"Tell me, quick, Effie! Where did he go?"

"W-west."

"Where out west? To Californey?" If California was his destination, he might never return, like Effie's father. More tears were in the making.

"N-no. M-my h-home."

"To the Territory of New Mexico?"

"Y-yes."

"Did he say when he would come back?"

"S-some-day." ·

Dessie carried the news directly to Martha, who bore the traces of worry on her face and had added strands of gray hair since Joseph's disappearance.

"Maw!" she shouted, triumphantly. "Effie knows where Joseph is! He told her where he was going before he left! He went on a trip into th' Territory of New Mexico to where Uncle Charles used to live." Dessie was ecstatic.

"He told Effie nothin' o' th' sort, Dessie!" reprimanded Martha peevishly. "When will you ever learn that Effie has no sane mind? You can interpret 'er grunts to mean anything you choose, which you have always done, but they mean absolut'ly nothin' at all. You could at least be reasonable, young lady, an' not add on to my grief. If'n Joseph decided to tell anybody 'bout his plans fer goin' anywhere, it would be me, 'is mother, not a witless child that couldn't even comprehend what he was talkin' about!''

It was fruitless to argue with Martha, so Dessie sought out Henry. "Papa, Effie says that Joseph told her where he was goin' before he left." Henry, with deep shadows under his eyes from lack of sleep, grasped at the straw. Joseph had always favored Effie; he had been overprotective of her when she was small. It was entirely possible that he had talked with her. "Where. . .where did Effie say he went?''

"Out west to the Territory of New Mexico to Uncle Charles' old homeplace. And he told her that he'd be back, too." Henry was comforted. Behind Effie's gnarled body lived a sharp mind, and she would have no reason to invent such a story. He slept peacefully that night fer the first time since Joseph's departure.

Joseph's exit served to increase Martha's animosity toward Effie. Joseph left home because he had no place to bring his teenage friends, she reasoned. He was ashamed to bring them to the farm house with a child like Effie in evidence. His friends would pity him, knowing that God had cursed the family to whom she was born, and now that curse had been passed on down to Joseph's home. She concluded that Effie had been partially, if not wholly, responsible for the loss of her son. Gertie Clark could rightly say that the evil spirits present in Effie had driven Joseph away.

The deacon's wife interrogated Henry repeatedly

about Joseph's whereabouts, and he managed to temporarily evade her prying questions and eagle eyes. But she was not one to be lightly put off.

"You say Joseph's not at home."

Henry groped for words. "He'll be back a'fore long, Sister Clark."

"Where'd he go?"

"Jest took hisself a little trip. We worked hard in th' fields this fall. Had a extry good crop this year, an' I's able to give 'im a little money. He needed 'im a vacation!"

Nothing escaped Gertie Clark's attention—or tongue. She knew that Henry was avoiding a direct answer and thought to call on Martha, but there was no illness in the family to warrant a call from a member of the visitation committee.

She cornered Matthew, reputed by Pastor Stevens to be the honest one and of late a frequent visitor to the pastor's home (which did not look good at all since the pastor had a teenage daughter).

"Where's Joseph?" she asked, point-blank.

"I dunno." That is all she could finagle from the unassuming Matthew.

At length, when Joseph did not return within the limits of her expectations, she approached Pastor Stevens. "Joseph Harris is run away, I 'spect to th' city," she informed, in her all-knowing tone of voice so offensive to the parson. "Prob'bly to Fort Worth er Dallas where all that wickedness is goin' on."

"That's likely none of our affairs, Sister Clark," Pastor Stevens cautioned, trying to avert a sticky discourse. He wished that Gertie Clark could get her tongue "on the altar," but alas, no altar would be long enough!

"Maybe t'aint," she conceded, "but I jest wanted to remind you o' what I perdicted a good piece back. I told you judgments was on their way from God Almighty. Now if'n a prodigal son, takin' his goods an' leavin' for th' city to spend his substance in riotous livin', sharin' his money with harlots an' republicans, ain't judgments, what is, may I ask?"

"Every man is a free moral agent and has to make his own choices for good or evil, Sister Clark. I'm not laying the blame on our good Brother and Sister Harris for the actions of a grown-up son."

"First you try to help em' cover their sins, then you try to pervert judgment. Seems we could use a more holy parson. The Good Book says train up a child in th' way he should go an' when he gets old he won't depart. An' Joseph has departed, so they must've not trained 'em right!" *A pity Sister Clark never had any children of her own, the way she could tell others how to rear theirs,* thought the parson.

"The Bible says judge not, Sister Clark."

"I ain't judgin', preacher. I'm jest tryin' to get you to face facts. You preach th' judgments o' God over th' pulpit, then when they get here upon some o' yore sinful church members, you choose to close yore eyes to 'em."

"Me and the Lord will pastor the church if you please."

"Humph! If'n th' Lord was anywheres in on it, a lot o' things would be different. You'd recognize that Martha's child o' sin is keepin' th' blessin's o' God away from th' Harris home. . .*an'* from our church. An' now we've lost *Joseph*, th' best one o' th' bunch!"

"The prodigal son came back. Maybe Joseph will,

159

too."

"An' I guess when he does come in after wastin' his youth on winin' an' dinin', you'll be th' first to kill th' fatted calf an' make him a hero!"

"That's exactly what the father in the Bible did." Pastor Stevens knew he was cutting his own throat, but he could not resist saying it: "And I guess you'll be the elder brother, with the Pharisee spirit, jealous and angry because the lost has been found!"

Chapter 14

Joseph's Journey

"*I* see you made it!" The driver hoisted Joseph's gunnysack onto the baggage rack.

"Yes, sir."

No guilt rode with Joseph. Indeed, a "peace that passeth understanding" settled upon his troubled soul and the brisk fall wind blew away his agitation as he joined himself to the coach driver at the main road and headed westward.

Joseph guessed the driver, a tall, lanky man named Jim Collins, with a moustache ready to dance to the music of any humor, to be in his early thirties. He liked Jim from the onset, taking the seat beside him by invitation.

"Is this the same coach Uncle Charles came to Texas on? Did he ride in this very seat?" Joseph asked when they had scarcely got rolling.

Jim laughed. "Drivers outwear coaches, I'm afraid! No, this isn't the same coach. We have to modernize to keep up with the times. We retired that old coach of which you speak about five years ago. Getting pretty ragged, it was. This one's got more luxuries, rides easier."

"How long have you been driving?"

"Started out when I was right young, 'scarce out of knee britches' as my paw would say. Means I've been driving nigh fourteen years."

"Like it?"

"Addicted to it! Meet all sorts of people. I've always liked to travel."

"And you're the one who brought my uncle back to these parts from the Territory of New Mexico in '78?"

"Yes, I remember Charles. Likeable chap. Didn't know him real well, but had met him several times at the stagestop out there in the territory. Got better acquainted with him on the journey."

"And you took him to California, too?"

"No. I took him as far as the main terminal. He took the southern route through El Paso. I drive the northern trail, up the caprock, and through Amarillo. I always favored that wide-open territory, though the other is pretty sparsely inhabited itself, I hear. Charles didn't want to chance getting stranded in the mountains; said he needed to make the best time possible. 'A man as barefooted as I am don't want to take no chances with a rocky road,' he told me. I was never able to forget it. I haven't seen Charles since I left him off at the stop. Where is he now?"

"We had one letter from him about a year or so after he left our place for the west coast to scout for gold. He wrote that he had made his fortune and said he would be returning in a fortnight, bringing all his riches with him. It was his plans to build us a new house. But we never heard from him again from that day till this."

"Ah. . .it's the eternal tragedy. Someone that he may have considered his best friend and absolutely trustworthy, found out about his gold, and coveted after it. The love of money is the root of all murder in that Gold Rush Country. That's too bad. . .too bad."

"Yes. He left an orphan child."

"I remember the baby, a girl if my memory serves me right?"

"Yes, sir. A girl."

"The little thing slept most of the way. Wouldn't eat nothing. She must have been exhausted, or missing her mother. I felt mighty heartsore for Charles; it was obvious that he was unaccustomed to caring for an infant. He kept her covered most of the time with the lap robe I furnish for the lady passengers on chilly evenings. The child didn't move about much and that worried me; I feared she was nigh dead. He said she'd been sickly all her life. She looked to me like rigor mortis was already setting in. I noticed your uncle gazing at every churchyard cemetery we passed. Didn't know if he was thinking about his wife, or a place to lay the child if she expired on the journey. I've always wondered what happened to her. She didn't live but a few hours after we left, did she?"

"Oh, yes, she lived. She's still alive. Very much so!"

"You don't say! Someone must have given her very good care to pull her through, as sick as she appeared to be."

"It wasn't that. She was born a cripple, all bent out of shape, but she's a spunky one. She has a will of iron, and is a princess in disguise!"

"Well, bully for her!"

"Mama has always been ashamed of the child's deformity. Mama is of the old school that believes in mothers marking babies before they're born, and sin causing physical mishaps. She's never allowed us to have our friends in, or invite neighbors over, for fear someone would see Effie and think someone in the family had sinned. Now me—I'd be proud to introduce Effie to the President of the United States as my *sister*. There's not many kids in the world with a mind as sharp as Effie's! And there's not *any anywhere* as brave!"

"You know what I always said about those kind?"

Joseph raised his eyes in question, not knowing what to expect.

"I said them kind are angels from heaven that was willing to get their wings all bent up just to get to earth and spread happiness down here! My sister had a little one thataway, and she brought more joy to all of us than all the others put together. We *called* her Princess! She didn't live long, though, unfortunately for us. I'd give everything I own to have her back. Them kind are made out of pure love."

Joseph choked back tears that he feared Jim would consider unbecoming to a traveling man. "I'm glad you feel that way, sir."

"You know, Joe. . .what's your name again?"

"Joseph."

". . .Joseph, I like you. You remind me a powerful lot of Charles. And Charles was a prince of a man."

"Thank you. I didn't have the opportunity to really know him."

"And you're going back to his part of the country just for a visit?"

164

"Well, yes, more or less. I'd like very much to find Rebecca's grave if there's any markings, or if anyone in the area knows where it might be. I'm doing this partly for myself and partly for Effie."

"I think you're in luck, Joseph. The stagestop is still operated by a part of the same family that had it when Charles homesteaded there. They should be able to give you a lot of help. They knew Charles quite well; he bought his supplies there, did his business transactions there and got his mail there. . .that sort of thing. The child knows of your plans?"

"Yes, sir. She's the only one that I told. She can't talk much. She has a terrible speech impediment, but man, can she communicate with those eyes! I told her if everybody talked with their eyes like she does, we'd have no need for the English language! The first word I taught her to say was 'thank you' and she says it every breath. You never saw a more grateful little soul!"

"She was too small to remember her mother at all, wasn't she?"

"She doesn't remember anything about her mother. Recently she found a photograph of Rebecca in an old Bible, though, and. . ."

"Say, now I recall the Bible. . .and seems there was something else, too. . . ."

"I've seen her kissing the picture of her mother at bedtime. Nearly tore my heart up!"

"Just hearing it tears me up."

"Did you ever see Rebecca?"

"I only saw Rebecca a few times. She was a regular homebody—the most perfectly content lady I've ever met. She *radiated* happiness. She was young and beautiful and obviously well educated, but then Charles wasn't bad looking, himself! She was from a city back east. I never quite understood what brought them to the territory. It was my own father who gave Charles the map of the area. But Charles and Rebecca certainly weren't the run-of-the-mill squatters."

"Papa says Charles was restless-natured, with no roots when he was younger. I guess maybe he wanted to get his own land and plant his own roots in a place of his choice."

"Yes, I recall him telling me something of that nature. It was a boyhood dream of his to stake claim on land of his own is the way he put it. And he was doing a bang-up good job of it, even through the toughest of days, until he lost Rebecca. That blew him out of the saddle."

"Do you know what took her?"

"Probably pneumonia, he said. Told me she was sickly and coughed a lot; that she had nursed the child until she got her own body run down. Pneumonia can take you fast if your resistance is low."

"And he buried her out on his land?"

"All by himself, they say."

"Then packed up and left?"

"Brought his nice Conestoga wagon and pair of horses to the stagestop and sold them cheap to a caravan headed out west. Got enough money out of them to take the child to your place and get on to California. The last thing he told me was that he was anxious to get back and make a home for his little daughter."

"When I make a home of my own, I plan to take Effie to live with me if she wants to go." Joseph lapsed into thoughtful silence.

They approached a settlement. "Ever drink sulphur water?" Jim asked.

"No, sir."

"They say it's good for what ails you."

"What does it taste like?"

"Rotten eggs."

"I believe I'll keep what ails me."

Jim's moustache danced. "Smells like rotten eggs, too, but every man owes it to himself to taste sulphur water once in his lifetime. Glen Rose is overrun with sulphur springs. It's down below the hill yonder. I stop there to water the horses."

"The horses like sulphur water?"

"No. There's a clear, bubbling fork of the Paluxy runs through. Easy to get to."

"Does sulphur water cure impatience?"

"Guess so. Most folks are not impatient for a second drink."

"Then I'm game."

Joseph weighed the advantages of being a stage driver. It would surely provide more excitement than planting corn or taking up peanuts. It would probably be more financially rewarding as well. Too many things influenced crops. . .drought, varmints, hail, rainfall. . . .

"Do you headquarter in the territory?"

"I call it home, though I'm seldom there."

"What's the country like?"

"We have it all, like Texas: broken mesas, deserts, mountain wildernesses with heavy forests, bare peaks, arid plains covered with cactus, sagebrush, and yucca. Depends on what part you're in. Your uncle chose rich land below the caprock with plenty of water for ranching, but luck was against him all the way it seems."

"Have any trouble with the Indians?"

"There's been bad trouble with the Apache and Navajo tribes in the past years, but the Apache Chief, Geronimo, surrendered a year or so ago and there hasn't been much conflict since."

"Do you think the territory will ever become a state of the Union, like Texas?"

"I expect so, eventually. May be several years yet. We're booming right now. When they put the railroad through—that was the year after Charles left—it brought people by the droves. I don't think Charles would have liked the change. Can't say as I like the congestion myself, but can't none of us stand in the way of progress."

The journey passed quickly. After several days, the vegetation became squatty and the trees sparse. "This is like a different world," Joseph said when the caprock was negotiated. The air was lighter, dryer.

"Nights in this part of the country intrigue me. The skies are infinitely clear, and the stars, flung across the heavens, look like dazzling jewels."

"Wouldn't Effie love to wish on a star out here?"

"She'd have *millions* of them to wish on!"

"There's a lake!" Joseph pointed across the high panhandle plains to the silvery mass, resplendent in the sunlight.

"A moving lake," chuckled Jim. "It moves back as we move forward."

"How's that?"

"That's a mirage. It just *looks* like a lake. Many a traveler has died chasing one."

"Could have fooled me!"

"You want to be careful, Joseph. You're young. Not only can mirages fool you, but people can, too. Watch your step, son."

"I'll try, sir. I've never been off the farm, and there's an awful lot about life I don't know."

"Stick close to the coach house people. They're honest and trustworthy. They'll take you under their wing since you're Charles Harris' nephew. They got a right pretty daughter, too, so you might watch your step there." Jim's mustache was dancing again, a jig this time.

"Well, sir, if I was out looking for girls, there's plenty of them back home. I got some things I want to do before I take on the responsibility of a wife. I'm not much on window shopping just for the fun of it."

"Ah, smart boy! But you do plan to return eventually to your parents' home and the orphaned child, don't you?"

"Oh, yes, sir. I won't be here long. I can't afford to spend up all my money and chance getting stranded. Little Effie would never stop worrying about me. I promised her that I'd be back. That's one reason I've got to be mighty careful not to get myself hurt in any way."

"The territory is Billy the Kid land, you know. When he was just a tyke in knickers, his family moved to New Mexico. Before he was sixteen years old, he had killed several men. Killed one of our own sheriffs the year I took Charles to Texas. They finally shot him in '81 though."

"Won't have to worry about him then, will I?"

"No, but there's still the likes of him."

"You might say some prayers for me. This is sort of a. . .a mercy mission, see."

"I see, Joseph. And, believe it or not, I am a praying

man. A life without prayer is like a wagon without springs
—mighty rough traveling."

"Do you drive the stage year 'round, Mr. Collins?"

"Just call me Jim."

". . .Jim."

"Depends on the weather. Some winters are real mild;
now last winter, the blizzards shut us down. Been many
a year since we had such a bad year for travel."

"I was hoping to catch your coach going back home."

"I'll be back through in about a month. That long
enough?"

"Just right."

"Got a goal in mind?"

"Yes, sir. I want to be back to Effie by Christmas."

"You're the one that sees that she has a little gift each
Christmas, aren't you, Joseph?"

"Yes, sir. You should see the mess I made of the first
corncob doll I tried to make for her! She wore that doll
out before New Year's Day handling it!"

"Pity she couldn't have a real doll. Say. . .that's the
other thing Charles had with him. What happened to that
fancy doll that was with the Bible? I remember it, because
I'd never seen a store-boughten doll like that one, and
I thought it was about the prettiest thing I'd ever seen
for a girl child. I was thinking he told me Rebecca left
it to the child."

"Mama took it for my two sisters. I don't think
Charles made it clear to Mama that it belonged to Effie."

"Oh, I see."

"Life's been mighty unfair for Effie."

"You think it'd be all right if I got her something for
Christmas, too, Joseph?"

"I don't see why not."

"She'd be sure and get to keep it for herself?"

"I'd personally see that she did."

"Then let's me and you make a pact to give Effie the best Christmas she's ever had. How about it?"

"Nobody deserves it more."

"I think you can fetch a room right at the coach house. They'll let you use a horse to ride out to the spread that Charles lived on, and do your sightseeing."

"You're mighty kind to me, sir."

"A fellow reaps what he plants; you've been kind to the child."

"And Jim. . ." Joseph hesitated, a great lump threatening to choke off his voice.

"Yes?"

"Please say a prayer for her too, would you? I've got a feeling she's going to need it mighty bad while I'm away."

"You have my word, pardner; my word is my honor."

Chapter 15

Good For Evil

"Joseph left 'cause he was ashamed of Effie!" Martha advised Henry, climbing higher up the stairs of agitation with each day of Joseph's absence.

"Now Martha, that's not one bit so!" he objected. "Joseph loved Effie, in fact."

" 'Twasn't *love*. 'Twas th' *gentleman* about him. He'd leave home a'fore he'd lay down his gentleman ways. If'n you warn't so blind on purpose, you could see that he never brought 'is friends here. We never had no parties for 'im. 'Twas more'n he could take! A mother knows what 'er children suffers. He went off to have some laughin' like all young folks hanker fer. Some o' th' othern's'll follow suit. An' all because of yore brother's child. Just you wait 'n see, Henry Harris!"

When reasoning proved useless, Henry went back to the field. "Do believe she's gettin' farther from God 'n closer to th' devil ever' day!'' he muttered, aware that Martha's frustrations would be hurled at the helpless child she blamed for all life's woes.

To counteract Martha's coldness, Effie clung to warm thoughts of Rebecca, delving deeper into her beloved Book to learn about the future blissful reunion with her immortal mother. The Bible became her textbook, and she spent days studying about heaven, a place where no tears would dim the eye, no one would be crippled or sick, and "we shall know as we are known." That meant, of course, that she would not be a spastic there, and could run all over the hills of glory at breakneck speed. . .and that Rebecca would know her as her own child!

Absorbed in the dream of a place of peace and happiness, Effie did not see Martha enter the sitting room. Of late, she tried desperately to stay out of Martha's path, slipping unobtrusively behind a curtain of silence and stillness.

Martha saw her as she pressed Rebecca's picture affectionately to her heart and moved her lips in a half-whispered, indistinguishable prayer: "Oh, Mother! Mother! How I long to see you!" Then she lowered the portrait so that she might look full into the angelic face smiling up at her.

Seeing the picture for the first time, Martha froze in her tracks. Her gaze took in every detail of the scene before her. Who could this elegant lady be, and where could Effie have gotten such an expensive portrait? To whom did it belong? The mumble-jumble of words and glassy look in Effie's eyes could be nothing less than a seance with evil spirits!

A reckoning of new dimensions startled her. Was it

. . .could this be. . .*Joseph's* girlfriend. . .? Had he rushed away to get himself married, leaving this lovely lass's picture behind in his haste? Dropped it as he left out maybe, and Effie picked it up? The girl in the picture looked young, no more than sixteen or eighteen. And alluringly beautiful! And obviously *rich*! The clothes she wore were expensive and tasteful, and she sat upon a velvet chair! This is the sort of girl she had imagined (and hoped) that Joseph would seek after.

This then, was likely the girl that Joseph was ashamed to bring home and introduce to his parents because of Effie. She, his own mother, had been denied the privilege of meeting her future daughter-in-law because of Charles' ill-formed child. Joseph could not be blamed! Any maiden that pretty would be offended by the presence of evil! Martha was convinced that the thing she had feared had come upon her.

Vivid mental pictures, taken with the camera of her inflamed imagination and developed in the darkroom of her backslidden soul, came out without a blur. Joseph had met this wealthy, popular young lady, Martha decided, in town. This is why he had availed himself of every opportunity to ride into the township with Mr. Gibson. He had spent these carefully plotted Saturdays making his plans to take a wife! She might even be the mayor's daughter. Why, Joseph probably lived within twelve short miles of them at this moment! He would have no problem landing a job in The Springs at the booming railroad shops. A young man with his intelligence would be hired on the spot, and work up to foreman in a few weeks. With a bit of sleuthing, she would locate Joseph and apologize for the anguish Effie had caused him, meet this beautiful bride of his, and. . . . How ironic that *Effie* found the picture!

A creak of the floor brought Effie from her netherworld of glory to the harsh world of reality. Martha glared at her. Effie quailed; what had she done wrong? "Give me that picture right now!" Martha demanded. "It belongs to Joseph!"

"N-no!" Effie clung to the "pearl of great price" with pleading eyes; her hands shook violently. "M-mine!" The words were distinctly clear, plain enough for Martha to understand.

At any other time, it would have been below Martha to try to communicate with the child whom she considered witless. But now blind anger controlled her. "What do you mean, it's yorn?" she yelled, convinced that her foregone conclusions were indisputable. "It belongs to *Joseph!*"

"M-my mother!" defended Effie, clutching her treasure with her wanning strength and sending up a desperate heart prayer that Martha would not take it from her. "S-see!" She pointed to the name "Rebecca Ann Franklin" below the picture.

The innocent face, so different from Martha's preconceived idea of Charles' "wicked wife" shattered her aplomb, chafing her even more. She slapped the photograph from Effie's grasping fingers, sailing it through the air toward the smoldering fireplace. Embarrassed at the mistaken identity and confronted with the disillusion of her deceased sister-in-law, her self-control—already in short supply—was bankrupted.

Effie gave a haunting cry and sprang toward the precious print, losing her balance and striking her head on

the stone hearth. She lay injured and sobbing noiseless-
ly, floating in and out of consciousness, her heart imploring, "Mother! Mother! Please let me come to you! Jesus,
please take me to my mother!"

Martha turned on her heels and left, seething. The
voice of her crusted conscience was talking too loudly,
shaming her for wrongly judging the guileless girl in the
picture. But she stopped her ears to the inner voice.

Dessie found Effie asleep on the floor, clasping the
picture. The great knot on her forehead had turned blue.

"Mama," she called, running to the kitchen where
Martha kneaded bread, "Come quick! Somethin's happened to Effie!"

"Prob'bly a fit o' her'n," Martha replied, back turned.
"She'll be aw'right."

Dessie helped Effie to her own bed, oblivious to Martha's rules, and covered her gently with a quilt, noticing
that when she tried to take the picture and put it away,
Effie protested. She left it in Effie's locked embrace.
"Poor little Effie! Misses her mother fierce!" she said,
soothing back the tousled hair and applying a damp rag
to the bump.

The lump on Effie's head went away, but the terror
in her heart remained. She must now guard the priceless
copy day and night with her very life. For whatever
reason Aunt Martha tried to fling it into the fireplace and
destroy it, she might try again. What had Rebecca done
to Martha to make her hate the sight of her picture? A
perplexed Effie could not comprehend malice, but the incident was indelibly tattooed on her mind. She sought a
place to hide the Bible and the picture.

The place she chose was the woodshed. 'Lasses kept

the shed free of mice; the enclosure was waterproof. And where Effie's treasure was, there her heart abode also. She spent most of her waking hours in the little log structure, often missing needed meals. Alas! If she *lived* in the woodshed, it would be a blessed riddance for Martha!

Effie tried hard to live by Rebecca's Book, applying its instructions to the fibre of her life. In pouring over its sacred pages, she found a command to "do good to them that hate you, and pray for them which despitefully use you. . . ." Thus, every day she prayed for Aunt Martha. . .while every day Aunt Martha seemed to become more spiteful.

How Effie yearned to do something nice for Aunt Martha to earn her love! Something. . .anything. . .to show Martha that she was a human and not an insensitive animal. Like the Good Book said: *returning good for evil.*

She watched for occasions to be helpful. Dessie came home from school to find the fresh washed clothes "folded" into indiscriminate shapes on the bed, a work of Effie's fumbling hands. She hastily refolded them properly and sought until she found Effie in the woodshed. "Thank you for foldin' th' clothes for Mama." She put a loving arm about Effie. "You have such a good *heart,* Effie!"

"T-thank you."

On a day when Martha was especially irritable, Effie searched for a means to relieve the agitation. Willing her hands to the good deed, she took Martha a cup of hot coffee. But she clumsily bumped against the chair, spilling the scalding liquid on Martha's feet. Martha yelled, assured that the devil had prompted Effie to do it. Effie took her freshly wounded heart back to the woodshed and wept a puddle of tears. Of what value was she, except to infuriate Martha? Oh, for a haven where she would no longer be a spastic. Or unwanted! Or a burden! And where she would be loved by a mother!

Still another time, Effie attempted to assist with washing the mountain of dishes for the weary Martha. Unfortunately, she broke a plate. . .just one. . .angering Martha farther. This accident forever removed her from the joys of helping Dessie and Sarah at the dishpan.

Was there *nothing* she could do?

Chapter 16

The Woodshed

"*E*ffie's asleep in the shed, Mama."

When Effie did not show up for supper, Dessie went looking for her. She found her in the woodshed, asleep. Her Bible was nestled on her breast and she was smiling peacefully. Dessie tiptoed out and returned to the house, not wishing to disturb Effie's rest.

"Fer as I'm concerned, she can *move* out there!"

"Mama, why do you feel so about Effie?" Martha's prejudices no longer escaped Dessie's notice; her twelfth birthday neared. In broaching the subject, she tread on fearsome sod.

"Effie's bad luck, Dessie. She's caused nothing but trouble since she came to live with us. Joseph left home 'cause he couldn't invite none of 'is friends here. Who wants their friends to see a. . .a. . .a. . . ."

"That's not why Joseph left!"

"Are you disputin' my word, Dessie?"

"No, ma'm, but. . . ."

"Then hold yer tongue!"

"But Joseph went west to see Charles' homestead, and he'll be coming back. . . ."

"He did no sech. But if'n he had'uv, that shore proves my point. Charles got 'em all riled up an' filled with wanderlust when he came to bring Effie!"

"Well, I *like* Effie."

"You'll feel different when you grow up."

"I won't *never* feel different, no matter how growed up I get! An' when I'm growed up an' have a home of my very own, I want Effie to live with *me* since you don't seem to want her to live with you!" There was a tattered edge to Dessie's voice that Martha did not approve of.

"Young lady, you'd best tame that tongue o' yorn 'er face th' razor strop!" Martha threatened, and Dessie walked away belligerently.

Ah, there went yet another thorn in the flesh brought on by Effie's presence: Dessie's impudence. Why, Dessie would never dare to speak to her mother in that manner were it not for the Effie-Martha conflict! Effie was *dividing* the Harris family. When would Henry recognize the irreparable damage being wrought by his unwanted niece? Well, things had gone quite far enough; it was high time to separate Dessie from Effie's company. Evil spirits were proving themselves contageous after all.

Dessie watched the back door anxiously, sullenly. But as the sun made ready to hand her duty of lighting the earth over to the moon, Effie still did not return to the house. Just before sundown, Dessie went back to the woodshed. Effie had not moved; she was still asleep, still smiling. Dusk settled over the farm and Dessie determined to fetch Effie to the house before dark.

"Effie. . ." she called softly so as not to startle the sleeper. But Effie did not stir or awaken. How long had she been napping? All day? Was she ill?

"Effie, wake up!" Still Effie did not rouse.

"Effie, you can finish yore sleepin' in th' house! It'll soon be plumb dark out here! Come on!"

There was no response. Dessie became alarmed. The last ray of sinking sun made Effie's wind-raveled hair seem golden; she had never looked more beautiful. She looked almost like a. . .a. . .fairy. Near panic, Dessie took her gently by the shoulders and shook her. Effie opened her eyes, registering surprise at finding herself in the woodshed. Her eyes focused on Dessie.

"Effie. . ."

"Oh, Dessie! Dessie! I saw Him!"

"What happened, Effie? Tell me quick! You're not stuttering one bit!"

A radiant smile of utter happiness—a happiness not of this world—lingered on the thin face, mystifying Dessie.

"I saw Him!"

"*Who* did you see?"

"The Jesus in the Book. He held me in His arms!"

"You were dreaming, Effie."

"No, I wasn't! It was real! Oh, *Dessie!*"

Could Dessie be dreaming herself? Effie was speaking fluently. What had *happened* to Effie? She stared at Effie from head to foot, fully expecting to see a transformed body, no longer crippled.

"Oh, Dessie! He's my Friend and I'll never be lonely again!"

Awestruck by the flawless sentences, Dessie hugged
Effie tightly. "Oh, Effie! I don't know what happened to
you, but whatever happened to you, I want it, too. Do you
think I could meet Him like you did?"

"Yes."

"But my heart is so black, Effie. I have bad thoughts,
especially towards Mama. Just awhile ago, I talked sassy
to her, an' didn't even care! I don't know much about God
'cept what I've heard at church; an' most of th' time I
don't even pay no attention at church no more. But oh,
Effie, I'd sure like to meet Him for myself like you did!"

"You can!"

"You'll help me pray, Effie?"

"Sure."

Martha's demanding voice pierced the calm of the
evening.

"Dessie Harris!"

"Mama's calling, Effie. We'd better get to th' house
quick."

"We're coming, Mama!" Dessie had never answered
with more reluctance.

"If Effie wants to stay with the cats all night, that's
one thing—but I expect you to have better sense than that,
Dessie!"

"Sorry, Mama."

"It's time I heard a little 'pologizing out of you. What
were you *doing* in th' shed?"

"Just talkin'."

"Talkin' about what? How can you talk to somebody
that *can't* talk?"

"Oh, but Mama, that's just what I was fixin' to tell
you! Effie can talk just as good as th' rest o' th' Harris

family now!"

Martha resented Effie being included with "the rest of the family" by Dessie, and looked from her daughter to Effie skeptically, sensing a difference, but not being able to identify it.

"I. . .I. . ." stuttered Effie feebly, thinking an explanation necessary.

"Pretendin' games again! Dessie, I do declare. You can 'magine th' weirdest things! I thought you'd outgrow it, but I believe yore gettin' worse 'stead o' better. I want yore foolish make-believein' to stop, D'ya hear? Now get ready an' go to bed!" Martha was peeved, and hoped Henry would not be snoring when she went to bed. She sorely needed to have a talk with him.

Dessie watched Effie closely. The garbled speech returned, but the peace stayed. Effie radiated happiness! Whatever the vision, Dessie longed for a small touch of it. She would not ask for a "double portion"; she would be satisfied with but a half portion! Furthermore, Effie was no longer afraid of Martha; she had a trusted Friend to care for her.

Dessie knew where to find Effie; she stayed hid away in her sanctuary more and more. Dessie became hungrier and hungrier to know Effie's newfound Friend. Could He still her inner turmoil as He had Effie's?

"Please ask Him to be my Friend, too, Effie."

"I-in y-your h-heart." Effie laid her hand on her chest.

"Yes, I want Him in my heart."

"A-ask H-him!"

"I'll ask Him, but you ask Him, too. You have a better heart than I do. You wasn't as bad inside as me!"

"A-all a-are b-bad! H-he f-forgives!"

185

"He'll forgive *me*?"

"Y-yes. H-he d-died for y-you."

Both girls knelt on the feedsacks, forgetting all else but Dessie's desire to make acquaintance with Effie's Saviour. And Martha found them there. What ritual they were performing she did not wait to find out, but she meant to put a stop to it! She hauled Dessie to her feet, forbidding her to ever be caught in the shed with Effie again. She determined to cut the thread of communication between Dessie and this insane child with her sharp scissors of judgment.

"Dessie, I expect you to be a proper young lady! There's to be no farther games in th' woodshed. You're gettin' too old to play silly riddles!"

"But, Mama, we wasn't. . . ."

"Dessie, you *shan't* talk back! I'm sick of it! D'ya *hear*? An' if'n you *insist* on disobeyin', I'll do whatsome-ever it takes to get Effie into th' asylum!"

The last sentence drove a knife into Dessie's heart. She became fearful to be caught near Effie, lest her loyalty should work adversely for her. Martha watched her closely, and when Dessie became withdrawn and introversive, Martha again placed the blame at the feet of Effie.

Undaunted, Effie shared each new complication with her new Friend, never losing the tranquility in her soul, nor her happy smile.

"Blessed are ye, when men shall revile you, and persecute you, and shall say all manner of evil against you falsely for my sake. Rejoice, and be exceedingly glad: for great is your reward in heaven. . . ." There it was in Rebecca's Bible.

Chapter 17

Bittersweet Fall

*T*he sun, confined behind the dreary curtain of clouds, emerged centerstage and spread its glow of cheer. Henry came in from town jubilant.

"Th' crops 'er all sold, Martha, 'n we're in pretty good shape. This was th' best year we ever had. Joseph saw to it that I was in good shape cropwise a'fore he left me. I 'preciate that."

"An' th' grievin' thought that he's not here to get 'is pay!"

"I paid 'im some earlier." The disclosure substantiated Martha's fancy; Joseph had taken his money and gone off to get married.

"You think we'll 'ave enough to buy a team an' wagon this year?" Martha's next ambition, rising with the leaven of homesickness for her son, was to locate Joseph in The Springs.

"We got enough. Won't have to bum a ride in to th' city with Mr. Gibson no more. Won't that be grand?"

"We gonna get *horses,* Papa?" Robert cut in. "Real ridin' horses?"

"Yes, an' I thought I'd git you to come with me to pick out a fine pair tomorra if'n yore Maw can spare us."

"Oh, boy, oh, boy, oh, boy, oh, boy!" Robert's oh-boys were punctuated with a face-splitting smile.

"Where you plannin' on goin' to get 'em at?" Martha asked.

"First off, we'll look at Cleburne. I been told that's a mighty good place. Parson Stevens is goin' thataway an' we can hitch a ride in with him. If'n we can't find *e*'xactly what seems fitted to our needs, we'll take on another day an' go clean to Fort Worth. Bound to find somethin' there. Buyin' a team is a big undertakin', so don't 'spect us back real soon like."

"Get a wagon big enough to hold us *all,* Papa." This from Sarah. "I want to go to town shoppin'."

"That won't be no problem. I'm plannin' on us takin' a whole Saturday on th' town when I git back."

Henry and Robert left at daybreak, catching a ride into the Johnson County seat with the parson, who was making the journey to visit his ailing mother.

"So you're getting you a wagon and team?" the pastor asked, adjusting his words to the bouncing of the shay.

"Yes, sir. Been needin' one mighty bad fer better'n five year. Jest hadn't had th' financin'. You know how that goes with a family size o' mine."

Not a penny had Pastor Stevens seen of the tithe money from the obviously prosperous fall crop. He suspected that Martha kept the purse strings tightly knotted and now that she had "fallen from grace," her desires would naturally be carnal.

"How's Sister Martha?"

"Worry-wartin, as usual."

"About Joseph?"

"About everything."

"We need to get her started back to church, Brother Harris."

"That's gonna be easier said than done, I'm afeared. I've been after her for more'n a year now."

"I'm sure she'll be wanting to come during the holidays coming up. We're having a real special Christmas program this year. My Pauline is donating her piano for that one night and your Matthew's playing carols on it while she sings."

"Matthew's *what?*"

"Playing the piano for the Christmas program."

"Matthew can't play no piano!"

"I'm afraid you're behind the times, Brother Harris. Matthew is truly an accomplished pianist—one of the best I've ever heard in my life!"

"Where. . . ? How. . . ?"

"My Pauline taught him all she knew, then he picked up on it on his own and out run her all to pieces!"

"Well, I'll be. . . ."

"Do you think we can get Sister Martha to come and hear her professor play?"

"We *got* to get her there somehow! Matthew playing the *piano. . . .?" Had he heard right?*

"Yes, sir!"

"Well, if'n that don't beat. . . ."

"He never told you?"

"Never cheeped a word! An' here I thought he was workin' Saturdays."

"Oh, he was indeed. I've been letting him off a couple hours early for lessons and practice. Don't take much practice for Matthew, though. Music just comes as natural as breathing for him!"

"Well, I never. . . ."

"Favor me one thing, Brother Harris."

"Yes, sir."

"Don't let Matthew know I told."

"I promise. An' that goes fer you too, Robert." *Matthew* a pianist?

Still scratching his head in disbelief, Henry climbed down at the auction barn, helping Robert from the chaise. Robert directed his absent-minded father among the animals looking for suitable horses. Only with considerable effort was he able to shift Henry's brain from pianos to the task at hand.

Robert's perception of animals was uncanny. In less than an hour, he ferreted out the two best horses in the lot. "These are th' ones we want, Papa," he said. Henry looked them over. "A good choice," he agreed, and paid cash for the horses.

The portly constable piloted them to the city's foremost wagon maker, and in a short half day, all transactions were complete. "We'll go by th' farrier an' get those horses a new pair o' shoes, then be ready to head home," Henry told Robert. "Yore Maw'll be mighty surprised that we killed our bear an' skinned it all in one day!"

The horses, from good stock, were gentle. "Well-trained an' well-mannered, ain't they, Papa?"

"Not a finer pair nowhere."

"What's their names?"

"Aw, I fergot to ask! Had too many irons in th' fire. We'll jest have to give 'em new names. Since you picked 'em, why don't you name 'em?"

"I'd need a spell to think on names. Names has gotta be *right* ."

"I 'spect there's no rush."

The new wagon pulled into the Harris yard before sundown. A limousine could not have produced more excitement. Chester, Alan, and Arthur clamored a straddle the good-natured beasts, with Martha fretting for their safety.

"What's um name?" Chester asked.

Henry laughed. "We fergot to ask. Robert's gonna name 'em."

"Jest 'member their *back* name is Harris!" reminded William.

"You mean their surname," corrected Sarah.

"One of 'em might be a *sir* name, but th' other'n is a ma'm name. Right, Papa?"

The horses were tethered in the back yard for the night. "I'll keep a close check on 'em, Papa," promised Robert. He could be depended on to arise at daylight. His frequent exits out the window throughout the night went undisclosed. He came to breakfast flushed and winded.

"What's th' problem, Robert?" Henry stood at the wash basin.

"Nothin' much. Just named my horses."

"What um names?" Chester's question again.

"Adam an' Eve."

"Good as any," Henry said. "What decided you on them names?"

191

"Had to run 'em out o' th' *garden!*" Robert's dry sense of humor brought a smile from Martha.

"Better keep 'em out 'o my garden, er I'll drive 'em out with a flamin' sword!"

Robert stopped Effie on her pilgrimage to the woodshed that morning. "Come see our horses, Effie!" Effie followed, but at the sight of the big animals rippling with muscles, drew back.

"B-bite?"

"They won't hurt you, Effie. They're very tame. I picked 'em with you in mind. Some horses kick 'n pitch 'n bite, but not these." He coaxed Effie to scratch Adam's neck. "This is Adam; the other's in Eve."

"O-oh. P-pretty B-Bible names!"

"You like those names? They got in th' garden an' I had to drive 'em out. That gave me th' idea."

"I s-see."

"We're all goin' to ride to town in th' wagon soon . . . an' have a grand old time! The whole family! Papa bought us a nice buckboard wagon. See?" Robert pointed with pride toward the vehicle; delight shone in Effie's eyes.

"I g-go?"

"Well, *of course,* Effie. I'll see that you're on board, cause *I'm* the driver!"

"T-thank you!" She continued to the shed, staying there the rest of the day while the Harris family made plans for the trip to town amidst a noisy melee of talk. Even morose Dessie joined the discussion.

"Let's take our lunch an' eat it down by Steele Creek," suggested Matthew, who agreed to give up his "work" with the parson for one Saturday to join the family venture. "I want Mama to see th' old Spring Hole. It's pretty, ain't it, Papa?"

"Jest right fer a picnic! But if'n I know Maw, she'll want to take along some tow sacks to gather some pecans an' walnuts."

"Are we *all* goin', Mama?" Dessie pressed.

"Of course, Dessie. What made you ask somethin' like that?"

"Even Effie?"

Dessie saw the blanched look on her mother's face; what to do with Effie had obviously not crossed her mind.

"Sure, we'll take Effie," Robert interspersed. "*I'm* th' driver of th' coach—and what I say about my passengers goes. . ."

"Whoa, now. . ." Martha started to object.

"He's right, Martha," Henry said, almost casually. "We'll *all* go, er none."

"But what'll we. . . ?"

"We can make Effie a pallet in th' bed o' th' wagon. It's cool enough so's she'll be comfortable whiles we're doin' our shoppin'."

"But if'n some'un sees 'er. . . ."

"They won't. She knows how to mind 'er manners 'n be still 'n quiet. She does it all time here at home. She'll be jest as well off in th' wagon."

"We *can't* leave 'er here, Mama." Dessie again. And before Martha could get words to the contrary out of her open mouth, Dessie quoted her mother verbatim: ". . .she might set th' house on fire while we're gone!"

"Then yore to make shore she lays on th' wagon floor, an' not let anybody see 'er." But Martha was not happy; as simple a thing as a family shopping trip had to be mar-

193

red by the presence of Effie!

"Each of you will have a quarter to 'blow', an' Maw'll have five dollars," Henry switched the subject. Dessie wanted to ask if Effie would have a quarter, but she knew the answer.

Martha made her list. Each of the children needed shoes, and she a pair of gloves. . .a hundred pounds of flour. . .black strap molasses. . .ribbon. . .saleratus. . .coffee. . . .

The big Saturday came. Before dawn, Martha busied herself frying several young pullets and making light bread. Sarah baked two cakes. "You're fixin' enough food to feed th' army!" Henry commented on his way out to hitch up the team.

"You'll be glad 'fore we get back ta'night!"

"I'm a'ready glad! Jest wish we'd hurry an' git to Steele Creek!"

Dessie slipped in an extra quilt from her bed and her own pillow for Effie's comfort. "More paddin'," she whispered. Effie rewarded her with a crooked smile. Robert drove the team; Henry noted his skill with fatherly pride. Picture perfect weather added to the day's pleasantness.

The spring-fed water at Steele Creek somersaulted over the pebbles with sparkling clarity singing a liquid song. Robed in late autumn colors, the plant life preened. Beneath a giant walnut tree on the sandy bank near the Spring Hole, the banquet was spread. Chicken, pickles, bread, cold yams, and cake tasted like heaven's manna. Dessie saw to Effie's welfare.

"Can we go swimmin', Papa?" implored William.

"Next summer, Will. The water'd be too cold now."

"Next summer seems like forever! Wish we could've got here in time to go in *this* summer," Robert said. "Next summer I'll be fourteen years old!"

"Nuthin' says it's again' th' law to swim when yer fourteen," laughed Henry.

"I'll be *six*." Chester sought a comment from Henry.

"Me, too," Alan said. "We can go to school pretty soon."

" 'N I'll be five!" Arthur added his postscript.

"Our family's growin' up, Martha." Henry winked at the tall, manly Matthew. "Matthew's past seventeen. He'll be hankerin' to get married 'fore long." Matthew blushed; Pauline had occupied his mind all day. He wished for her beside him now.

"Gotta find somebody to have 'im first off," teased Martha.

Sarah said nothing; no one must know of her passionate love note exchange with Hank Gibson after church services on the Lord's Day. While Martha missed church, she missed the budding romance as well. Henry seldom detected such things. Martha would surely say that Sarah was too young to know what love was all about. But Sarah knew better.

"I shore hope they have a medicine show goin' today," William fidgeted restlessly. If swimming was out, there must be another thrill to occupy his time. "That's where I'll spend my quarter!"

"*William!*" Martha gave him a shocked look of reproof.

"Yes'm?"

"Medicine shows 'er worldly 'musements. An' your pastor preaches 'gainst sech."

195

"Papa let Joseph go see one onct. . .Joseph told me all 'bout it."

"Henry, you know the Bible says th' very thought o' foolishness is *sin.*"

"Well, I didn't 'xactly. . .uh. . .he really. . .he went with th' Gibson boy." Henry sought to exonerate himself. At the mention of Hank, Sarah's ears burned. "But if'n we don't hurry up here, nobody's gonna have time to spend their quarters nowhere. We'd best be gettin' to yore gingham store, so you'll have plenty o' time to shop," he sidetracked the fracas. Hurrying hands helped to load the leftovers.

"Jest lay down flat on th' wagon bed under th' quilt till we're finished buying." Dessie whispered the instructions to Effie as Henry maneuvered the wagon to the main street, wanting to add, "Because Mama don't want nobody to see you," but saying instead, "So nobody will get you." Except for the fitting of shoes, she would have stayed with Effie herself. Her quarter would be shared with Effie regardless of the consequences.

Henry stopped the wagon near the windmill located in the center of the main thoroughfare, and the passengers tumbled out onto the board walk. Robert stayed behind to wrap the reins about the reincheck and pat Adam and Eve on the flanks, showering them with compliments.

Martha pulled William aside. "You're to go into th' barber shop an' inquire if'n anyone in there knows if'n a Joseph Harris is workin' at th' railroad shops." Martha would not think of entering into the presence of menfolk herself; only a brazen woman would do that!

The tiresome wagon ride left Effie exhausted; she missed her Bible, her picture. Burrowing her head into the feather pillow, she fell asleep.

Robert was not a city boy; he stashed his quarter in his pocket and wandered from store to store finding nothing worthy of its expenditure. In an hour, he had seen everything he wanted to see. Since no shoes could be found in his size, he returned to his beloved horses. Adam nuzzled him lovingly.

Robert had one foot on the tongue of the wagon, ready to climb in when it happened. With his back turned, he saw neither the shelter-seeking cat nor the dog in hot pursuit. Seeing Adam's leg, and mistaking it for a protective tree, the cat skinned up it, sinking her claws into Adam's flesh.

Adam bolted, throwing Robert off balance. His overalls caught on the hook of the doubletree, suspending him precariously beneath the wagon's tongue while the horses ran wildly! "Effie!" he screamed, as loudly as he could. Effie roused when the wagon jerked off at breakneck speed, sending shoppers fleeing to safety. She struggled up, still shrouded in the quilt. She could hear Robert calling her name, but could not see him. Where was he?

Chapter 18

A Night In The Wagon

"Stop them, Effie! Stop the horses!" Effie was Robert's only hope!

The reins unraveled from the reincheck and flapped crazily in the wind. She must get ahold of them! Bracing herself against the wagon's powerful forward surge, she held her hands up to catch the leather straps when they blew her way. Would her stubborn fingers hold them?

Here they came toward her. She grabbed, wrapping them, twisting them around and around her stiff hands, then fell backward, letting the weight of her body assist her in pulling the reins taunt. The leather cut into her tender skin. She had to stop the wagon!

The horses, trained in obedience, stopped. Effie disengaged the lines from her raw hands, laid them to one side, and proned herself quietly beneath the quilt as she had been instructed by Dessie to do. She wished to cause no trouble. She was terrified for Robert. What had happened to him? She could no longer hear his voice. Had he fallen from the wagon during the wild ride?

Stepping from the drug store with a stick of candy to share with Effie, Dessie was shocked to see the wagon hurrying away with Effie tugging at the reins. What was she trying to do?

The townspeople who witnessed the runaway followed hurriedly on foot. The city marshall, informed of the tragedy, mounted his horse and was the first to arrive at the scene. Henry, who discovered the wagon missing as he exited the general store, ran toward the team, not knowing that Robert hung battered and unconscious beneath the doubletree.

Marshal Rose lifted the limp body. "This your boy?" he asked Henry. Henry gripped a wagon wheel to steady himself.

"Yes, sir. Is he alive?"

"Barely. Let's get him to Doc Murphy's office! And pray that Doc's in!"

The town was in an uproar. "I seen an *angel*. Raised right up an' stopped them horses," vowed Mrs. Berry, the smithy's wife.

"Yes, I seen it, too," agreed Mrs. Rose, the marshal's wife. "'Twas nothin' short of a miracle!"

Martha and the scattered Harris children rushed to see what the commotion that centered around their wagon was about. Martha fainted when she saw Mr. Rose carrying Robert, still and white. Mrs. Berry ran for smelling salts to revive her.

Dr. Murphy put Robert in his special examining room adjoining his bottom-floor office. He was a new doctor, not acquainted with the Harris family. He watched pityingly as Martha wrung her hands. Henry refused to leave Robert's side.

"I'm afraid he has internal hemorrhaging," Dr. Murphy told them. "His body took quite a beating. Only time will tell. You might as well prepare to stay the night—if he lasts that long."

Mrs. Rose and Mrs. Berry offered to "put the children up for the night," but they begged permission to stay in the doctor's office near their anxious parents and critical brother. Their tears were quietly shed, their voices subdued respectfully.

Robert tossed and turned, moaning. Once he called Effie's name. The doctor gave him morphine. "All we can do is wait, and hope for the best." Dr. Murphy offered little encouragement.

The approaching night, with its finger of darkness, pointed the Saturday's milling crown homeward, or to the backroom dens of iniquity. No thought was given to Effie, alone in the wagon. She had heard the marshal say that Robert was "barely alive" and was sick with apprehension. She prayed desperately and felt the close comfort of her Friend. If only she had her Bible to clutch to her quaking heart! Even Dessie, in her deep sorrow, did not remember to check on Effie, and the night seemed cruelly long to the suffering child. Had she done all she could to save Robert? Would daylight never arrive?

The town sounds were strange: a bare tree limb grating on a tin shop roof sent chills up and down Effie's spine. The door to the doctor's office closed with finality, shutting the Harris family and Robert into a different world. A clock struck somewhere. Twelve times. The street was

201

dark and vacant.

Then the sound of someone talking in subdued tones reached Effie's sensitive ears.

"What if they come out?"

"We'll check at the back window and see if they're fixing to leave." The voices faded, but eventually came back into earshot.

"Fine pair of horses, ain't they?"

"Nice wagon, too. Can you drive a buckboard?"

"Nothing to it, man."

"What if the horses don't like us and decide to run away again like they did today?"

"Are you yellow, or something? These horses will bring a good price. . ."

"No, but we gotta be cautious. I don't hanker to spend the weekend in the hoosegow." The voices were getting closer.

". . the marshal's sound asleep. We'll have them fine horses in Iredell before anybody misses 'em. . ."

Effie panicked! These prowlers were plotting to steal Uncle Henry's horses and wagon—and with her in it! She raised up, quilt and all, and gave a startled, plaintive cry.

"Ghosts! Oh, I told you, Sam! That's a bad luck wagon. Run, Sam, run! Let's get out of here!" One of the thugs tripped and fell trying to get to the alleyway. He looked back in terror to see if the ghost was following.

The thieves did not return. Effie dozed fitfully, wondering what was happening inside. If only Dessie would bring her some news about Robert. . . A light norther blew in, causing Effie to shiver, renewing the dread of winter. She never had enough cover! How glad she was that Dessie put in the extra quilt. She pulled Dessie's warm coverlet close about her and lost the battle to stay awake.

"His pulse is getting weaker," Dr. Murphy told Henry in the morning's small hours. "Don't believe he can last much longer."

"Would an operation help, Doctor?"

"No. It would just hasten his passing. He wouldn't live through it."

"There's nothing you can do to save him?"

"There's nothing anybody can do but God."

"He has a lot of broken bones?"

"I'm afraid so."

"Effie was brave. She tried to save him," Dessie whispered to Martha. "She stopped the horses. I saw her do it."

Martha shook her weary head. "What you jest told me couldn't possibly be true."

"But Mama, I saw. . . ."

"Hush, Dessie. Hold your tongue."

Martha moved to Robert's side and took his limber hand in hers. It was the last time he tried to rally. "Effie. . . ?" he mumbled. "Thank you, Effie!"

"Is he calling for someone?" Dr. Murphy asked.

"A cousin." Martha was ashamed to admit that the child for whom Robert called was in the wagon outside, unattended and alone. But she allowed Dessie to slip out quietly to check on the object of Robert's concern; Effie was asleep.

Robert died early on the Lord's Day. The trip home was quiet, overshadowed by a dreadful loneliness. Most of the children slept after their strenuous night in the doctor's office. "H-here." Effie pushed her quilts and pillow toward Dessie for the comfort of the younger children.

"William, did you find out anything 'bout Joseph?" Martha asked.

"No, m'am. Th' foreman of th' shops came in th' barber shop an' he said there'd never been anybody by th' name of Joseph Harris worked fer th' railroad at Th' Springs."

"It's sure gonna be hard layin' away one o' th' family without Joseph here." Tears fell onto the yoke of her faded dress, and Henry layed a weathered hand on hers. "Th' year I tried to make th' best fer you has turned to th' worst," he said. "I'm sorry, Martha."

Robert's body stayed in the living room for two days. Effie was relegated to a back bedroom while neighbors came and went. Someone sat up around the clock, keeping the lamp burning. Robert was laid to rest in the cemetery beside the church; Pastor Stevens preached the funeral, which Effie was not permitted to attend. *"Why couldn't it have been me?"* she questioned.

Part of the profit from the crops went to buy a nice headstone for Robert. Martha was inconsolable. Robert, the future doctor of the family, was dead and Joseph, the politician, was gone.

Henry bore his grief silently. Effie cried in the woodshed. But life went on.

Chapter 19

The Territory

"This is Joseph Harris, Mr. Browning." The proprietor of the stage stop looked from Jim Collins to the youthful face of Joseph, studying it for a brief moment.

"Wait. Let me guess. You're a younger brother of Charles Harris!"

"I'm his nephew, sir."

"Pleased to meet you, Joseph." Mr. Browning extended his hand, and Jim excused himself to attend the horses. "We was mighty fond of that uncle of yours, and you're his spittin' likeness. Take a room with us here at the inn. Charlotte, fix the back bedroom up for Joseph."

"Yes, Father." Charlotte gathered her feminine charms into a coy smile and tossed it at Joseph.

Mr. Browning turned to his wife. "Gracie, this is Charles Harris' nephew, Joseph Harris." Grace Browning, slender and bearing the gracefulness that befitted her name, nodded. "Put another plate on the table, Gracie. You will be staying for a few days with us, won't you, Joseph?"

"That's my immediate plans, sir. I want to look around a bit if I may."

"Good! I'd been hoping to get some word from Charles. Have a pair of boots here someone left for him; a trade he'd made I believe they said. Hadn't seen him since he left. I was afraid he was staying away on account of bad memories. Where is he living now?"

"We haven't heard from him in years. He left for the west coast when I was about ten years old."

"Never did return?"

"No, sir. We got one letter saying he was coming back east with the fortune he had collected. We waited and waited. . . ."

"That's too bad. I don't like books that end like that. But it's life, especially if there's gold mingled in. What happened to the baby. . .let's see, I believe he had a little girl?"

"Yes, sir. Her name is Effie. She's still alive. She lives with us." The needs of a customer called Mr. Browning to the counter, leaving Mrs. Browning to converse with Joseph.

"I'm sure glad you looked us up," Mrs. Browning told him. "Your uncle left a barrel of belongings that were Rebecca's. I'm sure you will want to take them back to the girl. Even if Charles is alive somewhere, he will want the child to have what was her mother's. Let's see now. . . that was about eight years ago if my memory serves me right. . .she must be eleven or twelve years old by now."

"Somewhere thereabouts."

"If she looks anything like her mother, she's a beauty."

"Did you know Rebecca well?"

"I knew her better than anybody did, except for Charles. She didn't come in to the stage stop very often, but I always enjoyed our rare visits. I could tell right away she was from a high class family. . .well bred, I mean. . . she wasn't uppity. She loved the simple things of life. . .it sufficed her to be on the land with Charles."

"They say Charles was really fond of her."

"He was crazy about her. It like to have finished him off when he lost her. Rebecca went through a difficult childbirth, it being her first one and all. We wondered if she ever really got strong again after the baby came. Effie was so tiny, we all feared she wouldn't survive. After she was born, we didn't see much of Rebecca. Her death was a real shock to us. . .and to Charles, too."

"She is buried on the land?"

"Yes, her grave is there. Charlotte can go with you and show you the exact spot."

"Could. . .could we go today?" To visit Rebecca's grave for Effie's sake was one of Joseph's foremost goals.

"Why not? Saddle the horses for them, Dave." Mr. Browning had finished with the business. "They'll have time to go before supper."

Having spent many hours in the saddle, Charlotte was a better rider than Joseph. They rode in awkward silence, Joseph hearing only the voice of the wilderness that had called Charles. No words were exchanged until they came to the abandoned cabin.

"This is where they lived," Charlotte told him. "Rather remote, but they liked it that way. I was just a

207

small child, but I remember Charles saying he brought his wagon tongue west to escape waggin' tongues back east. He said there were two kinds of tongues. . .a wagon tongue and a waggin' tongue, and the length of both were about the same!''

"Makes sense." Joseph dismounted and went to explore the ruins of the deserted cottage. The very primitiveness of it gave him a sensation of being akin to the Maker. That was the only way he could describe the feeling to himself. If Charlotte had not been along, he would sit and meditate. . .maybe even say a prayer. . .and let life's turmoils wash away, leaving his mind as clean and clear as the atmosphere here in this virgin territory.

Charlotte was talking, but Joseph was not listening. Something about government rights, suggesting that he check into the claim for himself as blood kin and think about settling on the place. Lost in thought, he did not even detect her ulterior motives.

"Father said Charles was getting ready to build Rebecca a nice house on the land when she died. But Mother says Rebecca wouldn't have been one whit happier in a mansion!''

Joseph mounted his horse for the continuation of the tour. Charlotte took him by the spring that had influenced Charles' choice of location, still bubbling and clear.

"Charles had an ideal piece of property," she pointed out. "He just had a streak of bad luck. He kept saying, 'We have the rest of our lives on the land; eventually the tide will turn our way,' and he'd be here yet if he hadn't lost his reason for living. . . .''

The next stop was Rebecca's gravesite beneath a low, gnarled Mesquite tree. Charles had erected a crude stone marker.

"He buried her all by himself. I wasn't but about ten years old, but I remember how I cried about it. We'd 'a come if we'd known about it. He didn't tell us, or anybody, till it was all over. Seemed that's the way he wanted it. . . to be alone with his grief."

Joseph tried to step into Charles' shoes and feel the trauma that crushed him as he knelt beneath this unsympathetic tree with thorns as poison as those puncturing his heart, and laid his sweetheart to rest. Someday, when he was a stagecoach driver, he would bring Effie and show her how brave her little mother had been.

"Mother says Rebecca was kind of. . .religious," Charlotte said. "Course we're too isolated to have a church or a preacher out here in the territory. . . ."

"Some folks that have no church building are better Christians than those who do." Charlotte misrouted Joseph's remark to the doorstep of her own ego and parked it there. But Joseph did not have Charlotte in mind at all. He was thinking of Effie. . .and the deacon's wife.

Back at the stage house, Mrs. Browning had supper waiting. Charlotte bothered Joseph with questions about Texas, and Joseph answered them to be polite. He wished, however, that he could be in a quiet corner with his thoughts.

Joseph made it clear that he could not stay long. Mr. Browning brought out every lure he had to snag Joseph into staying on in the territory. "Group of us will be going up into the mountains elk hunting after the first big snow. That's usually in December or January. We'd like for you to winter with us and go along. Never been hunting till you've hunted for elk! You can delay your return to Texas until spring, can't you?"

"I thank you, and I'm sure I'd have a good time. But I need to be home for Christmas. I want to see that Effie has a nice holiday. I told her I'd be back. She'll worry herself sick if I stay away too long."

"I never did see the child but a few times," Mrs. Browning said. "She was asleep the day Charles left with her. I thought surely Rebecca would come in and show her off when she was newborn, but Charles said she was a sickly infant."

"I'll never forget the day Charles left us," Mr. Browning added his chapter to the history. "Sold his good wagon and team way too cheap just to get the money for that trip. Seemed in an awful hurry. Driven by grief, I guess. The wife and Charlotte would have been glad to help with the tyke if he had wanted to stay on in the territory, but I guess he just couldn't stand it without Rebecca. Can't blame him really. They were awfully close."

"Do you have brothers and sisters of your own. . .I mean, besides Effie?" Joseph kept the padlock on his heart, avoiding personal conversations with Charlotte as much as possible.

"Yes. Two sisters and six brothers."

"Younger or older?"

"All younger."

"But obviously you're partial to Effie?"

"She's just real special. . . ."

"Being an orphan and belonging to Charles and all?"

"She's real smart. . .and real lovable. . .and. . .and she *needs* me. Mama has her hands full. . .and. . .well," Joseph stumbled for words. "When I get a house of my own, I'm going to *adopt* Effie."

"I've always thought adopting an orphan child would be the nicest thing anyone could do." Was Charlotte throwing a not-too-subtle hint? "But won't your mother object? She's bound to be *attached* to Effie by now, since she's such a princess!"

"Truthfully, Mama has always resented the intrusion of an outsider into her own family. Besides having her hands full with her children, she has some funny ideas. She would never accept Effie as her own daughter. *Never*."

"Say, that's too bad."

"Unfortunately, yes."

"Can't Effie. . .uh, *feel* the rejection?"

"Sure. That's why I have to hurry home. I try to make life easier for Effie in small ways. . .like seeing that she has something special under the tree and doesn't feel left out at Christmastime."

"Will you take something to Effie from me, Joseph?" Charlotte, smitten by the handsome nephew of Charles, was more interested in reaching his heart than Effie's.

Joseph was getting fidgety before Jim returned; the nights turned to sleepless tossing. They would scarcely have time to make the trip and arrive by Christmas, even with the weather favoring them.

When at last he arrived, Jim apologized. "Sorry for the delay, Joseph. A swollen river held me back. But if the Good Lord will hold out the sunshine for us, we'll still make it fine. Predictions are for a mild winter. The animals haven't put on heavy coats this year. If we can get down off the caprock, we've got it made."

In vain, Charlotte tried to coax a commitment from the winsome Joseph. "You *will* come back to see us, won't you, Joseph? You won't forget us, will you?" She used her wide pretty eyes to their greatest advantage.

"I hope to bring Effie out here for a visit some day," he replied. "She'll want to see her mother's grave. But until then, I guess I'll have no call to return."

"Couldn't you come just to see old friends. . .the Browning family?"

"Thank you, but I don't know just yet what the future has in store for me. . .or Effie."

"At least you could send a post now and then by Jim and let us know how Effie is doing. . .and the rest of you." The charms were not hitting their intended target.

Unheeding, Joseph turned to Jim. "Is there room for Effie's barrel? I don't know what's in it. Some things Charles left here that belonged to Rebecca."

"We'll make room if we have to throw out a passenger!"

Jim was as impatient as Joseph to be on the road eastward, but another day was stolen from them in the delay of connections with a southern coach. Only one passenger joined them going east. Amarillo destined, the middle-aged man slept most of the way.

"Say, where'd you get those classy boots?"

"They belonged to Charles, and they're a perfect fit. Wanted a pair all my life."

"Nobody ever deserved them more."

"I don't know about that. I ain't much of a cowboy."

"I dare say the miles'll pass snail slow getting you back to the angel with bent wings."

"I'm right anxious to get back to her, all right."

"I got a nice surprise for her Christmas! You'll see that she gets it, and nobody else?"

"I promise."

"Look!" Grinning, Jim pulled a box from beneath the seat.

Joseph stared speechless. He had never seen such a delicate creation of ruffles and lace. The doll was too pretty to *touch*! "Where. . .where did you get such a. . .such a treasure?"

"It belonged to our angel. When I told Sis about Effie, she insisted on sending this doll for her. She said Princess would want someone like herself to have it. From one bent-winged angel to another."

"I don't know how to thank you. . . ."

"My pleasure."

"I saved back a little money. Thought I might find her something special myself in Amarillo. . .a book of poetry or something. She's big on reading. I got to work a little bit for Mr. Browning, so I'd like to get the rest of the family a little something, too."

"Oh, say, Joseph. . ."

"Yes, sir?"

"How'd you get by without Charlotte stealing your heart?"

"My heart's done occupied."

"But someday you'll want a wife. . . ."

"Someday maybe. But right now I have my hands and my heart full. I've got to know what's going to become of Effie before I can make any plans of my own. . . ."

At first, it appeared that Jim had abruptly changed the subject. "You want to stop back by and get another drink of sulphur water?" he asked.

Joseph made a wry face. "Man, if that rotten water was the 'Fountain of Life' and I was ninety years old, I'd

213

turn it down and die with a good taste in my mouth!''

Jim's mustache jitterbugged, then he sobered. ''Speaking of the Fountain of Youth. . .life has a way of tiptoeing out on you while you have your head turned. Take me for instance. I can't believe I'm looking *back* on thirty. You want to remember that when you're thinking about Charlotte.''

Chapter 20

The New Grave

"We'll be there before the day's out, Joseph."

"Couldn't have picked a better day to get home than on Saturday. The young'uns will be home from school. I'm anxious to see them all."

"I hope your parents haven't worried too much over you."

"I'm sure Mama has; she's that way. But it wouldn't have done to tell her my plans. She'd have set out to block them."

"You've never said anything about anybody but Effie. How many brothers and sisters do you have?"

"Six brothers and two sisters. That's not counting Effie."

"All younger?"

"Yes, sir. Matthew is just below me. He's steady and dependable, a lot like Papa. He likes music. I always wished he had the opportunity to study notes. He claims the preacher's daughter, but that's still a secret. I found it out by simple observation. Anybody'd have to be blind not to see those two have eyes for each other!"

"What's she like? Is she suited to Matthew?"

"Oh, yes. She has long eyelashes and blue, blue eyes. Her hair is gold colored and naturally curly. She's soft-natured, soft-spoken, and gentle with children."

"Well, you *do* notice girls!"

"Only when they're not noticing me."

Jim chuckled. "What about the rest of your family?"

"Sarah's next."

"I wondered when you were going to throw a girl in!"

"Sorry we don't have one old enough for you, Jim. Sarah's too young." Joseph could not resist a turn about in the teasing. "Sarah looks a lot like Mama. But she has a lot of advantages that Mama was never afforded in life . . .like schooling. She's a great artist; can draw most anything. And a good cook, too. Mama's bound and determined that Sarah's not going to marry young like she did. But I don't know about that. I think Sarah has a sweetheart behind Mama's back. The neighbor boy. They do most of their courting at church."

"Are they a good match?"

"They're a perfect match. Hank is a good worker and real handy, already looking toward land of his own. Mama would have a wall-eyed fit if Sarah falls in love, but my wind vane tells me it's going that general direction."

"How old is she?"

"Fifteen."

"Then. . .?"

"Robert. He's an outdoorsman. . .a real different kid.

He is more at home with animals than people. Smart as a whip, though. And after him is William. When he was little, he was the most religious of us all, but I think he's getting a bit worldly-minded lately. Mama declares he'll be a preacher for sure. . .and it wouldn't surprise me. He can preach about as well as Brother Stevens now!

"Dessie follows Robert. She's Effie's same age and a natural born teacher. She has more patience than anybody I ever saw. Taught Effie to read. I don't know what Effie would have done without a girl her age for companionship. Dessie really loves Effie."

"That's a blessing."

"Yes, I've thanked God many times for sending Dessie. She's a loving-natured girl. . .just what Effie needed."

"And three more boys if I haven't missed my calculations?"

"Yes, sir. Twins and then a single all packed in close together. Mama's political idol is Chester Alan Arthur so she named the three last ones Chester, Alan, and Arthur. Papa calls them 'the President's boys.' And they're live wires!"

"Who was the mite of a boy that came running out to the coach wanting to pet the horses when I brought your uncle and Effie to your place back in '78? Must have been five years old or so. . .impressive chap."

"That had to be Robert. He's drawn to animals like a magnet. Spends more time with the cow and chickens than he does with the family! Mama declares he'll be a doctor, the way he practices on the ailing animals."

"A vet, maybe."

"He'd make a good one! He has an incredible way with the whole animal kingdom."

217

"He loved the horses. Never had a horse of his own?"

"No, sir. Papa hoped to make enough this year to get a wagon and team. Don't know if he did or not; I didn't stay to see."

"I was just impressed by Robert; I expect he'll be my favorite. . .besides Effie. Maybe I feel that way because he's the only one I met, and I know him better. A lot can happen in a few days, can't it?"

"Yes, sir. I just hope Mama hasn't been too hard on the. . .bent-winged angel."

"Time hasn't softened her any at all?"

"I'm afraid not. Mama has a good heart, but she's had a hard life. Married when she was real young and had all us kids right off. She had no chance at an education, and Papa put all his resources into the land, leaving little for luxuries for her."

"Do you suppose she'll ever. . .treat the child any better?"

"It'd be a miracle. If she could accept Effie as a normal *human*, with emotions and feelings and needs like other children, the problem would resolve itself. She thinks of Effie as an *object*, incapable of thinking or responding or performing. She is so prejudiced. . ."

"What you say we make a pact to pray about it? The Good Book says where two or three agree. . . ."

"Sure! I just wish I had more faith."

The stagecoach approached Five Oaks. Back to the perimeter of his world, Joseph wrestled with a strange foreboding that he could not shake. Jim sensed it; they had grown close in spirit and soul.

"Something troubling you, Joseph?"

"Yes, sir, but I can't exactly place it. Both were silent

as the community church came into eye range, bringing both good and bad memories to Joseph. Flashbacks of fifth Sunday dinners, baptisings, Myrt's choppy organ music, and the smell of freshly mown grass intertwined with the precognition. As long as the whole family attended, he found comfort there, but then Martha dropped out. . . And for some undetermined reason, Deacon Clark's self-righteous wife had been eagle-eyeing them all ever since.

Lost in thought, Joseph's fixed gaze fell from the familiar milepost and caught on Robert's headstone. A new grave! Who had died while he was away? Why, the mound was on the front of his own family's plot! HARRIS, the marker said. *Oh, God don't let it be Papa!* He could not read the smaller engraving from the road. He gasped and turned white, causing Jim to rein the horses to an abrupt stop. Something was wrong with Joseph!

"What. . .what's the matter, Joseph? Are you sick? Is it your heart?"

"Someone. . .someone in *my family* has died since I left! There's our plot. . .our name! A fresh grave!"

HARRIS the tombstone read. "Joseph. . .I'm sorry!"

"Jim, if it's *Effie*, I'll never forgive myself for leaving her. . .never!"

"Joseph, it's not Effie."

"How. . .how can you be so sure?"

"Your mother wouldn't put such an elaborate stone on the grave of a child she doesn't even consider a part of your family!"

"You're right, Jim. It's one of the immediate family. But I've got to know who it is before I reach the house, so I can be braced for it. I can't go home not knowing. Could. . .could I have a minute of your time to go see?

Or you could just put out the stuff here and I could walk on. . ."

"Take all the time you want, Joseph. I wouldn't think of driving off and leaving you. Do you need me to go along with you to the grave?"

"No, I'd rather go. . .alone. . .if you don't mind."

Jim waited, hurting inside for his young friend. He had learned long ago that death was a foe that had to be faced individually, and he watched now as Joseph came to grips with life's darkest enemy. Near the mound, Joseph dropped to his knees and put his face in his hands, crying great body-shaking sobs.

"He's a good kid, that Joseph," Jim said to himself. *"Wonder which one it was? Strange that I get mixed up in this family's personal grief. First it was Charles. . .and now Joseph."*

Always aware of others and feeling that he was keeping Jim and the coach waiting, Joseph returned slowly, sadly to the vehicle, head bowed. "It was Robert," he said simply. "I wonder what happened? Died not long after I left. Like you say, Jim, a lot can happen in a few days."

Chapter 21

Homecoming

"*Joseph!* Here's Joseph! Mama! Papa! *Joseph's home!*" William shouted while Chester locked his arms about Joseph's legs in a legiron grip. "An' look at 'is boots!"

Martha hastened to the door, dabbing her eyes with her stained apron. "Tell 'im to bring 'is little wife right on in. Effie's out at th' shed. . . ."

Henry hurried out to greet Joseph, relief showing on his weathered face. Joseph swallowed hard. *Papa has aged ten years!* Missing from the reunion was Robert, but Joseph bore his grief in silence, smiling on the "top side" with roots aching.

"I need a little help unloading," Joseph said, and six assorted sizes of masculine hands offered their willing assistance. "A barrel and some boxes."

"He's got to unload her stuff, too," Martha said to

Sarah, while Sarah craned her neck to locate her new sister-in-law.

"What um is?" Arthur pointed to the boxes, full of questions.

"Surprises," Joseph answered.

"Goody! Um's surprises, Alan!"

"Is Effie in the house?" Joseph asked.

"No." Martha misunderstood Joseph's reason for asking. "You can bring yer new wife on in an' th' driver, too, fer a cup o' coffee an' gingerbread."

"My *what?*"

"Yer wife you married while you's gone. . . ."

"Mama, wherever did you get the idea that I was *married*? I don't even have a bonnie, much less a *wife*. I told Effie where I was going. Where is she?" His heart gave one quick, terrifying leap; suppose Martha had sent her "off."

"She's in th' woodshed. Don't worry, she won't be comin' in. . . ."

"In the woodshed? As cold as it is?"

"She has a nest o' feedsacks out there. Bring yore friend on in. I jus' popped th' gingerbread out o' th' oven. It's pipin' hot."

Jim, with no passengers and running several hours ahead of schedule, accepted the invitation, hoping to get to meet Effie.

"Where's Matthew?"

"He works Saturdays fer th' parson."

Joseph winked at Jim. "And Sarah?"

"She's helpin' th' Gibson young'uns decorate th' church fer th' Christmas program on th' morrow. They'll be home fer supper."

"What are you so quiet about, Dessie?" Dessie shrugged.

Warmed by the coffee and cake that Martha had fussed over to her satisfaction, Joseph stood up. "I want to show Jim about the little place of ours, then we'll all sit down and have a long catch-up talk."

"I'll show 'um horses!" Chester offered.

"No, Chester," Joseph denied him gently. "All of you stay here and help Mama. I want to show Jim about the place myself. I'll be back after a bit. . . Mama, could you put on a fresh pot of coffee. . .and Papa, will you keep the boys out of the boxes?"

Martha would have turned cartwheels for Joseph at that moment, so relieved was she that he had not married a stranger to whom she would have to adjust. How glad she was that Effie was out of sight so Joseph could freely bring his friend in for a visit! This is as it should be all time!

When the back door closed behind Joseph and Jim, Joseph lowered his voice. "We'll find her, if she's in the woodshed. But just in case the boys are watching, we'll circle the barn and see Bossy first."

Adam and Eve raised their heads, still munching hay. "Fine pair of horses," Jim admired.

"Pity Robert isn't here to humor them. I wonder if he even got to see them. . . ."

"Guess you'll find out."

"Isn't going to be the same around here without Robert."

A furry gray cat rubbed against Jim's boot, purring a welcome. "That's Socks, Effie's kitten. Named it herself."

"Where's the shed?"

"This way."

The door was closed; no sound came from within. Joseph knocked and waited. Effie, thin and gaunt, pushed against the heavy wooden door, trembling. Had they come to expel her from her haven, her last place of solitude on earth?

Joseph helped her by pulling from the outside. He stepped back in shock at what he saw. The sunken eyes, red from crying, registered happy disbelief. "J-Joseph!"

"My little Effie! I'm back!" He threw his big arms around her, holding her close. It was the first time Effie had smiled since Robert's death.

"T-thank you." The first words he taught her.

"And Effie, this is our friend, Jim. He drove the stagecoach. Took me all the way to Rebecca-Land and back!"

"J-Jim?"

Jim dropped to his knees and took both of Effie's bony, twisted hands in his own. "Effie, Joseph told me what an angel you are. . .and I couldn't wait to meet you!"

"T-thank you!" She looked from Jim to Joseph; her gratitude was meant for both.

"You see, we had an angel, too, in our own family. Her wings were bent up like yours. We called her Princess. But we weren't as lucky as Joseph. We didn't get to keep her long. The beautiful smile, created with great effort in spite of her spastic face muscles, brought back memories so tender that Jim turned his head away to hide his tears.

"Joseph's going to tell you all about the peaceful place where your mother awaits the resurrection morning. And someday, Joseph and I are going to take you there to see it for yourself!"

"Oh, S-sir. I-I l-love y-you!" He had to but close his eyes and roll back time; here was Princess back into his life.

"But Effie, you must start eating good and get real strong before you can make that kind of trip. It's a long, long ways. We couldn't take any chances on you getting sick!"

"Y-yes, s-sir."

"You've been worrying about something, Effie," Joseph said. "It wasn't me, was it? I told you I'd be back."

"N-no. R-Robert."

"What happened to Robert?"

"I t-tried t-to s-save h-him!" Effie started to weep again.

"I'm sure you did your best, Effie, whatever happened. Just remember one thing. God knows you did everything you could. He knows what's best, okay?" Joseph's way of lifting the crushing weight from the child's soul amazed Jim.

"I want you in the house for supper tonight, young lady!" Joseph's sternness was betrayed by his twinkling eyes. "And you are to sit by me so I can see that you eat *properly*." The girlish giggle warmed Jim's heart. Joseph was home; the world was topside up once more.

Jim took his leave, refusing Martha's invitation to stay for the evening meal. "I'd sure like to stay, but I need to be in Cleburne by morning," he said. "Sure like your place, Mr. Harris. Especially the little log woodshed. Wish I had one just like it!"

Now whatever could he mean by that? wondered Martha. That old woodshed was nothing but an eyesore. Joseph did pick strange friends!

Martha bustled about preparing a special menu. On the front porch, Joseph sat on the railing near the familiar posterior-shaped cane-bottom chair that supported Henry.

"Tell me about Robert. What happened?"

"How did you know?"

"Saw the headstone and new grave in the churchyard as I came in."

"I don't suppose anyone knows exactly what happened. Some said one thing; some another. We were in Th' Springs shoppin' an' th' horses. . . ."

"Start way back. . .when did you get the horses?"

"I forgot you left before we got th' wagon an' team. Soon's th' crops sold, Robert an' me went to Cleburne—rode in with th' parson—an' Robert picked 'em out. We bought th' wagon th' same day."

"Jim said you got a fine set."

"Robert named th' horses Adam an' Eve, cause he had to run 'em out 'o 'th garden right off."

"That Robert was sharp as a razor."

"Then we all went in shoppin' on a Saturday. Started out a perfect day. Had a picnic at Steele Creek by th' Spring Hole. Robert drove th' team th' whole way. Th' tragedy happened while we were all shoppin'. Somethin' spooked th' horses. Some say a dog chasin' a cat made th' horses bolt. How Robert got on th' underneath side o' th' doubletree an' got drug, I dunno."

"Who stopped the runaway horses?"

"Conflictin' stories. Women that's generally sensible said a ghost riz up in th' wagon an' stopped 'em." Effie's broken words about trying to save Robert tugged at the fringes of Joseph's mind.

"Where was Effie?"

"Why, she was in th' wagon layin' down. Martha insisted she stay out o' sight."

"Was Robert killed instantly?"

"No, he lived 'bout twelve hours. Died early on th' Lord's Day."

"Never regained consciousness, nor said anything?"

"Kept callin' Effie's name. Don't 'spose he knew what he was sayin', though. His last words was 'thank you, Effie.' " The puzzle pieces locked together in Joseph's mind; he was sure that it was Effie who halted the horses.

"Does Effie know that?"

"No, I don't 'spose anyone bothered to tell 'er. Things have been in a turmoil 'round here since we lost Robert. I don't guess it would matter one way er t'other to her nohow."

"I'm sorry I wasn't here for the funeral, Papa. But the trip I just took was something I had to do for my own peace of mind."

Joseph was the last to wash at the wash basin for supper, purposely stalling until Effie made her way to the table. Then he pulled his chair up between her and Sarah. "Thought I'd sit between a couple of my sweet sisters tonight!" he grinned.

"Dessie, trade places with Effie," Martha ordered. Dessie arose to obey, but Joseph held up his hand in objection.

"I'm happy with the seating arrangement just like it is. Please don't change it!"

If Martha noticed that Effie ate twice as much as usual, she did not mention it. She cooked an abundant amount for Joseph's homecoming, and the joyful reunion absorbed her attention.

"Sarah, I hear you've been getting the church ready for the Christmas program." Joseph caught Sarah's blush. He suspected she had been doing more courting than decorating.

"Yes, we're having our recitin' tomorrow. Will you come?"

"I'm mighty tired from my long trip. If you'll excuse me this time, I'll stay home with Effie and let Mama go. She'll want to see her stars perform!"

"No, I'll stay. . ." Martha began, but Joseph interrupted.

"No, you'll *go*." He left no room for argument. "I'll help Effie unpack the barrel of her mother's things I found out west."

"Then you really did go to Charles' homestead?" Martha seemed surprised.

"I did. It was quite an experience. These boots I'm wearing belonged to Charles."

"What's in the barrel?"

"I don't know. Charles left it at the stagestop with the Brownings, and they've had it in storage awaiting his return. Since he never called for it, they sent it to his next-of-kin."

"Couldn't be nuthin' of value. Charles brought all th' valuable stuff with 'em."

"Judging from the place they lived out there, I'd say you are right! And by the way, Papa, when are we putting up the Christmas tree?"

"Since Robert left us, we hadn't had much hankerin' fer happy times."

"If I know Robert, he'd want us to have a *great* Christmas. Let's not disappoint him."

"When can you get a tree, Henry?"

"Th' day after tomorra, Martha. Wouldn't want to chop nuthin' down on Sunday."

"Good. I've got lots of surprises to go under that tree," Joseph said. "This is going to be the best Christmas *some* of us have ever had!" Nobody saw him wink at Effie except Dessie.

Chapter 22

Rebecca's Barrel

"*I* told you judgments was comin' to that family sooner 'er later," Gertie Clark reminded the deacon on the way to church. "I knowed it'd happen. The Bible says be sure yore sins'll find you out. Well, they found out Marthy."

"The most uprightest families on earth lose children sometimes, Gertie. That ain't nuthin' to base yore judgin' on. Th' Bible likewise says it rains on th' just an' unjust out o' th' same sky."

"Don't look now, Clark. . .but ain't that *Marthy* goin' in th' church door? As I live an' breathe. . ."

"Yes, an' yore Christian obligation is to be kind to 'er."

"My Christian obligation is to keep no company with sinners!"

Gertie made her way to her pew near the front, keeping her head high and her eyes straight ahead. "Marthy's here!" she whispered to Sister Myrt. The whisper filled the building, reaching Martha's sensitive ears. As heads turned to look, Martha surpressed an urge to get up and leave.

Outside in the plummeting temperature, Henry was talking to Mr. Gibson. "I believe we're in fer a bad spell o' weather a 'fore th' night's out," he predicted. "Possibly one o' those blizzards what drops th' warmth 'bout forty degrees in an hour! It's been too warm fer this time o' year."

"Got plenty o' firewood fer yore family?"

"We're all set, an' Joseph's home safe. How about yourself?"

"We're ready. Th' children think it'd be right nice to have a white Christmas."

Back at the Harris homestead, Joseph pulled the clumsy keg into the middle of the floor. "Are you ready to see what's in your ship that just came in, Effie?"

"C-can't w-wait!"

Joseph pried at the boards on the top. "Everything should be in good shape. This was stored in dry country. They don't have mildew and mold way up there like we have here."

"Y-yes. H-hurry!"

Joseph laughed. "I've never seen you so bitten by impatience, Effie!"

"E-ex-cept l-learn-ing t-to r-read!"

"So you could read Rebecca's Bible."

"Y-yes."

"Charlotte, the stage stop owner's daughter, told me that your mother was a religious person. She had no church to go to out there in the wilderness, but she loved God."

"W-what e-else?"

"She was very pretty, but you know that by the picture. But besides being pretty, she was happy and content. She loved simple things, Charlotte said—her land, her husband, and her baby!"

"O-oh!"

"Well, young lady, you can give me the prize for being the slowest barrel opener on earth, but I have this lid off at last. Let's see what we have here. . .Looks like it's all stuffed in good and proper. Charles packed it, and sometimes men aren't good packers! We'll be extra careful in case there's breakable things."

Joseph carefully lifted a wrinkled white gown from the trappings. "Look here! Must be a wedding dress!" He shook the garment to release the folds and held it up for Effie to see.

"O-ohhh! P-pretty! O-ohhh, J-Joseph!" A robe from Heaven could not have thrilled Effie more than this confection of lace, tiny pearls, and exquisite satin.

"M-mother's d-dress?"

"I'm sure it was. She must have been a tiny thing; this dress isn't very big. You can wear it when you get married, Effie!" Joseph loved teasing her.

"N-not m-me. D-dessie!"

"Wouldn't fit Sarah, that's for sure!"

"There's a dish next. Charles laid it between the dress and the next piece of cloth so it wouldn't get broken." Joseph lifted a massive piece of purple carnival glass, heavy with grape and leaf design. He gave an approving whistle.

"Wow! I've never seen anything more beautiful!"

"F-from h-heaven?"

"I'd say that's exactly where it came from if I didn't know better. But my guess is that it was Rebecca's and she saved it just for you. Where shall I put it?"

"O-on t-the m-mantle."

"Mama might claim it."

"Y-you t-tell i-it's m-mine?" A worry sprang into Effie's eyes; she was depending on Joseph to protect her rights.

"I'll take care of it. Don't you worry."

"T-thank y-you."

"And here's a big, thick something soft." Joseph tugged at the tightly folded material. "It's a fat quilt, Effie!"

"O-oh! O-oh!" Effie gathered the answered prayer to her body and let her tears of thankfulness fall onto it. "H-him!" She pointed up.

"You prayed for a quilt?"

"O-oh, y-yes. . . .l-lots!"

A pain smote Joseph's heart; that Effie had been denied life's basic comforts had never crossed his mind. "You've slept cold in the wintertime, haven't you, Effie?"

"O-oh, y-yes!"

"Well, you won't sleep cold this winter, Effie." He helped her unfold the comforter. "Oh!"

"O-oh!"

With intricate embroidered work on each block, the lovely quilt represented its registry well. A flower garden of colors that once lay on Rebecca's childhood bed brought tears to even Joseph's eyes. Effie was still in her dream world, dazed over the quilt, when Joseph brought another dish from the bowels of the barrel. The stipple-ray bowl with fluted edges shimmered with rainbow colors.

"F-for *y-your* m-mother," Effie said.

"You're sure you want to give it away?"

"F-for C-Christ-m-mas!" Effie yearned to experience the joys of giving.

"I'll hide it in my room and wrap it for you."

"T-thank y-you!"

"And here comes *another* quilt, Effie!" The second blessing was appliqued with colonial ladies, wearing bonnets and holding umbrellas that matched their hoop skirts. "And it's a pretty one, too."

"I-I'll b-be r-real w-warm!"

"And another dish. . .two dishes. . .*two* dishes. . .one on each side of the barrel." They were golden goblets with singing birds on them.

"F-for s-sisters."

"Dessie and Sarah?"

"Y-yes."

"For Christmas?"

"Y-yes."

"Looks like this is about the bottom, Effie. We're ending up with another quilt. A patchwork quilt. No, wait. . . here's two little blankets or shawls for a baby beside the big quilt. Must have been yours. Probably something your mother made for you." He tossed the downy coverlets to Effie, who hugged them lovingly to herself. Without doubt, this had been a perfect day!

"T-thank y-you f-for a-all!"

"But they're yours, Effie. I don't deserve the thanks."

"B-but y-you b-brought t-them."

"It was I who was blessed."

At church, the program was underway. Gertie Clark, more curious to know who was in attendance than to absorb the service, kept glancing back over the congregation. All members of the cast sat together, leaving Martha unsuspecting when Sarah sat beside Hank Gibson and Matthew by Pauline Stevens. Perturbed by Gertie's backward glances, she failed to notice Sarah's eyes searching for Hank's approval during her recitation.

"And now," Pastor Stevens was announcing, "We have a special treat for you. My daughter, Pauline, has lent us her piano for this special occasion. She will sing 'Holy Night,' accompanied by Matthew Harris at the piano. . . ."

Martha looked to Henry for an explanation. Pastor Stevens, of course, had made a mistake. Why, Matthew had never played a note on the piano in his life! Henry sat smiling, unabashed; he must not have caught the error. He was certainly paying poor attention!

Matthew moved confidently to the round stool with its three fat legs, and positioned his hands to the keys. Martha leaned forward, as if to object to the mistake that involved one of hers. She wished to suffer no farther embarrassment from the scorn of Gertie Clark. But it was too late. The notes of the prelude filled the building, floating to the rafters. Martha had never heard such capturing music! Surely she was hallucinating!

"When. . . ? How. . . ?" she tried to whisper to Henry, but her husband was totally engrossed in the delightful rendition.

Sister Myrt, the organist, sulked. The young generation had too much rhythm, too many fancy runs, excess filler notes. Anyway, only *sissy* boys played musical instruments of *any* kind!

Pauline's voice rang clear and pure. Martha's befuddled mind thought what a fetching couple she and Matthew made, and wondered why they had never noticed each other. She had grown up to be a lovely young lady, and had smiled quite pleasantly at Martha this very night!

Gertie Clark's stares that held daggers no longer vexed Martha. Anyone who had a son with this kind of talent should take the tuck-head to no one. And to think she might have missed this event if Joseph had not come home when he did. . . . It was settled. Matthew would have a piano, even if part of the land had to be sold to purchase one.

The program completed, Matthew and Sarah sought out Martha. "The Gibsons are giving a party for the young folks. They want us to come."

Martha, proud as a strutting hen of her chickens, gave her permission. "Why, playin' like that deserves a party, Matthew. Why. . .when. . . ?"

"Brother Stevens has been letting me off for a couple of hours on Saturdays for lessons. I have an excellent teacher. One of the best."

"I dunno where he comes from, but he sure must be good!" Matthew, then, had been spending his hard-earned money for music lessons. Matthew saw the smile in hiding at the corners of Henry's mouth. How did his father know?

Henry, Martha, William, Dessie, and the President's boys rode the buckboard home in the crisp air, already turning chilly. "I believe we're in fer a big snow, Martha," Henry said.

" 'Cept fer Robert in th' churchyard, I'd be right glad!"

"Robert ain't in th' churchyard, Martha. Robert's warm up in heaven with God!"

"Then let th' snow come. Long's all my children's warm. . . ."

Deacon and Gertie Clark took their leave from church. "I think it's plum turrible th' way children flirt nowadays!" Gertie complained to her husband on their way to their house by the river. "Did you see how that Sarah Harris flitted them eyes at that Hank Gibson, an' how th' *preacher's* daughter. . . ."

"Didn't you never flirt when you's young, Gertie?" the deacon asked innocently.

". . .An' th' very idea of Nellie Gibson givin' a party to encourage that kind o' tomfoolery! No good'll come of these doins', Clark, you mark my word. You'll see!"

At the party, Sarah and Hank made secret plans to elope in the spring when Hank turned nineteen. Sarah would be almost sixteen.

Chapter 23

Martha's Announcement

"Snow's a'comin'!" Henry hurried the children through the door to shut out winter's icy breath. Effie heard without dread; she would be warm.

The contents of Effie's barrel dominated the sitting room. Martha, her eyes pivoting from the bowl on the mantle that would comfortably grace the china cabinet of a governor's mansion to the stunning beauty of the quilts, concealed her chagrin. What a shame to waste such luxuries on one who did not comprehend either their value or significance.

Dessie stood agog. "Effie, I'm jus' so *proud* fer you!"

"Q-quilts!"

"They're *beautiful!*"

"Y-you n-need o-one?"

"No, thank you, Effie. I have plenty o' covers. When two sleep in th' same bed like me 'n Sarah, they keep each other warm."

"O-others n-need?"

"No, everybody has their own quilts. . .an' now you have yours. You won't be cold never again."

"I-I p-prayed. H-he a-answered."

"You *prayed* fer th' quilts?"

"Y-yes."

"Well, God sure answered yore prayers *pretty*."

Just before the blue norther struck with its howling winds, Sarah and Matthew returned home. Sarah espied the wedding gown and squealed with delight, running her chapped hands over the smooth satin. "It's too small for you, Sarah," Joseph ribbed. "You'll have to marry in your feedsack dress!" The starry-eyed Sarah flushed, but hid her guilt well.

"It'll be at least three years 'fore Sarah'll even be thinkin' of a feller, much less gettin' married," Martha spoke up. "Don't want no girl o' mine marryin' as young as what I did."

"How old were you when you an' Papa married, Mama?" Sarah asked offhand.

"Fifteen, most nigh sixteen."

"Did you an' Papa elope?"

"Now why'd you ask a question like thet?"

"Just wonderin'."

Joseph's holiday anticipation was infectious. He wrestled with Robert's vacant place at the table in the private of his soul, but outwardly led the family from the bitter graveyard back to the land of the living, resurrecting Christmas, threatened by extinction at Robert's death.

However, when the holidays had passed over the Harris household, a regiment of nagging worries backed up to the wall of Martha's awareness and refused to budge.

One thing was Sarah. Sarah's grades at school took a nosedive and she lost all interest in her books. Never as studious as Dessie, she had nonetheless managed tolerable marks until lately. Her apathy caused Martha no small concern. Was she ill? Was she resting poorly? Did she eat properly?

Then, too, something about Effie's barrel from afar brought an abrasion to Martha's senses. Indeed, this indicated that Effie was moving *in*, when her long-range plans included moving Effie *out* into an institution as soon as Henry was agreeable. . .and he was weakening. She meant for the roots of permanency to spread no farther.

Matthew needed a piano so that the hours spent practicing at the rectory might be better spent at home. No child of hers would be accused by the deacon's wife of making himself a nuisance to the clergy.

And a someone named "Charlotte" had sent a tiny box of hair ribbons to Effie for Christmas. . .by Joseph. When she asked Joseph who this Charlotte was, he nonchalantly replied that her father was proprietor of the coach house in "the territory." How old was the young lady? Did Joseph stay at the coach house and fall in love with her perhaps? Obviously, judging by the gift, she did not know of Effie's condition.

That brought the list to Joseph, the prime target of the worries. As soon as the snow melted, he caught a ride into Cleburne with the parson. He was there now. Excuses of every sort were employed by her eldest to get away from home. This time he said he wanted to talk with Jim, the stagecoach driver. He would be back tonight, of course. *But he won't stay,* Martha told herself, *it's Effie*

241

go or Joseph go. Her home, like a too-short blanket, covered one member of the body while the other must needs be out in the cold. And she did not intend to sacrifice her own "flesh 'n blood" for a derelict child that was not her responsibility to start with.

Characteristically, Joseph's concern stretched beyond his own doorstep during the snowstorm; Jim was weathered in somewhere in these parts. The stagestop hands would give him the information he sought. Jim would be anxious to hear about Effie's Christmas. The parson's trip to town provided Joseph the transportation he needed. He located Jim with ease.

"Joseph! How'd you know where I was?"

"You can't hide! The man at the stagestop said you usually took a room here when the roads were untraversable."

"I'd hoped to make it back to the territory before the weather hit, but it's not that important. This often happens; Sis won't worry. The important thing was getting you home."

"You'll never know how much it meant to Effie, Jim."

"I've got to hear all about it. Here, let me put on a pot of coffee."

"Wish you could have been there Christmas and seen Effie's eyes when she unwrapped that doll!"

"I do, too. Did she like it?"

"Did she *like* it? If it had been alive, she'd have smothered it to death with kisses. She named it Becky, for her mother. The 'child' is never out of her reach!"

"And what did Charlotte send?"

"All colors of hair ribbons. Mama has been making Papa cut off Effie's hair like a boy's every fall when school starts, but I plan to put a stop to that. I want Effie to feel like a real little girl, and the ribbons will add the feminine touch."

"Was there anything she could use in the barrel that Charles left with the Brownings?"

"Man, that's a story too heartbeaking to tell."

"Even to a friend that hauls you around all over the country?"

"I found out just before Christmas that Effie has never spent a warm winter since '78. I had no idea she was short of covers and slept cold. I don't know what's kept her from taking her death of pneumonia! Her guardian angel, I guess. There were three quilts and two little soft coverlets in that barrel. She cried tears of joy."

"How'd you find out she had been cold all this time."

"She pointed up and said 'Him' when I pulled the quilts from the barrel. I asked her if she'd been praying for warm covers and she said she'd prayed *lots* for them. She admitted she'd been sleeping without enough cover all these years. Makes me feel guilty for every blanket I've slept under."

"Me, too."

"But get this, Jim. First off when Dessie got home from church, Effie asked if any of the rest of us needed her quilts to keep *us* warm!"

The mention of the unselfish offer hit too close to Jim's memories. He looked away. "What else was there?"

"Her mother's wedding dress. It'll never be of any value to Effie except sentimentally. Then there were some fancy dishes. Looked like they came out of a castle; Mrs. Browning said Rebecca was apparently from high class stock. Effie insisted on giving Mama and Dessie and Sarah a dish apiece for Christmas, she has a mighty big heart."

"The little angel! Did your mother accept it graciously?"

"I'm afraid not. When I told her it was from Effie, she turned and thanked *me* instead of Effie. When I told her it wasn't my idea, it was Effie's, she said she knew who brought it, wrapped it, and put it under the tree. She figured I was simply transferring it to her under the guise of a gift from Effie. When Mama gets locked in on a supposition, there's no changing her."

"Remember the pact we made to pray. . . ."

"I'll do the praying if you'll do the believing."

"And Joseph. . . ."

"Yes, sir."

"We don't tell God *how* to do things."

Business completed, the parson stopped by Jim's room for Joseph. Brother Stevens appeared to be deeply troubled, sparing Joseph the burden of small talk. He was grateful that the pastor did not ask any questions all the way home.

Effie greeted Joseph with her fetching crooked smile. *If the world was full of Josephs, it would be heaven instead of earth.*

Henry called Joseph aside. "Your mother's took real sick, an' I'm worried about her." Martha's nausea became violent and she was scarcely able to keep meals cooked for the family.

"School can keep fer a few days, Sarah," her father insisted. "Yore Maw need help in th' house." Sarah needed no prompting to quit school; she had been on the lookout for an opportunity.

Matthew, wearing a tense expression, beckoned for

Joseph to follow him outside. "Did Brother Stevens mention anything to you about the trouble that's brewing?"

"No."

"Pauline told me and I don't know whether to tell Papa or not. Deacon Clark has asked Brother Stevens to leave."

"To *leave*? To leave what?"

"To leave the church. They're fixing to put him out and find a new pastor more to their liking."

"But that's not fair just to kick a man out. What has Brother Stevens done to get turned out?"

"Pauline says they're accusing her paw of condoning sin and compromising."

"Brother Stevens. . .condoning *sin*?"

"It's all rabble-roused by Deacon Clark and his long-tongued wife. He's got the rest of the congregation all stirred up. . ."

There's wagon tongues and waggin' tongues and the length of both are about the same. That was Charles' way of putting it. "But what about Papa and Mr. Gibson and me. . ."

"You'all don't count much against all the rest."

"You're sure this is true?"

"Positive. Pauline heard them ask him to resign with her own ears."

"How long did they give him to get out?"

"Thirty days."

"Don't say nothing to nobody, Matthew. I'll handle this."

In late February, it began raining, and rained for days. Martha's nausea began to abate. "Henry, I think there's another little Harris on th' way," she told her husband.

"Th' Lord's gonna send us another'n to fill in Robert's empty space at th' table, Martha."

"This'n will be th' tenth child I've bore, Henry."

"This'n will be *special,* Martha. He'll be our *tithe* baby!"

Chapter 24

Flood

"*T*he river's flooding, Papa! We need all the help we can get!" Joseph panted, out of breath from running.

"Matthew!" Henry called, pulling on his ducking jacket. "William!"

"Who's in trouble, Joseph?" Martha asked.

"We'll have to move the Clarks out before night. The water's rising fast. If we don't get them out soon, the house will wash away down the river and they'll lose everything they've got."

Everything 'cept her tattlin' tongue, Martha suppressed an urge to say.

"We'd best go afoot, an' not chance gettin' th' wagon bogged down to th' hubs," Henry said. "That could cost us precious time."

"Are th' Gibson's all right?" Sarah held her voice even to hide her alarm. *What if something happened to*

Hank. . .?"

"Their place is far enough back for safety. . .unless the flood covers the whole earth!" Joseph assured her. "It may get the schoolhouse, though."

"Hey, that'd be okay," William said.

"What about the church and parsonage?" Matthew's worry was for Pauline's well-being.

"The church and churchyard are up on the hill. Pauline will be all right. . .as well as our Robert." Matthew turned a tell-tale shade of red, and gave Joseph a withering look.

Mr. Gibson joined the rescue crew. Brother Stevens was unable to get across the angry river to help the distressed parishoners; Joseph was relieved that the parson was spared facing his tormenters.

Gertie Clark had heard "by the grapevine" that the prodigal son was home, but had not seen Joseph personally. Now he appeared to help in her adversity.

The swirling waters surrounded the aging structure, climbing swiftly, eager to lift the cottage from its supportive posts. Muscled arms began to lift furniture and clothing, bearing them to higher ground.

"The furnishin's need in out o' th' weather, Deacon. Where do you want that we take them?"

"If'n we lived on th' *other* side, our church would be th' logical place. . . ."

"But since you don't. . . ?"

"Could store it in my barn, but my barn leaks bad," Mr. Gibson offered. "Wouldn't be much better off."

"I know all 'bout that barn," Deacon Clark reminded. "I'm th' one what sold it to you."

"Should'a sold 'em this place, an' kept that'n," Gertie complained.

"Tell you what. . ." from Joseph. "We can push things around at our house and empty a room for the time being. I'm sure Mama wouldn't mind. . . ."

"That's mighty kind of you. . ." the deacon started to accept Joseph's offer when Gertie Clark cut in, "No! I'd rather leave it sit out in th' rain."

"Why, Gertie. . . !"

"I ain't havin' *my* belongin's contaminated with evil spirits in a sinner woman's house! A flood's bad enough judgment without addin' more!"

Deacon Clark, normally patient with his unruly wife, found this a bit much for his constitution. "Gertie, I've a mind to dismiss these friends who've come to help an' let your stuff sweep down th' river. . . ."

"She's not responsible, Deacon. Probably not rational," Henry said. "Women tend to get all hysterical in stressful situations; I'm married to one o' them kind. Martha fainted when our Robert got drug by th' team."

"I'm in my perfect right mind, thank you, Mr. Harris . . .uh, Brother Harris. I'm sorry you don't understand th' situation at your own house. . .how your wife sinned right under your own nose, an' you not even realizin' th' retarded child ain't yorn!"

Henry had no idea what Gertie Clark was talking about, but perceptive Joseph did. And he was furious! "Where'll we put this *junk* then, Mrs. Clark," he fairly spat, and Henry gave him a reprimanding look.

"Take it to Sister Myrt's! She's a *Christian!*"

Embarrassed at Joseph's rudeness for the duration of the move, Henry worked as swiftly as possible; he had never seen Joseph act this ungentlemanly before. It certainly reflected on his and Martha's training here before the head deacon of the church.

The journey to Sister Myrt's house was long and the furniture bulky. Deacon Clark insisted that his contentious wife stay with Sister Myrt while the men shuttled back and forth. When they returned for the last piece, a heavy marble-topped washstand, the house was gone, retiring their aching arms.

Joseph sent Henry, Matthew, and William home, inventing a reason to drop by Sister Myrt's before returning home himself. He had a matter to settle with Gertie Clark. Sister Myrt, or whatever audience might be on hand to listen, was unimportant. Joseph, akin to Charles, hated waggin' tongues.

"I need to talk with you, Mrs. Clark." He considered that he held his temper in check admirably, and hoped that she noticed he failed to call her "Sister" Clark.

"Sure, young man. What can you say that's worth listenin' to? A prodigal son. . . ."

"Gertie! You could at least show th' young man th' decency of a proper thank you fer savin' your furnishin's." The deacon was visibly abashed.

"Never mind, Deacon, I'll handle this." Joseph was ready to flush the hornets from the nest. "This lady. . .ah, woman. . .your wife accused my mother of being a sinner. . .and in the presence of my father. . . ."

"I forgot Marthy asked me not to tell. I didn't know Brother Harris was ignorant of it. . . ."

"Ignorant of what?"

"Marthy's sin. . .her *unfaithfulness.*"

"Her unfaithfulness to church?"

"No! Her unfaithfulness to Brother Harris!"

"Mama has never been unfaithful to Papa in her life!"

"I'm truly repentant fer breakin' th' news to Marthy's own son, but to clear my own good name an' not to be accused of slanderous talk or lyin', I'll have to level with you."

"And that's just what you'd best do right now."

"Th' retarded child. . . ."

"Her name is Effie Harris and she's *not* retarded. She's smart as a whip, in fact."

"Well, what I mean is she's been cursed by being conceived in sin. . ."

"Mrs. Clark, what do you mean by 'conceived in sin'?"

"Son, you're gettin' mighty technical."

"I demand that you explain the statement you made about Effie."

"Don't be demandin' me, young man. I never could stand smart-alecky kids. If you must know, that child was fathered by your uncle. . . ."

"Charles."

"Charles. That's the name."

"And mothered by my Aunt Rebecca."

"By *who*?"

"My Aunt Rebecca. She died when Effie was about three years old."

"I don't blame Marthy fer tellin' you that little white lie, Joseph. It was kind of a mother to spare her son th' embarrassment an' cover her. . . ."

"Mrs. Clark, I was ten years old when Charles brought Effie to our house to live. I remember the day well. Effie was three years old. You can reveal nothing that I don't know."

"Well, I declare. . . ."

"And, furthermore, I have just returned from a trip to the territory of New Mexico. . .a business trip. . .where Charles and Rebecca lived legally married for two years when their only child was born. We have their records in a Bible. Rebecca's purity and high moral standards were unquestionable; she was a devout Christian, always minding her own business. The stagestop owner's wife was Rebecca's best friend. Rebecca was of small stature and Charles told Mrs. Browning that she experienced a difficult childbirth. The baby was damaged physically. . . ."

"Them kind o' children are possessed. . . ."

"Those kind of children are angels who got their wings bent getting from heaven to earth to bring happiness to us unworthy mortals!"

"Never heard sech. . . ."

"Suffer little children to come unto me, and forbid them not: for of such is the kingdom of God."

"Then why has Marthy tried to hide th' child all these years?"

Joseph was bluntly honest. "She's ashamed of Effie. That's because she is uneducated like many of your generation."

"How disrespectful!"

"That wasn't meant as disrespect, Mrs. Clark. It's cold facts. Your generation believes that imperfect bodies are caused by evil spirits. The gnarled peach tree in your front yard. . .does it produce peaches any less sweet than the straight ones? Is its fruit cursed because its limbs are twisted by the elements? Do you refuse to eat the peaches?"

"Gertie, I think you owe Sister Marthy an apology. . .

an' Pastor Stevens. . .an' anyone else you told your story to."

Pastor Stevens? So that was Pastor Steven's purpose for the unusual house call the night of the storm! And Martha had dropped out of church to escape Gertie Clark's gossip! And the whole sticky situation, promoted by Gertie's inflamed tongue, had goaded the church group to ask for Brother Steven's dismissal.

"And you are the one who is responsible for kicking out our pastor?" Joseph turned to the deacon.

"I. . .well, I. . . ."

"Unless you withdraw your demand for our pastor's resignation, I shall go before the whole church and announce publicly the black rumor spread by your wife. . . ."

"Uh. . .just as soon as th' river goes down to where I can swim. . .uh, get acrost, I'll make things right. . . ."

A wagon tongue had destroyed Robert, but a waggin' tongue had almost destroyed the rest of his family. With his mission accomplished, Joseph took his leave. The score was settled.

The Clark's never rebuilt their house. They sold their land and departed for an unknown destination. To ask forgiveness was beneath Gertie Clark. Sister Myrt said they located "farther on south" where the weather would be milder and they would have no fear of flood waters. But Joseph knew why they left.

Thus, Gertie Clark was not around to spread talk of "Marthy's reapin' God's judgments" when Sarah and Hank eloped.

Chapter 25

Jim's Visit

*D*ear *Mama: Hank and me have gone away to get married. I hope you won't be too mad at me, for I really love Hank. I can't live no longer without him. Your daughter, Sarah.*

Sarah left the note in the sugar bowl, knowing that by mid-afternoon, when Martha lifted the lid to sweeten her tea, she would be on her way to Cleburne.

Martha was crying when Henry came in from the spring planting. "Martha! Are you al'right? What's happened? Is the baby. . . ?"

Martha handed him the note.

"My goodness, Martha, you scared me! Is that all that's wrong?"

"Is that *all*? Ain't that enough?"

"Why, it's no great tragedy, Martha. Hank's a good clean, steady boy. From real good stock. Couldn't 'a picked a better husband fer her if'n I'd been pickin' myself!''

"But she's so young. . .just a baby!"

"Was you a baby when we married?"

"Well, no, . .yes. . .I mean. . . ."

"She'll make it, Martha. She's real smart for her age. Kids have to grow up sometime. We can't keep 'em on ferever. Be happy she got 'er a good man! An' if'n she loves him that much, that's what counts anyways!''

Sarah and Hank returned after a three-day honeymoon and lived with the Gibsons. Mr. Gibson bought the old Clark place, and Hank planned to purchase a corner plot to build a cabin for his bride. Sarah radiated happiness, and Martha adapted to her new son-in-law without trauma. "Sarah was just th' marrying-early kind," Dessie explained to Effie. "But I ain't."

Martha harbored needless fears that Sarah would avoid bringing Hank to her home because of Effie. But Hank accepted Effie as if she were normal; he was certainly an unusual fellow! He and Sarah often shared meals at the Harris table, refilling the quota left short by Robert's passing.

No one on the Harris side of the river could attend church until the flood water receded. Matthew walked the floor.

"Matthew, what'cha so restless 'bout?" his mother asked.

"Missin' my music lessons," he answered.

In early spring, Joseph got a job with "the project" building a new bridge across the Brazos River. Commended as a good hand, he transferred with his job to Cleburne during the summer months to help build yet another bridge. Effie watched him leave with apprehension; he seemed to be the only one who could handle Martha. Now that Sarah, Martha's right arm in the kitchen, was gone, Martha would bear a heavier load. And with another child on the way, she sorely needed help. Effie longed to be able to assist her in some small way.

Matthew spent more and more time at the Stevens'. "Might as well move yore belongin's over to th' Stevens', much time as you put in there," Martha scolded, her tone colored with jealousy. To Henry she said, "We need to be thinkin' on sellin' off some o' th' land an' gettin' Matthew a piano, so's he'll stay home now 'n then."

"That's on my list fer this fall, if'n th' crops prosper."

"An' if'n Joseph comes back to help you harvest!"

"He'll shore be back by then."

Joseph hoped that the job in Cleburne would bring him in contact with Jim. He left a note at the station: *Jim, I'm working in Cleburne for the next few weeks. Have a room at the Liberty Hotel on Main Street. I'd like to see you when you come through.*

Jim looked Joseph up the day he got the notice; they sat up far into the night talking.

"Charlotte's still moaning the blues over you, Joseph." Jim had not changed a bit.

"Don't give her any false hopes, Jim."

"She wants to know when you'll be returning to the territory."

"I want to make enough money to take Effie with me next time I go."

"Hope I'm your driver."

"Wouldn't trust her life to any other."

"Charlotte's eager to meet Effie. She asks about her

every time I go through. I told her Effie liked the hair ribbons."

"But Jim. . .I'd have to know that she. . .or any other young lady. . .accepts her. . .uh, not just for *my* sake. Do you know what I mean?"

"I get the drift, Joseph. Don't the Brownings know about Effie's physical problems?"

"They didn't say anything about it, and I didn't tell them."

"How's Effie doing. . .and the rest of the family?"

"Effie's troubled about something. She didn't want me to leave. I could see it in her eyes. They were kind of pleading like. Made it hard, but I had this good job offered to me and I've got to have money to carry out my future plans."

"No idea what's bothering the child?"

"The older she gets, the more she feels Mama's rejection I'm sure."

"Haven't seen any signs of the answer to our prayer?"

"Not yet. I got a new insight on some of Mama's bitterness though. I learned that Mrs. Clark, the deacon's wife as well as the community gossip started a vicious rumor about Mama in connection with Effie. Evidently, it's been flying around for years. She claimed that Effie was Mama's illegitimate child by Charles. . . ."

"Where on earth. . . ."

"I guess she concocted it herself for her gossip column. I feel sure Mama got a hint of it and was terribly hurt, because she quit going to church. I don't know how much she may have heard."

"How'd *you* happen to find out about the slander?"

"The flood washed it ashore! I went to help move the

waggin' tongue's furniture that was in danger of floating away. Even offered to store it at our house to get it out of the weather. She let me know right off, and in no uncertain terms, that she would prefer it to wash downstream than have it contaminated in a 'sinner woman's' house."

"Why didn't you just drop the furniture into the river?"

"It was the greatest temptation I'd ever had!"

"What *did* you do?"

"I held my anger fairly well I thought, but made an excuse to stay after the rest of the family left for home to settle the score with her."

"Did you really get it settled?"

"With dignity. She had the gall to tell me that Mama had *me* deceived, but luckily I was old enough to remember when Effie came to live with us, coupled with the fact I had just returned from visiting Rebecca's grave. I had enough ammunition to shoot all the skunks in the hollow log!"

"Did the woman apologize to your mother?"

"Not on your life. They moved clear out of the country. And we got to keep our pastor; they had even got up a petition to have him ousted because he 'compromised' with Mama's 'sin'."

"Did you mother return to church?"

"She goes occasionally now. It'll take awhile. She is still dead set that nobody find out about Effie. In a way, you can't blame her after all she's been through. It's just an ignorant notion of that generation."

"I'm glad the waggin' tongue is gone."

"I'm sure Brother Stevens is, too. Papa says he's been preaching like a cyclone lately!"

259

"How's Sarah's love affair?"

"Sarah eloped."

"You don't say!"

"Back in the spring."

"Married the neighbor boy she was secretly admiring?"

"That one. Got a good man and is happy. He's started on their little home on the land next over from his folks."

"How'd your mother take that?"

"Pretty hard at first. Sarah was a big help to Mama, and Mama needs help real bad right now. She's expecting another little one this fall. It'll probably help fill Robert's place."

"That's something I've been wanting to ask. Did you learn the details about Robert's death? That's been bothering me terribly, what Effie said about trying to help him. Did he die of illness? Was he killed?"

"It was an accident. The family had gone to The Springs on a Saturday to shop. They left Effie alone in the wagon while they went into the stores. Somehow there was a freak runaway. When the horses spooked, Robert got caught by his overalls on the doubletree hook and dragged to death. Two of the reputable town ladies said they saw a 'ghost' or 'angel' rise up out of the wagon bed and stop the horses. Dessie was watching; she says Effie stopped the wagon, though no one else puts any stock in her story. Robert was too far gone by the time Effie got the wagon stopped; I'm sure she lives the nightmare over and over."

"She was the angel."

"The little bent wings did all they could."

"How's Matthew's romance?"

"Getting serious, I'm afraid. We may have another wedding on our hands before long. He gave Mama and Papa the shock of their lives just before Christmas?"

"Announcing his marrying intentions?"

"Oh, no. They don't know anything about his courtship. He played the piano like a professional on the church Christmas program. They didn't know he knew a note of music!"

"Did you get home in time to hear it?"

"I stayed home with Effie and let Mama go. I've never heard Matthew play. But that's another reason I'm working. I want to see that Matthew has a piano of his own."

"Whose did he learn on?"

"The preacher's daughter's."

"He may just marry himself a piano and you can save your money!"

"You know, I hadn't thought of that!"

"Joseph, when are you going to start thinking about *you* and your future?"

"If God wills, Jim, I have many a year ahead of me to get my own goals in focus. Right now. . . first things first."

"Will you be going home in the next few days?"

"This weekend, I hope."

"Thought I might get a big box of candy and send it to Effie."

"It wouldn't do any good, Jim."

"Is she a diabetic?"

"No, but she's so big-hearted, she'd give it all away to the boys."

When Joseph returned to the farm for the weekend visit, he did not like what he saw. Effie was losing weight again; her sunken eyes haunted him.

"Effie practically *lives* in the woodshed," Dessie reported.

Just before he returned to his job, he found her clutching Rebecca's picture and crying. It was a revelation. He and Jim could never fill the void in Effie's life. What Effie needed was a *mother*.

Chapter 26

Sally

"*I* believe it's time fer th' baby, Henry." Fall's first frost blanketed the ground, putting the summer warmth to sleep for the winter.

"I'll send Matthew fer th' doctor. Which one shall he fetch?"

"Don't make much matter. Either'n. Th' one what took care o' Robert is okay."

All the children were enrolled in school now; Arthur made such a fuss when Chester and Alan left for classes that Henry convinced the school master to take him early.

Matthew borrowed a saddle from Hank, crowding Adam to his fastest lope. Two shirts beneath the buckskin jacket staved off the biting chill. He had made a commitment to Pauline; someday they would face a day such as this.

Nothing could be more breathtaking than the fall

foliage in Central Texas. There was no secret call upon Matthew's heart to investigate other areas, explore other lands. He was in love and content.

He especially liked The Springs. Rocked in the lap of his native state and nursed at the breast of natural springs, this young town had the potential of outdistancing Waco, Dallas, and Fort Worth. It had grown appreciably since he first started making infrequent trips in with Henry and Mr. Gibson. It now had fifteen business houses, a lumber yard, a newspaper, and—best of all—a college known as "Central College" had recently been chartered.

Unobtrusive Matthew's ambitions were known to no one save his Pauline. The measureless hours spent under the parson's influence left its indelible mark on Matthew's life. He, with Pauline as his capable helpmeet, would like to establish a church in The Springs. The college offered a course in Elocution (Martha would call it "speakin' "), besides the Fine Arts of Music.

Neither Dr. Brooks nor Dr. Murphy were in. Dr. Murphy's wife said that he "would be returning any minute now from a house call just a hand's turn away." Matthew drew a detailed map for the doctor, and reined Adam about the town, seeking a suitable location for his future "church." Only one church served the entire fast-growing city; it was Methodist. The populace might welcome a variety.

Dr. Murphy, detained much longer than his good wife predicted, arrived at the Harris farm just ahead of Baby Sally. "Yore tithe baby ain't a 'he', Henry!" laughed Martha. "It's a 'she.' " From the first gasp for the breath of life, Sally had both of her parents captured, heart and

264

soul. A roly-poly, delightful child, she became the favorite of all Martha's brood.

Henry took money that he had planned for other necessities and bought the infant a wooden crib that rocked and a wicker carriage; Martha made no objection. She spent infinite hours smocking satin dresses for this adorable bundle of curls and dimples.

Now that Gertie Clark was gone and forgotten, Martha loved nothing better than to "show Sally off" at church, and Sally performed well for her audience. "She's a regular heart thief!" Sarah chuckled. "I hope my babies are *half* that pretty!"

A nameless longing cast a spell over Effie as she watched Dessie play with the darling baby. If only once she could hold a real live child in her arms, feel the soft skin, kiss the fluffy curls! She made numerous trips by the crib that winter, peering in fleetingly. Sally sensed her love; she cooed at Effie, stretching her fat little hands toward her to be picked up. The sweet innocence of her smile soothed Effie's aching lonesomeness.

Effie brought the elaborate baby quilts from her quiltbox bed. "G-give b-baby t-these," she pushed them into Dessie's arms.

"Oh, Mama! Look! Effie wants to give these beautiful covers that used to be hers to Sally. Won't she look just *gorgeous* going to church in them!"

Martha eyed the expensive satin coverlets; such finery befitted her Sally. But in the event evil spirits still lurked in the fibers of the blankets that once kept a simpleton warm, she could take no chances with the apple of her eye.

"Sally has plenty of blankets, Dessie," she said curtly.

Joseph came to see Sally. "Say! I've got *another*

sister! That makes four!''

"Have you fergot how to count?" Martha gave him a scalding look. If he was counting Effie, he could subtract. Whatever she was compelled to do to protect this little idol from the stigma of Effie, she would bar nothing to do it. Her course of action was still on the drawing board, but Effie would have to be removed from the household. And this time, Henry would agree. Baby Sally was his one weakness; she had leverage now. Sally might not be old enough for the presence of Effie to matter at the present, but by next year. . . .

Joseph sensed the approaching day of abandon. Anxiety clawed at his mind. He was not old enough. . .not ready yet. . .to provide a home for Effie. If he could only have another two years! Would Sarah be willing to take her in the interim? But no, it would be several months before Hank could finish their cabin, and the Gibson house was too small for another occupant. Jim would have no answers; he lived on the trail and his sister who lost her own special child was in failing health.

In the spring, Joseph crossed paths with Jim again. "I know Mama's got in mind to find another place for Effie somewhere, Jim. She has room in her heart only for my new baby sister, who is 'too good' to be reared with Effie. I try not to hold it against Mama, but it's getting harder. I know it's just ignorance. . .the way she was taught. Something tells me time's running out. If I could have even another year. . . ."

"Wait, Joseph. . . . Remember our agreement to pray?"

"Yes, sir."

"I've kept my end of the bargain. I haven't missed

a single night praying for Effie. . .*and* your mother. God *especially* loves his impaired angels. He'll do something special for Effie."

"But in case He doesn't, I'll have to. . . ."

"No 'in cases' allowed, Joseph. . .He *will!*"

Effie paused to receive Sally's daily smile. It was while she stood gazing into the cradle that Martha put in her appearance.

"DON'T TOUCH THAT BABY!" Her words cut like a knife, her eyes crackled. "If you ever attempt to pick her up, you shall be turned into th' woods to *starve to death!"* Blind with hostility, she whirled and went back to her kitchen chores.

Effie turned to flee, her legs shaking so violently that they threatened to take their support from her. *Turned into the woods. . .turned into the woods. . .turned into the woods. . . .* The words bounced off the walls of her heart and echoed to her brain.

A recall of the terrible night alone on the riverbank made her break into a cold sweat; Matthew's long ago tale of the "bears an' things that eat you" in the woods still lived with her. Oh, she must *never* go near the cradle again, no matter how her heart hungered for Sally's happy response to seeing her!

"Pray for your enemies." Rebecca's Book said it; she must do it. She would go directly to the woodshed and pray for Aunt Martha now.

"Before another Christmas, Henry, I want something done with Effie. Sally'll be better'n a year old, an' I'll not have her bothered with embarrassment like th' others was. Joseph left home on account o' Effie, Sarah left, an' Matthew stays hid out most o' th' time. We've done our

Christian duty to Charles, 'n more, too."

"We can't just. . . ." Seeing Martha's irritation, Henry folded his sentence in the middle and put it away.

"Henry, do you love this baby best 'er Effie best?"

"Well, of course, Martha, if you put it that way, my own flesh an' blood. . . ."

"Then you'll do as I say! I caught 'er droolin' over Sally's cradle today with that twisted-up look on 'er face. I ain't standin' fer it no longer, Henry. Jest you make up yore mind what you plan to do, an' start lookin' fer a place. . . ."

Henry was troubled. Was Martha right after all? He thought he could depend on time to help Martha accept Effie, but time had let him down. He was convinced that Effie had a sharp mind, and hated to see her go to an asylum for children with no minds. He had heard that there was such a place in Fort Worth, but he had also heard that it was a deplorable lodging. Effie was not a human vegetable! However, if there was absolutely no chance of Martha ever learning to tolerate his niece, he would have to do *something* with her for the sake of the family.

Effie kept her distance from the heaven-sent child, fearful to even glance her direction, lest Martha mistake her glance and turn her into the woods with the wild beasts.

A few miles away, a troubled Jim rode in silence. He sought Joseph, finding him at his room in the Liberty Hotel. Joseph welcomed him warmly. "Predictions are we'll have a worse winter than last, and it'll get here earlier," he said. "I've got to be getting back west. Sis is in poor health and needs me."

"You take care of the Mexican Territory and I'll boss Texas, and we'll compare stories come spring!"

"I'll tell Charlotte you said take care of. . . ."

"Did I say that?" They both laughed, then Jim sobered.

"Joseph. . .I'm worried to death about Effie. I've just got this feeling. . .right here." Jim put his hand on his heart.

"Me too."

"Something tells me I've got to see her before I leave. Might be the last time. When will you be going home?"

"I'm ready when you are."

"Tomorrow?"

"Tomorrow."

Chapter 27

The Rescue

"*W*e'll be buyin' some new furniture, Martha. . .an' we'll get Matthew a piano fer his birthday come next month."

The calendar leaves were torn off to October, 1887. The Harris household had never seen a more prosperous year. Except for the irresolute problem of what disposition to make of Effie, Henry would have been a happy man.

Sarah and Hank had a baby on the way. Sarah bubbled with excitement. "Hank'll have our cabin built a'fore our new'n gets here," she said, "Hope I get one like Sally!"

"No chance," Henry told her. "Only tenth babies are this special. She's our tithe baby. . .a gift straight from Heaven!"

It was a balmy day with enough wind to antagonize the dry leaves to restlessness. Effie had not emerged from the woodshed to eat breakfast or lunch. Her lips moved with supplicating prayers. Prayer for Aunt Martha. Prayer for grace. Prayer for some form of relief from her intolerable life! The rejection was eating at her spirit like the dread consumption, destroying her slowly but surely. If only Joseph would come home!

She heard faint voices outside the shed. Since all the children were in school, it would have to be Martha and Henry talking. Fragments of the conversation, at first only a hum of inflection, became audible. ". . .to do somethin' with Effie!" Unmistakably Martha. ". . .kept her long enough. . . I'll give you one month, Henry. . . gone before th' holidays. . . ."

"Hold yer patience, woman. I'm checkin' around. Ain't found no institution'll take 'er less'n five dollars a month."

"Nigh on to ten years is long enough. . . ."

"I'll go next week an'. . . ."

They were talking about her; they planned to take her away! *Oh, Uncle Henry, please let me live in your woodshed! Or die here! It doesn't matter!*

Effie placed Rebecca's picture back in the flyleaf of the Bible and closed it, laying it aside. Then she cried until her eyes were bloodshot and almost swollen shut. Her head throbbed. She had never lived through a worse day— not even on the riverbank when she battled the dastardly water moccasin, or in the pantry with the hail bouncing off the windowsill, or the day Aunt Martha slapped the picture of her mother from her hands.

"Jesus. . .my only Friend. . .let me die!" she implored fervently.

This was Monday, and washday for Martha. Her ultimatum had been issued at the clothesline. With Henry's departure, Effie could hear Martha bustling about, stoking up the fire under the black washpot, shredding more lye soap, and preparing another load of clothes for their cleansing while humming and talking to Sally.

"Kinda windy today, ain't it, Sallygirl? This wind'll dry our baby's diapers faster!" She often brought the baby in her carriage outside with her for fresh air and sunshine. Martha had dropped any responsibility that she may have ever felt for Charles' child; it was as if the occupant of the woodshed did not exist.

When the sun peeped through the knothole in the west wall, Effie knew the children would soon be returning from classes. She was weak from hunger and her bones ached miserably. She wished she might slip into the kitchen and find a biscuit, fetch her quilts, and make her move to the shed unnoticed. She might freeze to death here during the winter, but freezing to death was the lesser of two evils. Three laborous trips would transfer all her earthly belongings to her new "home," and to get the job accomplished before dark would take nothing short of a miracle. But she must!

The dish on the mantle, she would leave for Dessie; her trembling hands would surely let it slip and break, calling farther attention to her clumsiness. The doll that Jim gave her, her hair ribbons from Charlotte, and the poem book Joseph brought from Amarillo, her quilts. . . .

She stepped unsteadily from the shed, but as she did, the wind caught the old door and slammed it shut on her hand, bruising her fingers badly. A sob caught in her throat as she turned toward the house, bracing herself for the task ahead, hoping that Martha did not discover her intent. Her impotent feet caught on a log of firewood that Henry had dropped and she fell on her face in the dirt.

She lay moaning for some time, then painfully gathered her body to a sitting position. With stiff fingers, she attempted to brush the dirt from her ragged dress, to which she had just added a jagged rip.

Her unseeing eyes fell upon the baby carriage not far removed from the washpot. Martha was nowhere in sight. Her numbed mind jerked to attention at the scene before her. The wind had caught a live coal from beneath the washpot and sent it rolling under the carriage. Hungry flames licked at the wicker bottom. She heard the helpless whimper of a baby. A nightmarish panic seized her! Sally was in the carriage!

Effie looked about frantically for Martha. Where could she be? Perhaps she had taken an armload of dry clothes from the clothesline into the house. But why had she left the baby, even for a moment? Effie stumbled awkwardly toward the carriage. In only a matter of minutes both pram and baby would be engulfed in flames!

Effie knew that she might drop the baby if she tried to lift her from the buggy. Her joints were stiff, her hand sorely bruised, and her legs wobbly from lack of nourishment. And whether she dropped her or not, she would certainly be turned into the woods to starve. . .or be eaten by a starving beast. *DON'T TOUCH THAT BABY*. . .was Martha's command. *If you ever attempt to pick her up. . .turned into the woods. . .turned into the woods. . .turned into the woods. . .*

Effie's love for Sally overpowered reason. She might die of starvation or at the fangs of a wild animal, but Baby Sally *must* live. She was brilliant and happy and. . .normal. She was worshiped by both Martha and Henry. If anything happened to Sally. . . .

Effie swept the baby into her uncooperative arms, supporting her back as best she could. She did not dream that a baby could be so heavy! Holding Sally tightly and praying, Effie fled from the burning buggy toward the house and safety for Sally.

Once inside the back door, she tried to call Martha, making only a frightened, garbled sound. Martha, having dropped the clothes on the bed, turned to see Effie holding the baby. Infuriated, she snatched Sally from Effie's paralyzed arms. The dirt on her dress and the fresh tear indicated that Effie had fallen. Had Sally been hurt in the fall? Effie's locked arms had been slow to respond in releasing the child, and Martha's desperate pull had thrown Effie off balance. She fell face forward, striking a chair and sustaining a blinding blow.

"I-I-I. . ." she stammered helplessly, as the world swam about her. She lay very still and wished for death's sweet embrace, the wound in her heart surpassing all other injuries.

"I-I'm s-sorry."

Chapter 28

Fire!

"*T*he wind's getting up pretty good. Must be going to blow us in some cooler weather." Jim goaded the horses on.

"I just hope it doesn't bring rain. We need one more good week on the bridge. Then we're through, and I'll get my pay."

"You'll get it."

"Hope so."

"What do you plan to do after that?"

"Need to help Papa in the fields for a few days. We got a bumper wheat crop this year and wheat's selling high. Pecan trees in the bottomland are loaded. Peanuts produced good. Cotton, too."

"You're just anxious to get back to the angel."

"I am at that!"

"She needs you, Joseph."

"What she needs is a mother. The last time I was home I. . .I got a revelation. I found her in the woodshed hugging her mother's picture and crying. She had a lonely look in her eyes I. . .I just couldn't stand."

"That 'mother' bit is out of our territory."

"Yes, Jim, I wonder if we're being *fair.*"

"*Fair* to go see her?"

"No, *fair* to want to keep her in our world. She would be happier in heaven with Rebecca."

"As frail as she is, it wouldn't take a very big chariot to carry her there!"

"As much as you and I love her, we can never fill the vacancy in her heart; it'll take a woman to do it."

"I hadn't thought of it that way, but you're right. Shall we stop praying our selfish prayers then?"

"I think we should. I'd rather see her dead than in a home for retarded children or an asylum."

"You don't think it will come to *that*, do you?"

"Yes, I do. I live with the fear that I will come home one of these days and find that Mama has put her in an institution."

"And there would be nothing you could do. . . ?"

"Absolutely nothing. Being single and underage, I couldn't get her out."

"Nor could I. I'm not a relative."

"Can you drive faster, Jim?"

"What'd the boss say about you taking off work today?"

"I told him it was an emergency. . .and I wasn't lying."

At the sound of pounding hooves, the President's boys, just dismissed from classes, clustered beside the road to watch, while William plodded on. Recognizing Joseph, the fun-loving three stuck up their thumbs for a ride.

"Shall we give them a lift?" Jim asked.

"They'd love it!"

Jim reined the horses in, hefting the boys aboard, then stopped for William.

"Where's Dessie?" Joseph asked.

"It was her day to take down th' flag, an' teacher let her go early. Dessie goes early ever' chance she gets!" William furnished the information.

"Yeah," Chester added, "Dessie likes school a bunch, but she's so worried 'bout Effie, she don't know if'n she's readin' er writin' half th' time."

"What's she worried about?" Chester shrugged his shoulders.

"Effie spends most of her time in th' old shed now," William answered Joseph's question. "An' she's got to where she hardly eats anything. I guess Dessie's afraid she's gonna get sick er die er somethin'."

"She's apt to take pneumonia this winter if she doesn't stay inside," Jim said.

"That's what's troublin' Dessie."

"Well, she won't stay in th' house!" Alan spoke up. "No matter how cold it gets, she goes out there anyhow. Last winter, she went out in th' snow."

"Mama don't act like she likes Effie too good. She probably goes to th' woodshed to get out o' Mama's way." This deduction came from Arthur. *Smart kid,* thought Joseph.

"Well, *we* love her, and we don't want her to get sick," Joseph said. "I've got some money saved up, and

I'll talk to Papa about building her a little warm room all her own on the house!''

"No kiddin', you like 'er, Joseph? But I thought you didn't like Effie neither!''

"What ever gave you that idea, Chester?''

"Mama said.''

"When did I ever tell Mama I didn't love Effie?''

"She said that's th' reason you left home. . .'cause you was ashamed o' Effie. . .an' that if Effie was gone, you'd come back an' bring your friends, an'. . . .''

"*Me*? Ashamed of Effie?''

"That's what I heard 'er tell Papa.''

"Why, there's been a bad mistake somewhere! I'll have a talk with Mama and get this all straightened out! Effie's a favorite sister of mine!''

"Really?''

"Sure. Just because she got her wings all bent out of shape coming down to earth doesn't mean she's not still an angel! She's *special!*''

"An' yore not one bit 'shamed of 'er?'' asked Arthur.

"Of course not! Would I be ashamed of you if you fell off the barn and broke your arm? Am I ashamed of the oak tree in the yard with the crooked limb? Would I be ashamed of the wagon if the wheel got bent making a trip to town? Someday when Effie is strong enough, I'm going to take her on a long trip with me and introduce her to all my friends!''

"Joseph, you're aw'right!'' Alan turned to Chester. "I wish Mama thought thataway.''

"Where's that smoke coming from?'' Jim pointed ahead.

Joseph leaned forward. "I believe it's on our place,

Jim!"

"It's not th' house; it's out back," William stood up as the house came into view over the rise.

"Hurry, Jim!"

"It's the woodshed!" Joseph gasped as they approached the farm. "Let me out!"

"Stay out of range, boys," Jim warned the three younger ones. "We'll get the fire put out."

Wild with panic, Joseph ran toward the shed, almost bumping into Dessie. "She's not in there! Effie's not in th' shed!"

"Are you sure, Dessie?"

"I'm sure. I just came out'a there!"

"Jim! Effie's not in there!"

"You're *sure!*"

"Dessie checked."

The old building yielded without a struggle to the devouring fire. Jim shoveled dirt, digging a trench to confine its spreading and throwing the earth onto the crumbling structure, while Joseph and William ran back and forth from the well with inadequate amounts of water until the fire was under control. Finally conquered, the blaze admitted defeat, sulking in smoldering ruins. The President's boys and Socks watched from their perch on a low tree limb a safe distance away.

"We're winning." Jim wiped a sooty sleeve across his forehead.

"We're winning. But Effie's losing."

"What's she got to lose? She's lived in this old hovel long enough! I'm glad to see it go. You said you had saved up the money to build her a room, and if you haven't got enough. . ."

"Even a new room won't replace what she lost."

"What are you talking about, Joseph?"

"She lost the dearest thing to her heart. . .her mother's Bible and portrait were in that shed. I would have gone in after them, but it was too late."

"But we can be thankful that *she's* still alive."

"Yes, sir. It's a miracle she was out of the woodshed when it caught. She wouldn't have had time to get out, as slowly as she moves."

"You know who got her out?"

"Who?"

"That *other* angel."

Chapter 29

The New Daughter

"*M*ama! Th' woodshed's on fire!"

"Here, Dessie, put down yore books an' hold th' baby, so's I can. . ."

"Joseph 'n Jim 'n William 'er puttin' it out fine."

"Then don't be a'frightin' me so. There's nothin' in there what matters nohow."

Effie stopped the ears of her soul, willing herself not to believe Dessie's news. It could not be true! It was more than her hurting heart could bear, the finishing blow.

Rebecca's Book, her consolation, her relief in affliction, her help in need, was in the shed! She could never hope to remember all those cherished verses about heaven and mansions and tearless eyes. Time would steal them from her memory. And her family records, written by the hand of the one who loved her, had perished. Her mother's portrait, in the flyleaf of the Book, would live only in her mind, growing dimmer with the years, when she went to. . .*where?*

A new and worse shock, like a black powder explosion, thundered through her mind, killing the last visage of hope. Her only *home* was burning to the ground. It was no bad dream; it was a living nightmare. Smoke tormented her nostrils with its telltale smell. The home she was moving into permanently this very day was gone. This meant. . .this meant. . .*turned out into the woods.* . . .

And Socks, was Socks trapped in the burning inferno? She was too weak, too benumbed to cry.

"Martha! Martha!" The frantic screams came from outside. Henry had seen the columns of bellowing smoke and hurried home from the nearby field afoot. Something was on fire!

He passed the firefighters in bounding leaps without even seeing them, crashing his way through the back door. Martha, holding the fretting child close and crooning, heard the desperate shout of her husband. With pounding heart, she started to the door with Sally against her breast.

Henry waved wildly toward the baby carriage. Martha had never seen Henry hysterical; had something happened to him?

"It's on fire! The baby. . ." The flames had eaten the wicker from the carriage, leaving a naked skeleton of metal and with hunger abated, were now licking the fragments about the fire.

Henry's voice trailed off when he saw Sally safe in Martha's arms. "Oh, Martha, I thought. . .Oh, thank God!" He sat down weakly in a chair and gave way to a sob of relief. Effie, in a heap on the floor, crushed to despair, went unnoticed. She could summon the inner strength to arise. *"Please take me away to Mother!"* she prayed.

"I thought. . .I thought the baby was. . ." Henry mumbled, still in a state of shock.

"She *was* in the carriage!" The voice was Dessie's. "I was comin' up th' path from school an' saw it all! I knew I couldn't make it to Sally in time. All I could do was pray! Effie's what saved Sally's life. She walked right up to th' carriage—right up to th' *flames*—an' got Sally out just in time!"

Henry caught sight of the bedraggled mound on the floor, her dirty dress rent and rumpled. And in the silence of the room, still permeated with smoke from the gutted shed, Martha's conscience went to work. How could any being as unselfish and self-sacrificing as the hurting child on the floor be possessed of evil spirits? She was no animal; she had just proven herself capable of thinking, acting. Public opinion? Hogwash! She had bowed to public opinion long enough!

I've injured this child at my own hands. . .I have returned evil for good. . .if anyone is possessed of an evil spirit, it is me! The dam of superstition broke, flooding Martha's soul with light.

Henry made no move, no sound. Charles' child, the object of Martha's bitter hatred, the child she planned to send away to a sterile home for senseless mortals, had risked her life to save Sally. A little mound beside Robert for their lovely tithe baby was averted by the unloved Effie. How would Martha equate this heroic deed with her own grudge?

Dessie said no more and stood waiting. Effie had longed to "do something nice" to prove her love for Martha, and she had done the most noble thing possible. Why, she would not have hesitated to give her life for Sally! Would even this alter her mother's attitude?

Except for the ticking of the grandfather clock, the room was quiet, suspenseful. Wordlessly, Martha placed Sally on Henry's knees and went to the suffering Effie. Kneeling, she tenderly gathered the frail form into her strong arms.

"Oh, Effie, Effie!" she wept unashamedly. "Why did you do it? Why did you save my baby's life? You didn't *have* to! After I've treated you like a dog all these years, you could'a let her burn to death an' let me go to my grave a'grievin,' payin' for all th' injustice I ever done toward you. Tell me, why did you do it. . .Why. . . ?" Martha spilled her heart with her tears while Dessie's tears made a trail down her grimy face, dingy from the smoke's carbon.

"Because I *love* you, Aunt Martha." The soft words, scarcely above a whisper, came out with neither lisp nor falter.

"If you can find me worthy, Effie, please call me *mother*!" Martha bent to kiss Effie's blue, swollen lips and a warm mother's tear dropped onto the bruised cheek.

Joseph and Jim emerged through the back door with a washbowl destination, brushing ashes from their hair. Joseph stopped short. The sight of Martha soothing Effie's puffy face and black eye, oblivious to those about her, took him aback. He must surely be dreaming! His father and Dessie were crying. Why, something dreadful had happened to Effie! But why should his mother care? She had never been concerned before.

"Joseph," Martha smiled through eyes brilliant with tears, and spoke in a new gentle tone. "You have a new little sister."

"*Another* one?"

"Effie!"

"Why, Mama, she's been my sister all the time in my heart. My favorite one, I guess. I was going to take her to live with me. . . ."

"No, Joseph, she needs a *mother* and God has just given her one."

Jim grinned. How was it Joseph quoted Dessie about the quilts? That was it: God sure answers prayers *pretty*.

Dessie had been waiting in the wings of life's stage for the cue. It was time for her lines. "Effie," she said, "Here's yore Bible. I got it out just 'fore th' shed burst into flames!"

Chester held the purring gray cat. "An' Socks got out all by 'isself."

The weight of the world lifted from Henry's shoulders. ". . .And I will restore to you the years that the locust hath eaten. . ." Pastor Stevens had preached it last Sunday. Henry felt the restoration coming. "Could I hug my new daughter?"

"My arms ain't wantin' to turn 'er loose, Henry!"

Effie smiled. . .that beautiful crooked smile. Her spastic hand trembled with emotion as she reached to touch Martha's face.

"T-thank y-you, *M-mother!*"